Acclaim for
The GoodLife

"[Combines] the grisly true-crime minutiae of Truman Capote's *In Cold Blood* with Robert Altman's screwball social satire. Like all effective satire, *The GoodLife* recognizes the pleasures of indignation."

—*San Francisco Chronicle*

"The movement of a novel, even one as finely written as *The GoodLife*, across five points of view is potentially disastrous. . . . But Scribner . . . handles this challenge, cutting the focus not only to the action . . . but smoothly away from it, too, into his characters' troubled histories."

—*The New York Times Book Review*

"Written with a deft hand and an eye for detail . . . Scribner takes his story down a path that examines the disintegration of moral values."

—*San Diego Union-Tribune*

"Scribner has written his way into the sordid center of a riveting, morally complex crime."

—Scott Spencer

"Gripping . . . Scribner has created wonderfully complex characters in a briskly paced narrative."

—*Booklist*

"[A] nightmare vision of the American dream . . . A–."

—*Entertainment Weekly*

"*The GoodLife* is a riveting, psychologically sophisticated first novel . . . told from several different points of view, which heightens the tension of the story considerably as we move from Theo to Colleen to their victim, who struggles mightily in his captivity with doubts about the women he has loved, the life he has led and the choices he has made."

—*Library Journal*

"*The GoodLife* explores how easy it can be to rationalize decisions, and how doing so can slowly and insidiously unravel a persona's perceptions of right and wrong."

—*The Stanford Daily*

The GoodLife

Keith Scribner

RIVERHEAD BOOKS

New York

Riverhead Books
Published by The Berkley Publishing Group
A division of Penguin Putnam Inc.
375 Hudson Street
New York, New York 10014

First Riverhead hardcover edition: October 1999
First Riverhead trade paperback edition: November 2000
Riverhead trade paperback ISBN: 1-57322-834-6

The Penguin Putnam Inc. World Wide Web site address is
http://www.penguinputnam.com

The Library of Congress has catalogued the Riverhead hardcover edition
as follows:

Scribner, Keith
    The GoodLife : a novel / by Keith Scribner.
      p. cm.
   ISBN 1-57322-143-0
   I. Title. II. Title: GoodLife.
  PS3569.C735G66   1999   99-34338 CIP
  813'.54—dc21

Printed in the United States of America
10 9 8 7 6 5 4 3 2 1

To Karen Robertson, with great thanks

Acknowledgments

I am deeply thankful to Wendy Carlton and Gordon Kato for their hard work and insight, their tireless commitment to me and this novel, and to Rachel Knowles and Jennifer Repo for their conscientious attention; to John L'Heureux for his confidence, wisdom, and sixth sense for what makes writing good; to Brenda Miller and Sameer Pandya for their kind careful readings; to Paul Russell for his many years of guidance and honesty; to the Stegner Fellowship program at Stanford University and to my talented fellow writers here who have been so generous with their support and criticism; to the many fine writers in Missoula, Montana; to my parents and family; and to my wife, Jennifer Richter, whose love is my blood.

The
GoodLife

friday

A screech—and Malcolm awoke. He was napping on the breeze-way, an afghan over his lap. He looked out through the screen, each wire so fat with corrosion that it shaded his yard with rust. He should have stretched new screen years ago, but he'd grown accustomed to the cobwebs and flecks of dried grass caught in the mesh. Outside, Theo and Colleen were shoving a heavy plywood box into a rental van—screws and corner braces sticking through the bottom of the box gouged the paint and screeched against the metal. Theo had backed the midnight-blue Ford Econoline right across the side yard. There'd be a rut.

Malcolm dropped his hand to the end table at his side, fingered his inhaler, and brought it to his mouth. He squeezed off three puffs, and the clench in his chest subsided.

His son, Theo, had constructed the box—a large footlocker

really—to hold life preservers. The whole project disgusted Malcolm. Three sheets of five-eighths plywood, the hardware, the van rental—it had to have cost Theo nearly two hundred dollars. This from a forty-five-year-old man who didn't contribute to the grocery bill for his own family. "Spend money to make money," Theo had told his father. The box was some kind of goodwill gesture to the owner of a marina who was considering taking Theo on as a partner. Yet Theo hadn't spent the extra few dollars on CDX plywood, and he hadn't put a coat of sealer on it. The wet life jackets would rot out the box within a year. "That's what the air vents are for," Theo had said yesterday, standing at the bench in Malcolm's work shed, "and we'll varnish it *in situ.* After it's bolted down. We're going to bolt it to the dock. Next to where there's a fire hose. And an electric box." It was the way Theo had talked since he was a boy—adding details that may or may not have been true.

"If you put a pitch to the lid, the rain'll run off," Malcolm had suggested.

"I appreciate you want to help, Pop, but I can handle this." Theo was screwing corner braces on the *outside* of the box. His cuts were crooked, so the seams weren't tight—gaps too wide even for silicone. "Anyway, it's gonna be under a roof."

Malcolm had tried to ignore it, leave his son be. An only child, Theo always had two parents butting in. Maybe he and Dot were to blame for Theo's troubles—good intentions crowding the boy. As Theo screwed in the braces, he said, "You'd love seeing those boats down there, Pop. Gorgeous. Like you always wanted."

Malcolm looked out the window of his work shed down the back lawn to his old boat—*Theo's Joy*—rotting year by year, sinking into the ground. He lit a cigarette. He wanted to tell Theo to keep up the good work—keep the faith, they said these days. But he turned around and saw Theo using one-inch screws; the points were sticking through to the inside and would tear the life jackets. He couldn't help shaking his head: "Half-assed."

Theo pointed the cordless screw gun at his father. "Out," he ordered, calmly. But the disgraceful beard he'd been growing twitched on his face with the same furious tics that Malcolm saw in his son at age four when it was bath time, at age eight on the Little League field, at age sixteen when Malcolm refused to buy him a convertible, at age twenty-four when Malcolm first suspended Theo from the police force. Theo's face grew redder, more frustrated, and when Malcolm didn't budge, Theo jabbed the screw gun forward and squeezed the trigger, holding it on Malcolm as he moved to the door, the whir of the Phillips tip spinning.

Now, from the breezeway, Malcolm watched his son slam the doors of the van. Why on earth would a man grow a beard when he was looking for a job? Colleen hopped into the driver's seat, and Theo directed her with sloppy signals around the boxwood tree and the concrete mother duck with her ducklings in tow. The smallest duckling, Malcolm noticed, was knocked on its side.

The engine was straining as they rushed away. Malcolm hated to see them go off with such a shoddy piece of workmanship. It violated everything he'd tried to instill in the boy.

He rocked in his chair, springs squeaking, and slipped a Tareyton from the pack in his bathrobe. The grass, wet from dew and disgracefully tall, showed a darker green where Theo and Colleen had trampled it down. Here it was Memorial Day weekend, and Malcolm hadn't cut the grass yet. The spring had been bone-dry, but even so, getting out the mower two weeks ago would not have been premature. The truth was Malcolm didn't think his lungs were up to it, especially now that the days were turning hot. He'd been hoping Theo might pitch in and cut the grass. Malcolm had mentioned it once or twice.

He set the cigarette between his lips and looked down the yard. Years had passed since he'd even thought of repairing the boat, but he kept it in the yard to spite himself. It was his reminder of the mistakes that we make in this life. She hadn't been a bad boat, but as Dot was quick to point out, she hadn't been a particularly good boat either. The twin Liberty V-12's had wanted regular tinkering, but when she was timed like a watch, he'd get the full 380 out of them and then some. For five years they'd motored on the river and down the shore. The boat had brought them pleasure—Theo, Dot, and himself—and Colleen had loved it too, posed like a magazine model in her bikini on the little bow deck that first summer she and Theo were dating. It was already a collector's piece when he bought it—a 1941 Chris-Craft barrel-stern runabout with triple cockpits.

Now the boat was covered with moss, not a lick of paint left on her mahogany hull, the brass railings black as iron. It was propped up on stilts in the backyard, the trailer sold out from underneath, the keel sunk a foot into the ground. Where Malcolm had been able to reach in with the mower over the years, the grass was cut. Not exactly a junk car with a sprung hood and shattered glass, but there was no denying it was an eyesore. And Colleen said there was a smell—the nose on that girl, God bless her, she'd know if you passed gas at the other end of a telephone wire. If there was a smell, then there'd be a smell. Because what was clear to Malcolm was that on the day of his funeral, *Theo's Joy* would be a bit more rotted, a bit deeper in the ground, and still sitting comfortably on that spot. The boat represented the biggest blunder of Malcolm's life. It was his penance to look at that decaying boat every day, and if it was an eyesore for anybody else, well, life was like that. One life spills over into others: The joy and love—we welcome that, but the rest of it spills over too. The pain, the stupidity, and the wreck of someone else's life splash like vomit on your shoes from some drunk you're hauling in for Disorderly.

Before long Dot was standing in the doorway wearing her housecoat, her face misty with sleep. Her stance was getting wider with time. She would ask him as she had every morning for the last dozen-odd years if he'd had coffee, then she'd ask him what he felt like for breakfast. He'd say yes or no, nothing or an egg. And this morning he didn't want to have that conversation, because his son was going off to make a fool of himself with this half-assed box and Malcolm was to blame. Before Dot could speak he said, looking out through the corroded screen, "I wish I never had to eat again."

Malcolm lit the cigarette he'd been worrying between his lips, and as he watched a squirrel dart in and out of a hole in the hull of the boat, he realized he couldn't remember what hunger actually felt like. But more, he couldn't remember when his hunger had passed—that bearlike hunger of two or three decades ago that had seemed to consume him when he was unable to satisfy it. He remembered feeling it on the boat—swallowing deviled eggs like grapes, gulping tuna fish sandwich triangles, the bread cold and moist from the cooler, swishing down cans of beer. Still hungry, he'd watch the paper plates and empty tin cans bobbing in the wake of the boat, the water churned full of air, the color of dishwater. He'd watch the trash as it floated away, keeping inside the neat track formed by the wake. The hunger of those days had never been satisfied. At some point, like a pain, he had stopped noticing it, and when he thought of it later, the hunger was missing.

Dot was gone from the doorway, and after three puffs on his cigarette a clench gripped Malcolm's chest. He crushed the cigarette in the pedestal ashtray he'd gotten at the ten-year service banquet of the New Jersey Patrolmen's Association, and took two more hits from the inhaler. Yesterday, it had been four puffs of smoke till he couldn't breathe; last week it was half a cigarette. This is what the doctors had told him about emphysema: in the end it comes on quick. This is what was happening. Finally, Malcolm was dying.

Colleen drove the van. She liked being out early, the dewy morning suggesting a fresh start. Before they went to sleep tonight, she and Theo would be financially secure. "Is that the traffic light by Bottle and Cork?" Theo asked her from behind the passenger seat. He was crouched on the steel floor of the van between the plywood box and a roll of carpeting. The carpeting was wrapped in brown paper and flopped over in the middle to fit inside the rear doors. To Colleen, the smells of freshly cut wood and a new carpet were the smells of an addition being built on a house, of dreams being realized.

"Bottle and Cork," she said. "Yes." He had it planned so well, sensing as he did exactly where they were even though he couldn't see.

"Don't forget your directional going into the park."

She clicked down the blinker, her hands sweaty inside her gloves, and turned left through the first parking lot by the tennis courts, where several people were playing. She gassed up the hill to the upper lot by the picnic tables, where, exactly as Theo had predicted, there were no cars, no people, nothing.

"Seven-twelve," Theo said, his voice with the engine shut off much closer to her, almost like her own inner voice. "Stretch for three minutes and don't forget to lock up."

Colleen slammed the van door and slipped the single key on its rental agency tab into the zipper pocket of her warm-up jacket; then she leaned into the hood, stretching her hamstring.

She stared at her watch. When the display turned to 7:15, she took off her gloves and stashed them behind the front tire. She clicked her fingernails on the van as a signal to Theo and jogged back down to Route 401. The traffic already seemed heavier—rich people rushing to work—a steel-gray Mercedes, a boat-sized white Cadillac. She might never work again. Or she might. What was important was she'd have the choice. A year ago, when she'd begun to set up a business selling GoodLife products, she hadn't had that choice. Their debts from business failures, credit cards, and Tiffany's hospital bills were growing by the day. She was hung up on devising the perfect GoodLife plan that would guarantee her Majesty Status in eight months. There was no room for error. She couldn't relax, set up a solid front line, and take her time to build a successful network. After tonight, she'd be able to truly embrace the GoodLife philosophy—helping yourself through helping others. That is, *if* she chose to.

There were two blocks of sidewalk to jog along before she turned onto Carnegie Lane. She'd chosen her pink warm-up suit—elasticized ankles and wrists, *Dior* discreetly embroidered on the left breast and hip, a very conservative collar, not at all blousy, no shoulder pads. Among her various suits it seemed the least likely to draw attention. It was loose-fitting, really rather plain. She had to admit she had a nice figure for a forty-five-year-old mother of two. Her face was youthful, her hair still naturally blond, styled with a subtle permanent wave away from her face with enough length that she could wear it up for elegance or down, say, held back by earmuffs for skiing.

The GoodLife philosophy had taught her to think about profits not in terms of dollar figures but what those dollars could buy. She thought of Brook's college tuition, his future. She thought of resuming therapy for Tiffany. She thought of the relief to her twenty-five-year marriage staggering under the burden of debt. She rounded the corner onto Carnegie Lane and pushed easily up the small hill.

The corner lots along 401 were landscaped *natural;* ivy crawling up cedar plank fences, overgrown privacy bushes. As Colleen topped the hill, the sound of traffic on the main road was washed away by the steady hush of automatic sprinklers. The low sun fingered its way through the trees, lighting the mist that sprayed from invisible nozzles hidden in the plush carpets of grass and projecting rainbows across the freshly paved winding lane. It was a sight.

She checked her watch—7:19. Theo had figured six minutes to the foot of the driveway, and by her own estimation—the bend in front of her and then one more—that seemed exactly right. She jogged on the side of the street, looping around several half-circles of water sprinkling over the curb.

The houses on Carnegie Lane were mostly hidden from the street. Long driveways wound up through the trees, which seemed to be the originals—the actual trees that were there before the houses were built. In a few weeks when the leaves were thicker, the houses would be completely hidden behind the natural foliage—intimate and private.

She saw the mailbox, russet with a dark blue flag. Nice simple taste. A vine rose was tacked to the red cedar post. She could see the newspaper at the foot of the driveway. She slowed her pace, took a deep breath, then stopped to stretch her quads as if she had a cramp. She stood two steps into Stona Brown's driveway, as if she were concerned that a car hugging the curb too closely—someone late for work, moving too fast—could hit her. *Not even trespassing. The town owns thirty-three feet from the center of the road.* Theo had told her this, and it was his reassuring voice she heard now. She pulled an ankle up to her bum while standing on a single foot planted firmly next to the rolled-up newspaper.

But now she actually had a cramp, a spasm that made her leg shake. She dropped the leg, but the muscle pain shot into her hip. *Jogging on a quiet street in a free country.* She had a simple task: she kicked the newspaper across the driveway, where it nestled against the puff of English ivy encircling the roses.

Done.

And she was jogging again up Carnegie Lane, but the spasm in her hip and thigh didn't pass. She tried to run *through* the stitch, to run it off, but her stride was all wrong—her leg kicked out from the hip—and at that moment she looked off to her right, up through a stand of pine trees where two white birches caught her eye, and she saw a flash through the leaves: she saw a woman in a royal-blue bathrobe holding a hose dribbling with water, a woman looking directly at her. In half a second she was hidden again behind the trees.

Colleen jogged faster until she reached the cul-de-sac. The cramp passed. She turned around, jogged in front of the house again, this time on the far side of the street, looking to her left through the trees. When she caught a glimpse of the porch, no one was there.

She jogged back past the tennis courts. Inside the van Theo told her, "Two minutes late."

"Sorry, I had a cramp." She sat on the edge of the plywood box and slipped gray coveralls over her jogging suit. Theo opened the rear doors and unfolded the rolled-up carpet so that it stuck out the back, a red flag dangling at the end. Then he swung the doors tight against the roll of carpet and held them fast with bungee cords.

Colleen started the engine and eased down through the park past the tennis courts, gunned into traffic on 401, then took a quick left on Carnegie Lane. Now she slowed the van to an idle, rolling as slowly up the street as she had jogged it. When she passed the house, she tried not to look but couldn't help herself. She searched through the trees for any signs of life. All she could see was a second-long flash of sunlight shining silver off a stream of water running down the front-porch steps.

She looped around the cul-de-sac and brought the van to rest on the side of the road halfway back to the mailbox. From this spot she could see the top of the driveway and just glimpse the garage doors. She turned off the engine.

On the seat beside her was the *Asherton Gazette* and a bag from Dunkin' Donuts—a coffee and a cinnamon cruller. "Anything?" Theo's voice as soft and close as pillow talk. He was still crouched in the back with a blanket at the ready to throw over himself if there was trouble.

"Nothing," she said, looking into the bag. The cruller was half eaten, the coffee half empty, which was a relief with her stomach all butterflies as it was. She laid the newspaper across the steering wheel, put the coffee in the dashboard rack, and set the cruller on the pullout tray above the radio. *Just killing time before an eight o'clock install,* she practiced, saying it in her head. *Oh yeah, goes down quick. We'll be in and out in an hour tops. It's good work. Real steady.* At the top of the driveway everything was still. She looked at her watch—7:40. The

doors should open any minute. She had to say it casually. She had
to flirt. But there wouldn't be any police—all of this was backup.
The coffee and newspaper were props, her script was for the
unlikely event that the police happened to cruise Carnegie Lane and
stop to question her. But Theo had it all worked out. It wouldn't
happen, he promised her.

And she went through the lines once more—*eight o'clock install*—trying to hear her voice say it naturally. But when she spoke
she could only hear Theo, coaching her in bed in the grim dusty
room where they slept—the same room Theo had slept in as a
boy—under the rotting eaves of his parents' home.

S tona was late. He'd spent too much time fiddling with his new
ship's clock. But what a beauty. You can take the sailor from the
sea, but you can never take . . . et cetera, et cetera. This was neat. A
ship's clock for the house.

He pressed the garage door button, opened the car, and set his
overcoat and briefcase on the front seat. He started the engine. An
Italian voice blared from the tape deck . . . *"molto piccolo."* He'd been
trying to learn Italian for years. He turned the knob two clicks
down. The clock in the stereo read 7:56. *"Il fratello è molto forte."* He
hated to be late. It was one of the things that mattered—being in
the office before his subordinates. It seemed rather unsubtle to tie it
all to money, but he earned a more generous salary at Petrochem
for a reason—he worked better and harder. He would not coast as
some of the others did. *"La sorella è molto bella."*

You set a standard of attitude and behavior at the top. Then down the line that standard was emulated by management, and before long, right down to the secretaries and janitors you'd find professionalism and competence. Stona would never wear sunglasses, for instance, walking from his car through the lobby into the office. He would never sit in conferences eating pistachios, cracking the shells open like a chipmunk, as one of his colleagues did on a regular basis. Eating pistachios was an affectation. Like zinc oxide on the nose when sailing, half-glasses on anyone under fifty. They were unnecessary markers of a contrived self-image. Vacationing in Turkey, doing yoga (anything to do with India for that matter), solar power, feather beds, wood stoves, expensive cutlery . . . The list was always growing and changing in his mind. Basically, Stona didn't understand what was wrong with the classics.

He backed out of the garage a little faster than usual and swung into the turnaround. It was a sunny morning. In the rearview mirror he watched the familiar quick-spinning pivot of the pines, a flash of the Japanese lantern, and a pan of the house coming to a jerky stop at the front porch. As he shifted into drive, something caught his eye: a glint in the mirror, or was it sunlight reflecting off the lens of his glasses? *"Il padre è molto intelligente."* He looked over his shoulder through the rear window. Water was running off the edge of the porch and down the steps. The garden hose wound from the spigot to the porch. Nunny must have been watering this morning. How unusual for her to leave the water on. To forget like that. Stona hated the waste—the water and the water bill both: $38.58 last month and rising fast with the arrival of summer. Chimes sounded from behind the dash as he popped open his door. He glanced at the clock—7:58. He wouldn't take the extra minute to turn off the water. Nunny would notice in no time. She was very good with those things. He slammed the door and gunned down the drive. *"La madre è molto simpatica."*

When he saw the newspaper on the wrong side of the drive, he decided to let it be. An extra half-minute to stop and walk around the car. There'd be no time to look at it this morning anyway. He had a working lunch, and the afternoon was booked. Marilyn would give him a copy of the media brief at noon. He could leave the paper for Nunny. He pulled the seat belt across his chest, and then he hit the brakes hard. That's right. Haircut at six-thirty. He'd want the paper to keep that barber from chatting him up, the inanity so tiring at the end of a day. *"La famiglia è molto contenta."*

He hurried around the front of the car, pivoting on two fingers pressed to the cool steel hood, slouching as he knew he did when he rushed. He straightened up consciously. He'd always had good posture. He remembered taking Bob Hogel aside when Bob first came on at Petrochem and telling him, "If it cleans out your family fortune, donate your every suit to charity and go to Brooks Brothers and buy five of the most conservative suits they have. Get rid of those tinted glasses, and for God's sake, Bob, stand up straight." Bob was a little stiff at first, but in a week he was a new man and was now VP for International Oil Production.

Stona bent down in the shadow of the car and squeezed his fingers around the newspaper. He noticed a strange noise. Was it his car again? He hunkered lower to listen at the wheel well. He hated to put Nunny through the nonsense of another day at the Mercedes dealership because of a noise they could never diagnose. With one hand holding the newspaper and the fingertips of his other hand on the tire, he turned.

Still crouched, he saw the van first, dark blue with its rear doors open. Then, as if avoiding a swooping bird, he recoiled and would have fallen backwards had he not grabbed the edge of the fender: there was a man between himself and the van. Stona strained his eyes against the sunlight to focus on the man, who seemed to have been standing there a long time, waiting. And it did not occur to Stona—as the man came at him—to be frightened.

Theo was cramped. Damn it to hell. He had staked out Brown six mornings, and he always left the house at 7:45 plus or minus three minutes. Now it was 7:51. This was the kind of frustration the world was dishing out to Theo. Brown didn't have the personality makeup to call in sick. He got sick on vacation or saved it for retirement. Theo knew the type. Maybe Brown had a business trip today. "Make sure he's alone when he comes out. And if a limo shows up, get us out of here."

Wearing gray coveralls like Colleen's, Theo straddled the roll of carpet extending out the back doors to hide the license plate. The ski masks were in his left pocket—black acrylic masks that would cover their entire heads, orange-trimmed holes for the eyes and mouth. His .45 was strapped to his calf in a holster.

Seven fifty-four. He peered around the driver's seat. Colleen's mouth moved like she was saying the rosary. "You look tense," he told her. "You look guilty."

"I'm practicing," she said. "In case of the police."

"Watch the garage door. That's your job. That's your focus. And hold the newspaper up higher on the steering wheel."

Theo knew a bit about cops. Thirteen years on the force stayed in your system. Cops were blue-collar-type guys less apt to hassle people working for a living, like carpet layers in a respectable van, a clean-cut, nice-looking woman. "You should seem bored. Tired of the routine." This was no different from a bust . . . easier really. Collaring a man who's not looking over his shoulder.

Seven fifty-five. In ten minutes they'd scrub it for today. He was sweating now, bad sign, his nerves getting the upper hand. His nerves could take control of what he did: his suspensions from the police force—a shoplifter resisting arrest and the suspect's mother screaming obscenities at Theo, clawing at the sleeve of his uniform, obstructing. It was not until he saw the woman doubled over with her face in her hands, not until he had the kid in cuffs, and noticed the mother's teeth covered in blood, that he'd realized his revolver had come into contact with her face. The same phenomenon—nervous excitement controlling him—had caused the boating accident so many years ago. His father had never forgiven him, and Theo wished he could've explained, but now he'd make it up to his father, make his father proud . . .

"Oh, my God!" Colleen said. "The garage door's moving."

"Start the engine, little girl." Theo felt a rush from the base of his spine—adrenaline for showtime. This was it. He jumped up and threw open the lid of the box. He drew the .45 and went down on one knee behind Colleen's seat.

"Foot on the brake," he whispered, his mouth just inches from her ear. He'd told her not to wear perfume—it was the kind of thing he planned for, the minutiae of perfect preparation. Still, he could smell faint traces of Obsession on her clothes. Well, she wouldn't get that close to Brown. "Mask on." He tugged them from his pocket, and they pulled them over their heads.

Through the windshield he watched Brown's Mercedes back out of the garage and into the turnaround.

"Drop it into drive."

The transmission clunked. In gear now, poised like a panther—nothing would throw him off.

He watched the car, stopped in the turnaround, as he tugged on Colleen's mask, tucking in a few locks of blond hair that flicked out the back. The car crept forward, then suddenly shot ahead. "He's really moving," Theo said. "Now, ease off the brake."

He had timed Brown down the driveway at nine seconds, but he was moving much faster this morning. Theo estimated his speed at twelve miles per hour. Their van was six seconds up the street.

"A little gas now."

The vehicles were converging. It would all happen automatically. The actual moment was beyond Theo's control. He had done the drills, but the outside force that carried him into the zone had taken over.

Brown stopped at the foot of the driveway. He scurried in front of his car, and Colleen hit the gas. Theo went to the rear doors, gun in hand, and released the bungee cords. The rumble of the U-joints and the ping of stones in the wheel wells sounded like noises heard underwater. Insulated, calm . . . The world was pausing for a moment so this one act could expand and fill the space.

"Go!" Colleen said as the tires scraped over sand. Theo slammed out the back. His feet hit the pavement heavy, and immediately he adjusted the picture in his mind. He had seen it a hundred times—the angle of the van, the position of Brown, the distance between the two. Now he adjusted it to reality in less time than it took to take his first stride. Momentum was on his side.

Brown turned from his squat over the newspaper and seemed stunned as Theo's arm shot out and pulled him to his feet. Theo held him by the knot of his tie and pointed the gun at his head.

Already he could see that Brown was older and smaller than he'd thought. This would be tit. "Move, Mr. Brown! Into the van." It was Theo's command voice. He hadn't heard it since he left the force.

Brown resisted, tried to hold his ground like any punk Theo had arrested. And Theo was surprised for a moment—that Brown's face was so disbelieving. Didn't the man know that Theo was in charge now?

"I said *move!*" Theo shook the man so hard his glasses popped off his face.

Theo dragged Brown into the van, pressing the barrel of his gun against Brown's ear. "Go! Go! Go!" Theo shouted, and the van started rolling.

He was hunched over, his head banging on the roof of the van, pulling Brown by the necktie down toward the open plywood box. So easy—it was nearly over. "In the box, Mr. Brown," Theo said. He glanced out the windshield for a second, and Brown spun around. His arm clipped Theo's face. The ski mask twisted over Theo's eyes, his vision was completely blocked. Brown clawed at the hand clenching his tie, and Theo tugged at the mask with his gun hand. Everything was black. Brown kicked him in the shin, then again, and Theo stumbled over the roll of carpet, swinging the metal grip of his gun like a punch. The gun fired. *Nobody gets hurt.* Brown grunted like a man lifting a heavy weight. Colleen screamed. The van swerved. *The perfect plan.* Brown's fingers loosened. Theo yanked off his mask, and Brown was looking at him—an arm's length between them—the two men staring straight at each other; the entire world compressed into the space where their breath collided.

"You shot him!" Colleen. Shrill. "I can't believe you shot him!"

Brown's hand squeezed his forearm, blood seeping between his fingers. And in those few seconds of shock Theo forced him into the box, slammed down the lid, and sat on top while he hooked the latch.

The van halted abruptly—the stop sign at the bottom of Carnegie Lane—and the rear doors bounced against the carpet.

"Why did you have to shoot him?" Colleen pounded the steering wheel.

"I didn't shoot him. The gun discharged. Accidental. Take off your mask. He just got scared. It didn't hit him." Theo desperately wanted to believe he was telling the truth.

"It didn't hit him?" She screeched into traffic on 401.

Theo folded the roll of carpet back into the van, now at full speed, and slammed the doors shut. "He didn't get shot."

"You're sure you didn't shoot him?"

"I know how to handle a weapon." It was the first time he'd shot anyone. As a cop, he'd shot three times and missed.

"It really didn't hit him?"

Brown was shouting angrily, stomping his shoes at the bottom of the box. It was just a flesh wound.

"You hear that? He's fine," Theo said. "Full of piss and vinegar. Nobody shot him."

The faucet handle squeaked when Nunny opened it, and she thought, *That's a squeak everyone knows, the squeak of a garden faucet opening.* She turned it closed, then opened it again, teasing the loose handle back and forth. And how about the squeal of the pulleys when you slide the laundry out on a line? She hadn't had a clothesline for years, but she'd know that squeal in an instant. Some things were universals.

On the front porch Nunny dribbled water into the flowerpots arranged in semicircles around the carriage seats. She liked to water early before the sun got too bright. Holding the hose in the big pot, the cherry tree they had grown from a seed, she looked through the pine trees, past the Japanese lantern and the half-completed rock garden, toward the road. At the foot of the drive she saw a pink flash, a blur at first as she looked into the rising sun. She dropped the hose in the big pot. A bell was ringing. On the road by the mailbox, she could make out a pair of legs scissoring—the body above the waist hidden by the bough of a tree. Then the jogger was gone, and an image rose up from Nunny's past, something buried in her memory. The bell rang again. She threw open the front door and there was Stona down the hall in his study, turning the key at the back of his new brass clock.

Straightening the knot in Stona's tie, Nunny thought, *I love how he loves this tie;* a burgundy foulard, a gift from their son, Victor. She adjusted the hankie in his breast pocket. "Ahoy matey," he said. "The ship's clock is operational as of oh-seven-hundred. Have the eight o'clock watch swab this rust heap stem to stern." A kiss on the lips.

"I love you, Captain," she said. The gentle scent of his lime water aftershave.

"I love you, Admiral."

And a second kiss—never a peck between Stona and Nunny— fleshy and wet, embracing lips. She righted his glasses. As he stepped from the kitchen down through the verandah to the garage, she plucked two stray hairs—longish (he needed a haircut)—from his shoulder. Pinched between her thumb and forefinger, the hairs ribboned across her palm.

These were the rituals of Nunny's life—fixing his tie and hankie, the kiss, *I love you*. Sending him off in the morning, receiving him home at night. A glass of wine on the sun porch after work, dinner at Marcelle's, long walks on weekends.

It made her think of what Stona said about the Catholic Church: its rituals, steeped in tradition and history, were what made it so meaningful. The repetition of prayers. The ringing of bells on the altar. Nunny remembered that as a little girl she'd wanted to be an altar boy, dressed in the starched white smock, kneeling at the feet of the priest ringing the golden bell. She knew she wasn't allowed. She sat stiff in the pew between her parents. Something to do with goodness, sitting up like that, sitting straight.

Still holding Stona's two hairs, she moved through the kitchen, thinking she'd had too much coffee, fluttery hands and heart. As she stepped down to the sun porch, she remembered— no, she'd had only two cups. Maybe she was coming down with something. She picked up the toast rack from the breakfast table, thinking of Stona's heart, when the remains of his grapefruit moved across her field of vision: not that her eyes scanned the table, but that the hollowed-out half of fruit slid across her field of vision. Its color was pink. She closed her hand around Stona's napkin, staring into his grapefruit rind—knife marks inside the skin, cut-down membranes, the meat scraped away. She reached for the saucer with the hand that held his two stray hairs, intending to drop them into the rind, then clear the saucer from the table.

But she stopped. She stared at the pink grapefruit. She knew something was wrong. Sniffing for fire, she walked from the sun porch to the living room. She clicked down a checklist—burners off, nothing in the oven, bath not running. Then she remembered the garden hose and heard the squeak of the faucet inside her head. That was it. The source of her unnamable anxiety. The water left running. She passed Stona's study and sensed the bell inside his new clock still faintly resonating. When she pulled open the front door—standing on the threshold, relieved—she heard water dripping and saw the doormat half soaked as if stained.

She leaped over the puddle on the porch and twisted the nozzle closed. Water specked with potting soil gently flowed over the edge of the big clay pot. Her eyes snaked along the garden hose, down the steps and brick path, then across damp grass to the two birches they'd planted for their two children. Through the pine trees beyond—she couldn't discern the shape or outline, only areas of color between the limbs—she saw the unmistakable green of Stona's car.

A football field away. This was her first thought. It was the way Stona visualized. The practicality of the man. Their drive was a football field long. Forty-one cents per square foot they paid each winter to have it plowed.

She did not run. She stepped over the garden hose, walking very quickly. It was nothing. He was probably talking to Don Stern. That man could chew your ear off given half the chance. But Stona was never late for work. Dear Lord, his heart. Why hadn't they taken the thrombosis more seriously? Was he slumped over the steering wheel? She moved faster, a stiff-legged jog from the hips. There was a stitch in her own heart. A knot tightening. She could see the car clearly now along the curve of the driveway. Stona's door stood open. Did she hear the engine? Not sure. She looked past the car into the street hoping to find him chatting with Don Stern, trying to tear himself away. But he wasn't there. She was running now. Any moment his head would pop up. Pulling up weeds or a problem with the car. Tromping through the bushes for the newspaper. How many times had that happened? That damn delivery boy. A man, really. Coming to the house at Christmas and requesting a tip.

She ran faster, becoming angry. Stona did not have time to bushwhack for his paper on the way to work.

The engine *was* running. A liquid heat cloud of exhaust. She touched the trunk of the car with her fingertips, Stona's napkin still twisted in her palm. *Not* slumped over the steering wheel. Down on the seat? No. Not there. "Stona," she spoke. She heard it, her own voice mixing with the sound of the engine and birds with scratchy calls. In front of the car now—he'd be down, fallen to the pavement. "Stona!" Her voice sounded farther off this time. Another cloud of heat rising from the hood, her hand and the napkin dragging along the metal. Around to the far side of the car, and he wasn't there. But the newspaper was. And his glasses! They lay on the drive beside the tire, lenses facing down, temples pointing up.

Nunny rounded back to his door, and with the napkin open in her hand turned off the ignition and pulled out the keys. Stona's overcoat was folded on the passenger seat. His briefcase was on the floor. His commuter cup was on the dash—the steam lapping quickly disappearing shapes on the windshield. His Italian lesson was playing on the tape deck, and his lime water aftershave lingered in the car.

With his keys wrapped like jewels in the napkin, she ran up the drive, splashed through the water on the brick path, and bounded up the porch. Her hips tightened as she ran in wet slippers across the marble tiles in the front hall and turned sharply into his study. From his phone she first called the police, and then the Code Blue number at Petrochem. She called Jane and woke her up, and left a message at Victor's office. She told them all the same thing: "Stona has been kidnapped. Hurry!"

Then she sat down sideways in his desk chair and pulled her knees to her chest, her wet slippers on the seat. She buried her face in the back of the chair where he had rested his head. The smell of his scalp was the smell of love. Then Nunny realized she was still holding the two hairs she'd plucked from the shoulder of his suit coat. She drew them between her thumb and forefinger, and she began to wait.

A red-hot spike pounded into Stona's arm. He had given up struggling before he'd felt the pain, baffled that a bullet could pass through his forearm, then clatter like spilled coins on the metal floor of the van. He would have vomited from the pain had his body not shut down. His heart and breath, his digestion and his mind slowed to the torpor of sleep. A deep freeze crept over him.

After they raced away from Stona's house, the lid of the coffin-like box opened, and now the man, wearing the black mask again, was pointing his gun at Stona, warning him not to resist. Stona's ears still rang with the gunshot. He could still feel the man's grip at his throat. And he could still see the man's face—a large meaty face, small eyes, and coarse skin. He had deep pores around his nose, very little color in his lips . . .

Stona knew the man. He had seen him before, more than once, but without the beard. And now, as the man taped Stona's eyes and mouth closed, Stona remembered the gunshot again, the man pulling off his mask. He was certain he knew him. The man handcuffed Stona's wrists, bound his ankles and legs with tape; then Stona felt the lid of the box close down again.

The van stopped. The man and woman moved around inside, doors slammed. Then nothing. Stona heard voices and cars starting. They were in a parking lot.

Time passed before they drove on. The lid of the box opened— fresh air filled his lungs, light seeped around the tape covering his eyes. It was the woman this time, whose perfume smelled like running into CVS for a birthday card or a bottle of aspirin. He listened as scissors cut through the cloth of his suit coat and shirt; then his sleeve was pulled away from the elbow. She poked at the wound with something cold that sizzled on his flesh. She wrapped his arm with gauze, patted it when she was finished. "There there," she said, as if she'd slipped a thermometer from under his tongue and pressed a cool washcloth to his forehead. Stona hoped with all his heart that after she was arrested and convicted and in prison, when a guard finished raping her and she was bleeding, the guard would kick her aside and say tenderly, "There there."

Then the lid of the box was closed down on Stona again. He was bound inside it, his body buzzing at highway speed. The hole in his arm tearing larger under the bandage with each bump and sway. He was cold. The box felt like a freezer. He couldn't get a breath of the frosted air curling around him. Inside his chest, the valves of his heart creaked like frozen knuckles. His blood hissed with a chill through his body, spitting through the thin gauze wrapped around his arm. His arm was throbbing. Infection. It would spread past his elbow to his shoulder. Amputation. There was a scream locked inside the box with him, growing so large that in the darkness he could see it. His heart was too weak. Would he die like this, bound inside a box? His heart clenched tighter. The tape stuck to his eyelids, pulling them away from his eyeballs, which were drying out, which he couldn't moisten even by rolling his eyes wildly, madly. Lunacy. If only he could vomit, he'd choke and they'd have to release him . . .

And then a beep. The double beep of Stona's watch on the hour—merciful and mundane. The scream vanished. He heard his struggling breath, felt a healthy heartbeat preceding each throb in his arm. He began to weep, syrupy soothing tears washing over his eyes. He was handcuffed and wrapped like a mummy. He could not see the bullet wound, nor open his mouth for a gulp of air. He was locked in a box, but his watch had beeped with such normalcy he knew he would live.

Unless he'd been unconscious, it was nine o'clock. The seven o'clock beep had come as he finished his toe touches. The eight o'clock beep came just after the bullet—the echo of the gunshot bouncing off the sides of the van, the bullet rolling around on the floor, the woman racing down the street yelling hysterically, the rumble of the engine curling up through the open doors with the exhaust.

Stona had not seen the woman's face, but he was sure he knew the man. He held the picture in his mind. This afternoon a police artist would draw a likeness that would make tomorrow's papers, and the sons of bitches would be hunted down. He would scour photographs of people with whom he came into contact. In his mind he would walk through his days, examining every face. He would find that face. The money would be recovered.

It was insurance company money, he knew. Petrochem executives were good for twenty or thirty million, but out of principle

Stona wanted the money returned. He wanted these swine in prison. The man had shouted something about environmental crimes, but Stona knew he was lying. He'd been kidnapped for money.

Although Stona had never dealt directly with environmental radicals, whether they were Greenpeace or Earth First, they tended to be a class of people who could have made something of their lives, but for one reason or another they'd ended up failures or academics or journalists. Their politics were sour grapes. That was not these two. These two were all about greed. She was certainly his wife. Stona couldn't decipher a word through the box, but the rhythm and urgency of arguing, ordering, accusing, betrayed the dynamics of marriage. The man smelled of a horribly spicy stick deodorant and Irish Spring soap. Stona knew the smell. For a while, he and Nunny had—

Oh, Lord. Nunny. How was she taking this? Surely, she and half the street had heard the gunshot and the commotion. Did someone get the license plate? Were the police trailing the van this moment? Setting up a roadblock around the next bend in the highway? It wouldn't be long now. Whether they'd be forced to the side of the road by a fleet of cruisers and a helicopter, or whether they were driving now to pick up a briefcase of cash, it wouldn't be long. Jane would be with her mother now. Rock-solid. What a head on that girl. Nunny would make it fine if Jane could distract her. She could be too easily affected by emotion, the poet in her. Just a few more hours. Could he stand it that long? The burning in his arm and the deadly chill through the rest of him. Panting through the tape over his mouth.

It was quarter past nine by now. Fifteen minutes since he thought he was losing his mind. There would be the ten o'clock beep. And, realistically, two more. But that would be it. By one he'd be in a warm hospital bed. Nunny and the kids would be there, Foster and Sanford from the office. Bradford Ross from Petrochem security. Police, FBI, the press. He'd play it all down. He'd been shot, for goodness' sake. No one would expect that. He'd never been shot before. He'd never hit a man or ducked to avoid a blow. And he'd done all those things today. *His swings at my head with the butt of his gun were telegraphed.* That wasn't how it was phrased. *He telegraphed his blows, and I ducked.* He wanted to say it right, or would the reporters fix up his quotes as usual anyway? He would thank God and Nunny and everyone. He'd have a sling and a scar. He'd completely recover. Although he was shivering in the box and his mind was slurring his thoughts, although he'd been shot in the arm and was struggling for each breath, life had not ended or even changed. He'd take a vacation day tomorrow. There were things to look forward to. He could make it till one o'clock.

The storage locker—a little larger than a one-car garage—had trapped the cold night air. Colleen stood by the door, which they'd left open a few inches. A band of sunlight shone off her white tennis shoes. In the center of the unit, Mr. Brown stood in the open box, supported by Theo, who spoke gently: "I'm going to take the tape off your mouth, and it's important that you don't make a sound. It's important you don't speak. You won't be hurt."

Colleen was afraid of what they had done. The perfect plan worked out between the two of them, lying in bed whispering in Theo's childhood room, had seemed flawless and instant. But now she was standing with a ski mask over her head and watching her husband remove duct tape from the mouth of a man nearly the age that her father would be. Now there was the reality of this man they had put in handcuffs and wound with tape, a man her husband had shot in the arm. She'd had to run into a drugstore, she couldn't even think of what to buy. She'd had to cut the sleeves off his suit coat and shirt while Theo drove. She'd tried to clean the bullet hole in his forearm—not even a hole but a mess of tattered flesh. "Apply pressure," Theo had kept repeating, looking back over his shoulder, but the bleeding wouldn't stop. Each time she released the pressure, blood seeped from under the soaked gauze.

"I'll need you." Theo's voice startled her. "Over here."

She had wrapped his arm around and around with a bandage, and finally the bleeding had seemed to stop. He'd bled for at least an hour. It was hard to know the quantity. A pint? Two? His suit was stained. Ruined. She hadn't thought anything would be ruined.

"Close it all the way," Theo said, and Colleen stepped on the handle of the steel garage door and pushed it tight to the concrete floor. The battery-powered lantern gave off white, almost silver, light. In Theo's plan it was only an annoyance in Mr. Brown's day, a shift of actuarial figures in the insurance company's books. The three of them stood together, and Theo slowly peeled the tape from Mr. Brown's eyes. Blinking and squinting, he twisted his head toward Theo, then Colleen. His breath quickened. He grunted—

"Quiet," Theo cut him off.

But he still made noises like the gasps and moans of tortured sleep. The way he squinted, Colleen realized he must wear glasses. Had they fallen off in the van? How awful to lose the man's glasses.

Mr. Brown looked down at the bullet wound, and in trying to raise his arm to see it, he pulled against the handcuffs and tape. Fresh blood seeped from the gauze. Colleen laid a hand on his shoulder and said, "Most important is relaxation," but when she touched the skin on his arm, she gasped. She looked to Theo. *He's so cold,* she mouthed. *Freezing.*

"It's a mild shock, Mr. Brown," Theo said confidently. "Completely normal. What you're experiencing."

Mr. Brown panted. Again he tried to speak, but Colleen couldn't decipher a word.

"We just have one thing to do, then we'll get you taken care of double-time," Theo said, and he handed Colleen the microcassette recorder. Mr. Brown's face was pasty and damp. He was shivering. His breathing had no rhythm.

Colleen felt herself beginning to panic. Theo had shot a man. He should be in the hospital. She focused on the circle of her breath, trying to remain calm.

"Mr. Brown," Theo began. "We are representatives of the Rainbow Warriors." He held up a sheet of paper. "We'll need you to read a statement." Mr. Brown tipped his head toward the paper, but then his chin dropped to his chest. Colleen touched the back of his neck. His skin felt like a steak just out of the fridge.

"We need to get him warm," she said. The comforters were in the bottom of the box, two of them. "Lift him up," she told Theo. She slipped one of the comforters out from under Mr. Brown's feet and wrapped it around his shoulders.

Theo was getting impatient. His lips pursed through the orange-trimmed hole in the mask. Hairs from that awful beard spiked through the black acrylic weave. She held the tape recorder below Mr. Brown's mouth. A dank cold sweat—like the smell of Theo's parents' basement—came off the man.

"Okay, let's go," Theo said. "Mr. Brown, you'll read the paper on cue. . . . And set?" Colleen nodded to Theo. "Begin."

Colleen hit Record with her thumb. Mr. Brown dipped his head closer to the paper, squinting. He rocked forward and Theo held him up. His voice cracked. "Let . . . me . . . go."

"Stop," Theo said.

Mr. Brown looked at Colleen in her mask. He was a man whose nostril hairs and eyebrows were trimmed. Despite its pastiness at the moment, his skin had a healthy golf course glow. His hair was vibrant and black and maintained. He looked at her with his squinted eyes, and she could tell he was not a man used to being helpless. He leaned toward her, and said quietly, "Let . . . go of me, bitch."

"Okay, that's enough!" Theo pulled Mr. Brown away from her by the collar. "The quicker you read this, the quicker we get you out of here."

"My glasses . . . idiot."

"Where's his glasses?" Colleen said. "Are they in the van?"

"In my driveway."

"He needs them," Colleen said.

"The hospital."

"Double-time," Theo said. "They'll take you when we're done."

"My heart . . ."

"Don't try to tell me." Theo's jaw clenched and his voice rose. "*I* tell *you*, is how this works. You've got a mild shock, which I've seen plenty of."

Colleen lifted the comforter tighter around Mr. Brown's neck, tugging at it as if straightening his coat. Draped in the old comforter he looked smaller, less powerful.

"Please," Mr. Brown said, and Colleen knew they had to move quickly. They had to make this tape and get him to a hospital. The plan had been to drop him by the convention center in Newark, where the streets were deserted at night and it would take him some time to find a phone. But they could just as safely drop him around the block from Samaritan Hospital.

Theo held the paper inches from Mr. Brown's face.

"Can you read it like that?" Colleen asked. "Up close."

He leaned his face closer. Touched his nose to the paper. "This is Stona Brown," he read. "I'm . . . I'm being held—"

"Good," Theo said. "Start the tape."

Colleen pushed record.

"This is Stona Brown. I'm being held by the . . ." He cocked his head. ". . . the Rainbow Warriors for my crimes against the environment. If at any time . . ." Then he collapsed.

Theo reached out the window of the van with the magnetic card that opened the gate. They hadn't had a gate since Hilton Head. They hadn't had a proper home since Hilton Head. Colleen's hands were shaking.

"Even a flesh wound, there's some shock. Police officers, guys I know personally, they got shot, and the body goes through trauma. It's an involuntary response."

"But he looked so *awful*."

"And these were younger and stronger men. Nothing can be done."

"I know, but—"

"If you know, then you know it's normal. Who was a cop for thirteen-plus years? Who's had the training? Who's a step ahead? Who *knows*?"

She was silent.

"That's right. Pale. Sweaty. Disoriented. Confused." He ticked them off on his fingers. "Symptoms of mild shock. It's not the bullet wound per se. Just the body's reaction. Shortness of breath. You didn't know I checked his pulse. A little weak, but rapid. I could go on. Anxiety, depression. Textbook case. I'm on top of it."

When the gate swung open, they rolled past the sign for American Mini-Storage: a fierce bald eagle clutching a padlock and an American flag in its talons. Should they have left him there like that? Wrapped with tape, locked in the box. Had they done the right thing? She trusted Theo, but she also was learning to trust herself. Her stomach had turned sour.

"It's just, I don't think I'll feel better till he's in the hospital," Colleen said.

"This is my meaning, exactly. We'll all feel better. But I've taken measures. I know how to treat for shock. Stop the bleeding, accomplished. Keep him warm, he's cozy. Plenty of rest and fluids, he'll get them—"

"Okay," she cut him off, her voice sharp. The swampy warning signs of a panic attack bubbled up from her stomach and through her chest.

They sped along the Parkway. Theo gulped down the cold Dunkin' Donuts coffee and started snapping off chips from the lip of the Styrofoam cup set between his thighs. The plan had been to get the tape with the payment instructions delivered by noon so the insurance company could pull together the cash before tonight. But Colleen knew, as she watched Theo break down the sides of the cup, he was already considering whether Mr. Brown would come out of shock in time to make a tape. He was working through their contingency plan. After the last couple hours, Colleen could barely think at all. The only way through this, she knew, was to let Theo take control.

At the carpool lot their car was parked where they'd left it beside the pay phone. Colleen's initials were spelled in nautical flags on the bumper. They'd owned his-and-hers white Mercedes in Hilton Head, but now they were down to hers.

Still wearing gloves, Colleen brushed bits of styrofoam and doughnut crumbs off the driver's seat. God, she hoped they'd done the right thing. In the back of the van she swept out slivers of plywood and shavings of blue paint where the box had scraped the metal.

Theo took the broom, snapped the handle over his knee, and dropped it in the garbage barrel. Colleen waited in the Mercedes while he opened the hood of the van and yanked out the wire that powered the engine fan.

Over the rush of cars on the Parkway, and the smell of blacktop and exhaust, she listened to Theo at the pay phone chewing out the clerk at Garden State Rentals: "It's been overheating all morning. No, I'm through with it. No. The keys are under the mat. You come get it." He hung up the phone, squinting against the sun, flashing Colleen a smile.

The house was full of men. Nunny moved between them as if moving between men on the railroad platform in Sorrento. Men standing around and waiting. The strange insistent odors of men. She moved through the dining room—the Queen Anne table covered with tape-recording equipment, headphones, maps, and files, telephones lined up like an office. She moved past a young policeman in uniform, his face still shiny from shaving. He jumped out of her way— "Excuse me, ma'am," the leather squeak of his gun belt, the smell of his spearmint gum. She moved through the smells of the other men, smells of bacon and eggs escaping from their coats and mouths, of cigarette smoke, aftershave, acrylic and metal. She pushed through to the kitchen.

"We need a case of Coca-Cola from the basement," she said to Jane.

"You should sit down, Mother."

"And in the meat freezer there's bags of ice."

"If a phone call comes, you should be ready." Wearing sweatpants and running shoes, a black turtleneck, and silver button earrings from her fiancé, Jane stood on a chair and searched through the cupboard above the microwave for ashtrays. Her brown hair was pulled back in a pink and white scrunchie. The microwave clock read 10:49. Nearly three hours and still no call. Nothing.

Nunny pushed a tumbler against the ice dispenser in the door of the fridge. She filled the glass and dumped the cubes into an ice bucket and filled the glass again, the groaning motor spitting out fewer and fewer cubes. "We'll definitely need a bag from downstairs."

The cupboard door clapped shut, and Jane stepped down from the chair with a stack of brightly colored ashtrays that Nunny hadn't seen in years. They'd quit smoking in the mid-seventies. There was a cartoon golfer in tartan knickers on each one, and jokes about slices, sand traps, or the nineteenth hole—jokes that Stona had found so charming he bought the whole set. "Yes, lay them out," she told her daughter, and an empty groan sounded from the ice dispenser. "Then the ice. Better bring two bags."

Instead of distributing the ashtrays, Jane set the stack on the counter, opened her arms to Nunny and hugged her. "I know you'll handle this however you need to, Mother, but if you just sit down you'll be ready." Nunny was looking over Jane's shoulder at the ashtray on top of the stack—feathers flying as the knock-kneed Scotsman's drive beaned a pigeon in flight. Written below was something about hitting a birdie. Suddenly she could see Stona—his cautious laugh and honest eyes—sipping a vodka tonic and poking out a cigarette in that ashtray twenty years ago.

"We'll make it, sweetheart," Nunny said. Her daughter's hug was the hug of a woman, not a girl.

Jane slowly stepped back from her mother, took up the stack of ashtrays—a hollow ceramic clatter—and pushed through the swinging door to the dining room. As the door flapped back and forth, Nunny still felt Jane's arms across her back, she smelled her daughter's hair, felt Jane's body pressed into her own. It brought her back to a time when Jane always turned to her to dry tears, bandage scrapes, or soothe hurt feelings. Jane had depended on Nunny in a way that Victor never had.

Now, Nunny wrapped her own arms around herself, one hand touching her collar and the other at her abdomen as she listened to Jane's voice in the living room. It rang above the hushed voices of the men, above the scratch of radio static and the squeal of tape yanked from a roll, the beep of strange telephones, and the weighty sound of heavy shoes. She was struck by the complete foreignness of the sounds in the household she had run for twenty-seven years—dinner parties, birthday parties, sleepovers, receiving hours for Stona's father and a year later for Binny. She had stood in this kitchen for years, sensing her guests in the house, familiar with their sounds. Her home was a part of her and its sounds were harmonious with the rhythm of her own body. But the sounds today were strange, unexpected—wrong in pitch, in tone.

As Jane's imprint lifted from Nunny, as Nunny's body cooled, she felt pain in her breast and tried to breathe it away—phantom pain in her left breast, the one they'd removed. The masseuse at the spa had told her to breathe over the pain. Or through it. To rinse the area with breath until the pain dissipated. She laid her hands flat on the counter and stood straight. A deep breath, eyes shut. Do not cave in to the pain, but open the chest. Open.

She touched her forehead, then her cheeks, like feeling for fever. She pressed on her chest, her ribs, then she moved her hand through the pain that hovered like electricity in front of her body and laid it firmly over her heart.

The bell startled her. The ringing was familiar even though she couldn't place it. She was looking at the kitchen counter, at the pink tiles along the edge, and she suddenly remembered. Stona's ship's clock had been ringing. How could she have forgotten? With the phantom pain fading, she dropped the ice bucket on the counter and hurried into the dining room through the crowd of men and a cloud of cigarette smoke, a young man's hand waving to disperse the smoke as if sweeping Nunny a path. Bradford Ross, the head of security at Petrochem, was leaning on his fist against the windowsill. "There *is* something," Nunny said as she reached the window. "There's something I didn't mention."

Bradford Ross squared himself to Nunny as if to hear her better. He held up a finger, and the two detectives who had questioned her earlier, as well as the police chief and the insurance man, gathered around her in a loose semicircle. "I was out front watering, and someone jogged by, an odd stride. Awkward. Was it a woman? I think so, yes. Pink jogging pants. She paused right at the foot of our drive. While he was setting his new clock."

"What about her face?" Bradford Ross asked her, the men scribbling in notebooks. "Her hair?"

"There were only the legs."

The men stopped writing.

"Did you see a vehicle?" asked Dave Tomkins, the chief of police.

"Have you seen her before? Anywhere? Was she alone?" Bradford Ross touched Nunny's elbow.

She closed her eyes. She saw only the legs, the pink flash through the leaves, the jerky stride, frighteningly familiar. She saw the trickle of water on the steps. She heard the scratch of birds and the bell. The ringing of Stona's ship's clock.

Nunny opened her eyes to the faces of the men, looking at her expectantly, pens halted over little pads, radios fastened to hips, wires snaking from ears, guns bulging under suit coats, and she realized they were completely helpless.

They had only two leads: a few scrapes of blue automobile paint on the road and a tire tread in the dirt beside the mailbox. They'd taken a plaster mold. They'd identified the tire. It belonged to a van or a pickup. They'd start, Dave Tomkins told her, with stolen vehicles, then rentals. He had five detectives on it. For two hours men, dogs, and machines had searched the drive, the yard, the street. They dusted Stona's car for fingerprints. They questioned the neighbors. Nothing. They had essentially nothing. They hadn't told Nunny this, but she knew. From their expectant, forward-tilting heads, from the eager pitch of their pens, she knew that just like her, they were waiting for the phone call. And until then, they were only waiting.

Malcolm held a firm grip on the railing while he caught his breath. Across the cellar, on the other side of the furnace, Theo was hunched over his family's cartons of belongings. Theo's figure seemed to shift from side to side as the bare lightbulb swung above him. The pull chain ticked on the frosted glass. Taking a shallow breath, Malcolm let go of the railing. "What do you need, son?"

Theo jerked around. "Chrissake! You don't sneak up on a guy."

Malcolm ducked under a low asbestos-wrapped pipe, pulling the invisible threads of a cobweb from his face. He coughed up phlegm and spit in the bucket half full of swampy water below the bleed valve at the base of the furnace. "I would've thought you'd heard me on the stairs, huffing and puffing the way I do. These damn lungs."

Theo turned back to rummaging through the cartons. "So how'd they like that life jacket locker?" Malcolm asked him.

"They loved it," Theo answered without turning around. "Said for their purposes it was perfect. Strong and simple. I know you could've made something prettier, but for this kind of thing they don't need fine furniture."

"That's good then." Malcolm cleared his throat. "There *was something*," he said as Theo pressed flower-print ruffles of cloth to his face. "Something I wanted to talk to you about."

"Jesus. Colleen'll be bullshit about these pillow shams. Totally mildewed."

"Nothing a little airing on the line won't fix." Maybe this wasn't the best time to discuss matters with Theo, but if not now, when? "The thing is is—"

"Oh, no!" Theo had popped open another box. "No, no, no." He flung a magazine, its pages chattering open as it flew across the cellar and hit the asbestos insulation. Fine white powder sprinkled to the floor.

"My *Sail* magazine collection. Four years. Totally ruined! Everything down here is wet." With a box in his arms Theo turned angrily toward Malcolm. "You know, we put stuff down here because the rest of the house is so dusty. Plus the cigarette smoke."

No. Now was not the time to discuss matters. Theo dumped the glossy magazines onto the floor and sent the empty carton tumbling into the corner; then he ripped open another one.

"What is it you're looking for? Is it something I might have upstairs?"

Theo tore through extension cords and telephone wire, barely taking notice as an electric pencil sharpener fell to the concrete floor, shattering its plastic top. Malcolm's son was a man without respect for the value of a thing.

Malcolm didn't want to make a big deal. He just wanted to explain to his son about the CDs and the IRAs. He wanted Theo to know about the stocks and his share of the fishing cabin. Any week now Malcolm could go the way of Raymond Kowalski: they'd shove a tube up his nose and another in his arm, put him in a nightgown under a plastic tent, wait for his lungs to shut down tight.

"How'd that van run?" Malcolm asked his son. "Any power?"

"Yeah. Good, Pop." Theo pulled a telephone from the tangle of cords.

"Sounded like the four-point-two-liter engine. Not worth much if you're hauling a load. People think they'll get better mileage dropping down to a V-6, but I don't believe it. Not if the vehicle is underpowered."

"It ran fine."

There was a time Theo had an interest in cars. But now, unemployed and without responsibilities, Theo was losing his drive for living. Malcolm was desperate to see the boy in a job before he died.

"I heard a two-oh-seven come over the scanner," Malcolm said, pressing two fingers on the brittle insulation. Theo dropped the phone. "Over Asherton. Sounds big," Malcolm continued. He couldn't leave this asbestos for Dot to contend with. One more task before he died. "Petrochem security was all over the scanner too. More than likely it's one of their people."

"They onto anybody?" Theo said. Malcolm looked down from the pipe, and Theo was facing him. "Are the Feds in yet?"

"Not that I heard. They're still trying to find which way their butts are pointing. Calling it a missing persons, but I can't think anybody believes that."

"Any leads?" A nonchalance had settled over Theo's voice. He calmly folded his arms across his chest. He rocked on his feet. Malcolm leaned the heel of his hand into the pipe elbowing between them. A rare moment with Malcolm and Theo: two men talking.

"Didn't sound like it. But Dave Tomkins is at the scene. Do you remember any higher-ups at Petrochem living on a Carnegie Lane?" Police work was something they could always talk about. Theo had seemed so promising those first years on the force.

"No leads, then?"

"Tell you what. We'll get Dave Tomkins by for coffee and pick his brain—"

"Don't do that! No." Theo ducked under the pipe. "I'm much too busy. This yacht club thing falls through or flies big-time next couple days." He was halfway up the stairs with two pillows clamped under his arm.

"Don't you want to repack your things?" What had been neatly stacked cartons now looked like a Salvation Army drop-off.

"All I want is these pillows. Colleen needs them to prop herself up in bed to read. She can't take the smoke in the living room. The rest of it can go to the dump."

Malcolm watched the floor joists give as Theo pounded across the kitchen.

He stood alone in the cellar adding up how many feet of asbestos he was dealing with. The discussion with Theo of financial matters couldn't wait more than a few days. If only Malcolm's own father had been a little more explicit before he died, if he'd just taken the time.

Malcolm ducked around the far side of the furnace and picked up Theo's magazine from the slab. The magazine had punctured the insulation's paper shell, exposing the powdery corrugation inside. Malcolm would take care of it. After fifty-plus years of smoking, a little asbestos wasn't going to make any difference now.

He had to do something about the back steps too. He thought he might sweep up Theo's mess in the shed and see if he could use the scrap to shim the stringers, just rig the steps for now and cheat another year out of them. He wondered what they were getting for vertical-grain stair tread these days.

Malcolm stood among Theo's belongings—towels, blankets, a camera, pot holders decorated with nautical flags—all lying in a heap on the damp slab. He took a breath, deeper than he could usually get—must have been the cool cellar air—so he lit a cigarette and held it in his lips, letting the thinnest traces of smoke seep in with his breath. The nicotine enlivened him. He went down on a knee and started putting things back in their boxes.

This kidnapping would be fun to sit up late talking about with Theo, who was never as busy as he said he was. Policing didn't leave a man. They'd discuss the case, all the angles. Just the thought of it brought Malcolm back to busy days, father and son in uniform, out in the world, making things happen. And Malcolm had to admit, as he picked up pieces of the electric pencil sharpener, that before they plugged him up with tubes and started waiting for him to die, he wanted a good talk or two with his son.

When Theo came up from the cellar, he and Colleen went back to American Mini-Storage with the pillows. Theo sat Brown up in the box, and Colleen held a bottle of spring water to his lips. The man drank the entire liter. Evian. A buck eighty-nine. He'd be all right. His body temperature had risen to normal. His breathing was steady. Theo tried to record a tape, but Brown was still too disoriented.

Before he locked Brown back up, he rewrapped the duct tape more loosely around the injured area and elevated the arm on a pillow. With another pillow he propped up Brown's feet, then covered him with a comforter. Treating for shock was a no-brainer. By later this afternoon, he'd be his old self.

They drove back to the house, and Colleen got in the bath. His parents were out running errands, so Theo dashed up to their bedroom and turned on the scanner. He sat on his father's side of the bed, watching the lights run through the channels. A smell like the river in summer rose from the blankets and pillow—damp, heavy, pleasant, and tinged with something sharper like gasoline. This had always been the smell of his father, and Theo had come to associate it with humid summer afternoons, the two of them side by side, boating on the river as if the day could go on forever.

For ten minutes he listened to the police radio. There were three transmissions about the kidnapping. All routine. The cops didn't have a clue.

Downstairs, he paced through the kitchen and out to the breezeway. Theo hated waiting. He looked out through the screen at the thick grass. He'd been meaning to cut it for weeks, to help his father out. But damn. It was already past noon. The plan was to get the ransom tonight at Riverside Marina, which would be packed with the Memorial Day weekend crowd out to see the flame-jumpers. If Brown didn't pull out of shock so Theo could record a tape by two o'clock, they'd have to go to the backup plan. Theo swatted at the corroded screen. Maybe he'd mow the lawn.

In the kitchen he stared into the fridge at a tub of leftover pierogies, milk that nobody drank, ketchup, a head of lettuce, cans of Ensure lined up in the door, Slim-Fast on the bottom shelf, a jar of dill pickles . . . He let the door swing shut. God, he hated to wait. Whenever traffic stopped dead, Theo was the first driver to shut off his engine and get out of the car. He'd lean on the front fender, arms folded over his chest, until another man got out of another car. Then he'd walk over to commiserate. Theo could always strike up something with a stranger, find some common ground.

In the living room, next to a shelf with snapshots of Tiffany and Brook in Vail, there were two shelves of his mother's Hummels. Dozens of them. Worth hundreds. A little porcelain choir girl, a boy throwing a stick for his terrier, arranged just the way they were twenty-five years ago. Theo shook his head thinking how many times she'd lifted each one to dust it and set it back. The futility.

As he turned a Hummel over in his hand—a barefoot boy fishing off a bridge—he heard Colleen's bathwater clatter down the pipes. He put the figurine back in its spot, then lay down on the couch and clicked through the possible variations in the plan one more time. Brown had tossed a turd in the punch bowl getting himself shot, but the plan was adaptable. The glitches were tiny blips. The soundness of the plan was bigger than a few mishaps. If Brown wanted to slow things down a day, it was no skin off Theo's teeth. Theo had built in a margin of flexibility. Variations were accounted for. It was the point of his preparation. Separated the pros.

Colleen's bathwater was still draining when she came down the stairs in her robe, her hair up in a towel. "Has to be Sunday night," he said in a low voice, linking his fingers behind his head. "Has to be."

"I hate to think," she said, her face flushed from the bath, her cheeks and forehead oily with lotion.

If Brown hadn't gotten shot, he'd have been released tonight. But tomorrow night the marina was having a classical music concert, which it didn't take a rocket scientist to figure out was no diversion. If not the flame-jumpers tonight, it would have to be the Blue Angels flyover, Sunday night at ten.

Colleen paced the length of the couch, back and forth in tiny steps, wrapping her robe more tightly and cinching the belt. "It's just I'm so worried. His condition—"

Heavy steps pounded across the breezeway and through the kitchen door. Colleen stood still. Halfway across the living room, in front of the buffet crowded with more family photos, Tiffany suddenly sensed her parents and glanced over her shoulder. "Oh," she said, and kept walking toward her room.

"Why are you home so early?" Colleen sat on the edge of Theo's mother's chair, her knees pressed together, her hands clutching the robe at her throat.

Tiffany stopped. "Guess what? Erica got a job at the mall, so we're going to pool our savings and take a trip at the end of the summer to Saskatchewan." She fingered the hair hanging over her eyes until she found a split end. "Anyway, you're home before I am."

"Did you go to all your classes?" Theo said.

"I'm working from three to five-thirty." She ripped the strand of hair up the middle.

"Stop that!" Colleen snapped, then softened. "Sweetheart."

Through the dry hair hanging in her face, Tiffany eyed her mother's robe and towel. She fidgeted with the big clacking beads around her neck. "Maybe it's just me, but does it seem weird that you guys take baths all afternoon? I mean, don't like most adults usually have jobs?"

"That's enough, young lady," Theo said.

"Hello. I'm not being confrontational. It's just I know we never mention it or something, but I'm perceiving a certain financial crisis, and I was discussing with Erica today that you should grow hemp."

"Honey," Colleen burst out. "You're not."

"What?"

"Smoking . . . grass?"

Tiffany laughed. "No, Mom. But groovy. Mellow yellow."

"Happens to be illegal," Theo said.

"It's the most totally random law. And it's hemp, not pot.

You'd have to smoke about a thousand joints to catch a buzz. Which, by the way, turpentine isn't illegal, but a couple whiffs—"

"Did you have lunch?" Colleen interrupted. "Can I fix you something?"

"I'll eat at work." Tiffany worked the counter at Joey's Tacos after school and weekends. Despite her claims that she ate at Joey's, Theo didn't believe her. Her hipbone seemed to protrude through her stretchy black pants, skintight except at the bottom, where they flared out above her chunky-heeled black shoes. Eighty-nine bucks at the Kenneth Cole outlet in Estes Park. But what was money for if not to spend it on your kids? Especially for quality shoes. Tiffany ground the edge of her heel into the carpet like she was trying to make a hole. "Hemp is the oldest crop in the world," she said. "It's our only hope. The planet's, I mean."

"We weren't really planning on being farmers," Colleen said, the towel around her head beginning to unravel. "Do you have homework?"

"All the multinationals are getting in on hemp. They're keeping it illegal until the corporations can get geared up to grow it and cut the farmers out. That's the point. It's never the farmers."

Colleen retucked the corner of the towel at the nape of her neck. "Don't you want a bite to eat? You look a little pale."

"Oy," Tiffany said.

"Don't talk like that," Theo said to her back as she clomped into the den, which for now was her bedroom, and closed the door.

He looked at Colleen. She lay back sideways in the chair, exasperated, pulling her knees to her chest. She closed her eyes. When the money came through, Theo would take care of it all. He was a man who did the right thing. He would pay for Tiffany's and Brook's educations and help them get started in careers. No more daughter of his working in a taco shop. He'd torch this ratty house and set his parents up in a brand-new fully serviced condo. And the things he'd buy Colleen—a Cartier watch, getaways to Paris where she'd be pampered, a new wedding ring that reflected who they'd become and not who they'd been at age twenty. She'd forget all her money anxieties, forget about selling GoodLife products. He'd provide his wife with true financial security, as any man should. And give his family nothing but the finest.

It baffled Theo how some rich people didn't spend their money. What was the point? Or why some people chose careers that they knew were financial dead ends. He knew personally of an elementary school teacher who was easily smart enough to do something more lucrative. Fear and lack of self-confidence caused people to limit their success and pleasure. In Vail, when their sex life fell off for the first time in their marriage, Colleen had said she was "too vulnerable for sex." What did that even *mean*? If she was anxious or stressed and she had a husband who loved her and was happy to fulfill her every request, why deny herself?

Colleen's breathing became heavy. She'd slept like hell the last three or four nights. She didn't have the constitution for a plan so expansive. Stress got the best of her.

But Theo knew that Brown was recovering. The wound was clean and bandaged. He'd had plenty of fluids. He was resting.

Theo shook her foot. "Why don't you go up and lie down. Nothing to be done but wait."

Maybe he'd mow the lawn.

On the breezeway his father's work boots stood behind the couch on a newspaper crinkled with salt residue from the winter. Stupid to ruin his Tretorns with grass stains the very last time in his life he would mow a lawn. He laced up the stiff black Thorogood boots, from the police supply catalogue, looking out the screen at the side yard. His father would appreciate the gesture. He wondered if there'd be gas in the mower.

It had been years since he'd mowed a lawn. The Hilton Head house and the apartment in Vail were both fully serviced. Damn, he didn't think he'd used a mower since they left New Jersey more than three years ago. He wasn't going to be one of those sheltered rich people—he thought of President Bush not knowing about super-market price scanners—but the simple fact was there'd be business to take care of, and Theo's time would be worth more than the twenty bucks an hour he'd pay a lawn service.

The yard sloped downhill from the side of the house, making it pretty unusable. It was surrounded by chest-high chain-link fence, rusty, the color of burnt toast, and in places completely humped over with weeds. The yard behind used to be the Harrig-ans'. Andy Harrigan had been in Theo's high school class. He'd always been a whiz kid, talking with a self-assurance that seemed to impress teachers and parents, Theo's father included, who called him "the All-American Harrigan." It seemed like Theo's father secretly wished his own son had been more like Andy, who went off to Rutgers and then to business school. He'd gotten into commer-cial real estate in Hartford, selling, then financing like crazy in the eighties, making truckloads of money. When the market collapsed, he took a bath on every property he had. But last spring in the Klub Klondike in Vail, Theo ran into Harrigan. He had started his own consulting firm in Hartford, advising companies who had overex-tended in the real estate market of the eighties. Pulling in mounds of dough again. The guy got knocked down but came back strong. Just as Theo and Colleen were doing. Theo's father would see that his son was leaving the All-American Harrigan in the dust.

The Harrigan parents had moved to a planned community out toward Bishop Hill nearly ten years ago. They'd sold the house to a black family, and now on the other side of the chain-link, a corrugated fiberglass privacy fence was already falling apart. Sheets of green fiberglass slapped against the chain-link with the slightest breeze. They had a pool. Aboveground. In one of the second-floor windows a venetian blind was hanging at an angle. In another window there was only one half of a curtain.

Theo walked out toward the shed, built by his father from recycled wood he'd scavenged over the years. The shed was solid and practical, like his father. Nothing excessive. It was constructed of old-time quality materials: solid-wood window sashes, hand-built casings, full-measure studs. There was no particle board or aluminum, but thick wood siding that gave the shed a kind of weathered dignity. But in the end, Theo thought, it was still an old musty shed smelling of grass clippings, sawdust, and gasoline.

He paused in the middle of the yard, looking from the shed to the old Chris-Craft, rotting away, worthless. In the years when Theo was first a cop, he and his father had both tried to start a new relationship, focusing on the good times—from a proud little Theo who'd visited his dad at the station as a boy, right on through Theo's confiding that there wouldn't be another girl like Colleen, that she was the one. They'd talked like the two cops they were, jovial and easy, ignoring the scabbed-over anger, resentment, and disappointment. But after Theo's first suspension, a sharp edge in the voice or the eyes was always knifing up between them. Theo knew it was his own fault as much as his father's. After the money came in, and with it a feeling of relief and success, those old wounds would heal. They would become father and son in every way.

It would be sad to see all this go, he thought, looking out over the yard. Of course it *had* to go, they all had to move on, but this house, this yard, this neighborhood, had been the homestead for Theo's entire life. Forty-five years of this sloped patch of crabgrass. Sleeping out in a tent, burying hamsters and turtles, taking batting practice with his dad, working on cars in the driveway . . . And here he was, standing in the middle of the yard they'd sell off to a black family in a few months, Theo wearing police-issue boots that he'd sworn off a dozen times. But this time was for real. He imagined eighteen and a half million one-dollar bills swirling around him like snow in one of those plastic-domed scenes you shake, the money settling over this house and yard, the shed, the boat. Colleen's GoodLife sponsor had given her a cassette called "Letting Go of Stress" about picturing your perfect life and going there "in your mind," but now Theo and Colleen were going there in reality. No more looking at the boat he wrecked. No more damn police shoes.

Theo tugged open the padlock on the shed. He thought of the American Mini-Storage unit—eighty-two dollars for a one-month minimum, which was your higher-end storage, but Theo believed in high end. There was clipped shrubbery at the compound entrance, a locked gate accessible only with a magnetic card, a heavy-duty metal door.

He tried to remember the evolution of the box concept, the idea to restrain Brown with cuffs and duct tape, to weave ropes through the airholes a few inches above him so he couldn't kick the lid. At first he'd planned to keep Brown in an old shack he'd discovered by an abandoned factory twenty miles south off the Parkway.

But there'd been problems about guarding him, about someone seeing a light or the car. And then, a couple months ago when Brook was home from college for spring break, Theo was helping him look for his cleats in all the boxes in the cellar. The dog had followed them down there, and Brook went down on all fours, playing with her. The dog ran into her canine carrier and Brook crawled in after her. As a joke, Theo kicked the door closed; then it hit him. Perfect really, an elegant solution.

He'd be able to pull this off where others had failed because he knew exactly what the cops would be looking for. He knew how a case was built. He knew about evidence and paper trails. The plan had evolved so that there would never be a single shred that could be traced back to him and Colleen.

They would succeed because most people, Theo understood as he got older, weren't all that smart. Most people who you think are on top of things are in fact working double-time to keep up appearances. Most people—their basic skills of analysis, their insights and instincts—were extremely limited. They operated in their own sandbox universe, and tried to get everybody else to play along. Theo was a big-picture man with a mind for details.

There was a power at work while he slept and drove and watched TV, leading him to the right thing. Two nights after Brook followed the dog into the carrier, Theo was watching a late-night movie on TV. An inmate working in a prison mortuary escaped inside a casket in which he'd drilled tiny airholes. Everything was pointing Theo in the right direction. A problem had presented itself in their lives: they needed cash. And the solution was unfolding before him with equal insistence.

He'd thought about it years ago, when he was earning sixty-one and change a year at Petrochem with two kids and a mortgage, and the company shelled out millions for one of their vice presidents kidnapped in Argentina. Theo's job was fine, supervising nearly fifty uniformed watchmen. He and Colleen had had enough money, they'd been comfortable. They'd never been poor. But something was missing in their lives; there was a hunger, a lack of purpose. They were stuck in the small-time. They needed to jump-start a new life. Listen to any of the call-in radio shows. You've got to have capital to get going. Shit, the eighties were a bounty with everyone from Reagan on down forcing money on you. They'd have been fools not to go after everything they wanted. Thirty-two hundred square feet in Sea Pines Plantation; "Insiders" of Hilton Head; their own furniture and home-decorating business; a thirty-eight-foot sloop. They were working night and day, but their feet were planted in the life they'd dreamed of. Then they fell a few payments behind, and the bank chopped off Theo's nuts. He'd gotten started too late in the eighties boom. Theo blamed Bush.

Even the All-American Harrigan, the M.B.A. networker, got slammed. Hey, it couldn't be avoided: bankruptcy was part of the system. Colleen and Theo had taken their hits, and now they were coming out on top. Theo remembered the last spring of high school. His mother and father were real proud that he was accepted to the police academy. But Colleen was going away to Providence College. He'd gotten so nervous about losing her, a girl who imagined herself with a college man, a future investment tycoon like Harrigan. Why would she want to come back to Ludlow to marry a town cop? But Theo had won her, and now he was going to win again.

In two days Theo would be a different man. He would be someone people like Harrigan would come to for a break, for fast cash to turn an overnight real estate deal and a quick twenty percent. Theo would be firm, but because he was someone who had worked his way up, someone who knew about pouring every ounce of his energy into his own business, only to be forced into bankruptcy by the very bank that had pushed them into twice the loan he had asked for . . . because he knew about supposedly reputable creditors like MasterCard and Macy's phoning the house at all hours, harassing his wife and children, until finally they were locked out of their home . . . because he knew the humiliation of a foreclosure sign pounded into the lawn . . . because Theo knew what it was like to punch a time clock, first for the Ludlow Police Department, then for Petrochem security . . . because Theo knew about grocery bills and a family depending on him and arriving in Vail in the middle of the night and staying with two kids and his wife in a Motel 6 while they started over again . . . because of Theo Wolkoviak's unique history he would not become an asshole. He'd be tough but magnanimous. He'd be known as a son of a bitch.

As Theo was rushing through the half hour they'd given him to collect his personal effects in Hilton Head with the bank man and the cop in the hall, he'd thought back to the months of layoffs during his time at Petrochem. *He* had been the cop swooping into offices with a lawyer from personnel, ruining people who'd dedicated their lives to Petrochem. A pencil line got drawn across a list of names by men like Stona Brown, and if your name fell below that line, you could kiss everything good-bye. Dedicate your life to Petrochem, but as soon as they can save five cents by slashing you, don't expect a shoulder to cry on.

As fast as he could, he'd filled boxes with files and records, their wedding album and photos of the kids, a maple jewelry box that Malcolm had made for Tiffany. In tears, Tiffany had begged Theo to get it from her bedroom. And then he pulled open the bottom drawer of his desk and saw the *Reader's Digest*—sized book with the white cover and logo he knew well—the directory of Petrochem personnel—staring at him like a message.

A single big haul was the ticket. Hey, he wasn't a scumbag. He was a committed family man, an honest businessman. A man who wanted no more than to provide for his wife and children. He'd given Colleen a home, a sailboat, and a comfortable life in the country's most desirable real estate market. But he'd never been able to give her real financial security. It had all been snatched away. Theo and Colleen were creative, hardworking entrepreneurs who played by the rules. They epitomized the American ethic, and the time had come for their taste of the American dream.

In the work shed, he saw that his father had cleaned up. The scraps of plywood were leaning against the wall under the rack of clamps. The circular saw and screw gun were back on their shelves, yellow cords coiled and hanging from hooks in the rafters. His father had swept up the sawdust, the scattered cardboard, and the shrink-wrap packaging of the corner braces, hinges, and latch. Theo imagined his father in here this morning: shaking his head at the mess: *When will Theo take some responsibility?*

At the far end of the shed next to the mower, Theo unbolted the side door—a paneled door with a brown porcelain knob that used to separate the kitchen and living room. He unscrewed the gas cap on the mower: not a drop of gas in it. Along the wall next to a bottle of GoodLife Degreaser and two cans of oil, there was a red plastic tank. He sloshed it around. Plenty. With the gas in hand, he dragged the mower out the door.

It felt good to be outside—a warm spring day, pouring gas in a mower for the first mow of the season. Gas rushed down the transparent green spout with a smell like high school: working on his cars, mowing the lawn. The gas overflowed the tank, spilling over the mower and evaporating in the heat.

Damn hot, really. Brown was surely warm by now. He tightened the gas cap, punched it up to half-throttle, then put his foot—his father's boot—on the mower and yanked the cord. Nothing. He yanked again. The gas line was empty, so it needed a few pulls to suck some fuel through; he pulled again and again, and the next time, he pulled so hard his foot slipped, and he picked the mower up off the ground.

Then he realized the spark plug wire was disconnected, dangling from the block. Theo was down on a knee, pinching the metal clip between his fingers, then bringing his face against the mower and biting the clip small and round—a scratchy metal taste on his molars. Maybe this wouldn't be the last time he mowed a lawn. There'd be gardeners at the yacht club and marina. "Is that what you call weeding a bed, Juan?" Theo said aloud. He would reach down behind the bougainvillea and pluck some hidden weeds. *I'm sorry, Mr. Wolkoviak. It won't happen again.* And the gardeners might be having trouble with the mower, but hell, it was a five-horse Briggs and Stratton that Theo could tear down and put together in an hour. "Give me half a day, Juan, and I could rebuild the motor in that old Chevy of yours." And Theo would discover the blocked fuel line, then start the mower and cut the lawn along the seawall, an ocean breeze keeping him cool, the American flag and yacht club ensign flapping on a white pole, fully rigged with a spreader and shrouds. The gardeners, the office staff, certain members and VIPs, would see Theo, a tan and powerful man who isn't afraid to get his hands dirty, who wasn't born with a silver spoon in his mouth. A man who knows how to work. The wives of Philip Morris executives would gossip: *He was a police officer years ago.* A North Carolina senator sipping a glass of Dom: *I heard he worked covert ops with the CIA.* There'd be a certain mystery about the rich and powerful Theo Wolkoviak.

As he fitted the metal clip over the spark plug, his father's brown Plymouth Fury came backing into the driveway, as if he were still a cop on call.

When Theo rose to his feet there was a sweat spot at his gut, red on his pink Lacoste shirt. He pulled the shirt over his head and hung it on the porcelain doorknob. He bent over the mower again, reaching for the cord. On the first pull, the engine sputtered, and in the corner of his eye, he saw his father getting out of the car. On the second pull, the sucker fired up, an unmuffled four-stroke internal combustion engine. Hardly been improved upon in all these years. He'd pay his gardeners well, but he'd expect top-notch work.

Theo hammered the throttle to max, and decided to mow the front first. He cut a beeline across the side yard toward the boxwood tree, the concrete ducks, and his father leaning a hand into the side of his Plymouth, watching Theo with his head cocked to the side. *Is my son really cutting the grass?*

The vibrations and the blast of noise were working Theo like a shiatsu massage. He cut a swath straight for his father, who was still giving him a look, raising a hand, turning his head as if to listen more closely. Theo tried to imagine Donald Trump popping in on the parents for the weekend and firing up the mower. Then the engine started to buck—the grass was too thick—so Theo slowed his pace. But it bucked worse, and his father was waving his arms now, and he thought the blade must have caught something. He popped the mower back on the two rear wheels. There was a terrible screeching, strangling sound and a hot, burning smell. The engine cut off midgasp.

Coming slowly at him, his father paused to pick up a duckling that had fallen on its side. He set it in line behind the others. He was holding a green and white paper bag from CityLine Discount Drugs folded over and stapled with a copy of his prescription. Theo turned the mower upside down to get a look at what had bound it up. He grabbed the blade but couldn't budge it.

"Seized up," his father said, touching Theo's shoulder. "You couldn't've known."

"I'll figure it out," Theo said, tipping the mower on its side. The smell was awful. "Maybe the belt to the blade got fried."

"Son, it *seized*."

Theo could see the blade had seized. Christ, nothing had changed. Whether it was mechanics or carpentry, assembling a bike, finding a short up under the dashboard—his father always knew it all.

The blade wouldn't budge. He flipped the mower back on its wheels and jiggled the spark plug wire, and—"Damn!"—burned his knuckles on the engine block.

"That'll be hot," his father said.

"With you looking over my shoulder, how can I diagnose anything here?"

"You ran it dry, Theo. I drain the oil every fall. The engine seized."

Theo dropped his eyes from the mower to his father's boots.

"It was an old machine anyway," his father said. He was wheezing.

Theo had destroyed the motor. He looked back toward the shed at the strip of cut grass slicing through the overgrown lawn. His father was looking at the remains of the boat, and Theo knew what he was thinking.

"Anyway," his father said, "I thought I'd have that kid down the block mow this year. He came by with a flyer."

His father was thinking that Theo couldn't even mow a lawn right.

"A nice kid. Very neat."

The boat sat there rotting to remind Theo every time he looked at it how reckless and irresponsible he'd been. But starting tomorrow, Theo was buying a little respect.

"The kid's got a new Toro. Self-propelled. Looks you in the eye. Says 'sir.' "

Inde Deus Abest. Heat radiated off the inside of the box. A smell like a sauna—dry lumber and sweat. For hours he'd been cold, but now the steam from his body condensed inside the lid of the box and dripped hot on his face. The comforter bunched up under his chin so heavy and hot he had to fight to breathe. It was like the hot packs he'd been wrapped in for polio as a boy. He tried to twist his head away. He tried to wriggle the comforter down with his shoulders, his fingers, the tips of his shoes. But his ankles were bound together tightly, his bony knees scraped against each other, tape bound his arms and held down his hands. When he tried to roll up on a hip, to roll on his side, he came against rope strung taut between himself and the lid of the box from his feet to his chest. It was a heat with weight and bulk. A furious heat. Rabid.

Walking his mind through a maze of distraction. It could be as easy as cooling down a horse around the perimeter of a ring. But now Stona was too tired to rein in his mind; it shot off, wild and unstoppable, and he had no choice but to hang on as it raced down treacherous steep trails.

Blood splattering the sidewalks. Blood streaming in the gutters. His mind raced through a business trip in Kuwait City during the Bayram slaughter. Sheep, goats, cows, swinging from their hind legs, swinging from balconies and tree branches. Animals bleating, screaming. Sparks showered from grindstones and scrabbled on the streets through the city for days, electric grindstones spinning on tripods, screeching against the edge of a blade. Throats slit for Allah, the distorted call to prayer warbling from loudspeakers, echoing from every direction. The smell of blood, the reek of decaying flesh. And now the pissy animal smell of fur and sweat was his own. *His* blood, *his* flesh rotting in the heat. The smell of his own death.

Stona reeled his mind around, and he was sitting in a meeting with the Kuwaiti oil minister, who offered 19.5 percent, but Stona held firm for two days at 16 percent, knowing he could go to 18.25, wanting 17. Then, as Stona sipped that god-awful desalinated water, he heard amid a stream of Arabic the words "F-18," and before his interpreter spoke Stona realized the negotiations would have to broaden. He'd have to call over someone from the embassy.

He took a commercial flight to Rhodes, where Nunny was waiting at the hotel. When he stepped from his car and spotted her by the pool, she was wearing her white bathing suit and a floral cloth knotted at her hip. Now, under the tape Stona's eyes were soothed by tears that rinsed the sting of sweat, and he would spend the next hours remembering every inch of Nunny, beginning with her toes. He saw them clearly, the smallest three toes on each foot curved under from years crammed into elegant shoes that did not resemble the shape of a foot. Three or four hairs, fine as eyelashes, sprang from the joints of each big toe. In the summer when her feet were golden tan, two white sandal lines—as white as the flesh on the underside of her breast—converged in the crotch between her big toe and the next.

He saw Nunny's feet as they were walking on top of a wall in Turkey, at the Crusader Castle of St. Peter in Bodrum, where they'd gone by ferry from Rhodes. "I chose the wrong shoes," Nunny said, kicking pebbles out of her sandals, leaning on Stona as they dropped down steep stairs, dangerously pitched blocks of stone that became more massive as they descended inside the castle wall. Their view of the Aegean Sea gradually disappeared, and the air became cooler. They pushed through a small door, from blinding sunshine to darkness, to a cramped stone room, to moans and red flashes of light. As their eyes adjusted, they saw skeletons shackled to the wall, mannequin arms reaching through a black iron grate in the stone floor with abrupt mechanical movements. They heard the tape-recorded shrieks of the victims, and the deep-voiced commands of the torturer: a beefy wild-eyed statue of a man with an animal's hair and beard in full Crusader costume adorned with the emblem of Saint Peter, and a whip that jerked in his mechanical arm. Above his head, in a block of marble chiseled as precisely as the names on a gravestone, were the words *Inde Deus Abest*—Where God Does Not Exist.

Inde Deus Abest. Stona would not believe it. He would not believe that God did not comfort the Muslims starving in the castle dungeon. He would not believe that God was not with him in this box. How else could he be keeping his sanity? What else could explain the moments when he slept and was released by his dreams? When he walked and stretched and brushed Nunny's ankles with his fingertips? Her ankles had always been fragile. A weak link. She sprained them constantly on the tennis court. Her skin there had become loose, betraying her age, but still they were delicate and thin as a wrist.

Inde Deus Abest. No. God was with Stona. How else could he forget the heat, his thirst? He'd thought the heat of the day had peaked, he'd thought he felt the heat pull away like one blanket of many peeled off the top. But now he heard the metal garage door creaking, contracting from heat, the oven turned higher. He struggled for a breath, and realized the moaning must have been his own. He saw the mechanical Crusader again, the crest of the Knights of St. Peter on his chest, and the head was the head of his kidnapper.

To rein in his mind. Walking a horse around the ring, cooling him down. With the kidnapper's face clear in his consciousness, he began to walk through his day and the faces he saw. He'd seen the man before. He'd spoken to the man, perhaps a tollbooth collector, a maintenance man at the office, a valet at the club, but he had spoken to that man, and the man had spoken to him.

Stona got up from the box as naturally as getting up off the couch after a nap. He got into his car and drove home with all the windows wide open to drown in the crashing waves of wind. Nunny was out shopping for dinner, so Stona sat at the foot of the drive and thought about a typical weekend. He put the car in gear, took his foot off the brake, and headed to the hardware store. Behind the register ringing up spackle and a putty knife was the owner, Mike, who had curly red hair. Stona examined the regular customers: the old man, a Yankees fanatic, who lurked in the paint department dispensing free advice; a young professional in over his head with a fixer-upper asking Mike about sanding-belt grits. Stona walked up and down the aisles, looking at every face: Mike's son Rodney who had Down's syndrome weighing out nails in the back; the blond kid who cut electrical wire, rope, and chain. He calmly searched for the man with the small eyes and big face, the porous skin and colorless lips. Stona wandered back in the corner by the rakes, shovels, and bags of cement. He watched people come and go, but his kidnapper was not among them.

He had parked his car with the windows open in the shade of a maple tree so it was cool when he returned. He drove slowly down Main Street, looking at each store and asking himself if he'd ever been inside. Clothing stores, shoe stores, a toy store, Hallmark—he hadn't shopped in any of them. Then the CVS—yes, many times. He pulled over, put a quarter in the meter, and went through the automatic doors. The affront of cheap drugstore perfume made him think of the woman who bandaged his arm, and Stona's mind began to race again. He felt his heart working harder, struggling in his chest. He forced air out his nostrils to clear them but couldn't fill his lungs again. He thought he was suffocating. If God were with him, why wouldn't that hand pinch his nostrils for the few seconds it would take to let Stona die?

You shot him. I can't believe you shot him. When Stona heard the woman screaming, he'd known what amateurs they were. The woman's hysterics betrayed them, and the look on the man's face when he'd yanked off his mask: he was biting his lower lip in an adolescent rage. His hair stuck straight up from static, blond hair edging toward red. And now Stona could see the man with hair combed and parted, cut short and choppy. He *knew* he'd seen him before, but in a jacket and tie, a light blue dress shirt. He struggled to hold the image in his mind.

He returned to the aisles of CVS: clerks in red smocks, mostly young girls. Not a single face coalesced. He picked up a bottle of Grecian Formula, on the left side of the aisle, hip level; he passed the walkers and canes, silver aluminum, which reminded him of his polio braces when he was a boy. He admired the pharmacist, Ricki, a gorgeous girl with blond ringlets and just the right balance of perky and professional. The two assistants, a small black man and a young guy right out of school, filed computer printouts in the glassed-in office. On the blue vinyl bench, everyone waiting was at least ten years older than Stona. The kidnapper wasn't here.

He drove to Rosenblatt's and entered quietly through the side door. He brushed his fingertips along the rows of dark suits lined up on their hangers. He squeezed the soft leather cushions of the club chairs under the stained-glass chandelier in the middle of the store. He pulled a deep drawer from the mahogany-paneled wall and sank his arms into stacks of cotton boxers, no packaging, no labels or price tags—there was a dignity about Rosenblatt's, the smallest purchase boxed with tissue and tied with twine. He stepped into a waterfall of neckties, cool silk flowing over his face and down his back. And when he approached the salesmen, all of whom knew Stona by name, he examined their faces: fastidious, tidy men . . .

Voices! A child shrieking. An idling car. Stona's body shook. Fitful, epileptic. He screamed from his gut, piercing screams that scraped his throat raw and emerged through the fistful of cloth taped into his mouth no louder than his tortured breathing. The voices were closer. He fought against the tape and the rope, jerking, writhing, yanking in every direction. The garage door rolled up. He'd been found, praise God! He rocked and lurched. He pounded his forehead on the lid of the box, pounded until he felt his skin tearing. Let the blood flow! Let it stream down his face, because he'd been found.

Then he fell still and listened. The voices were sporadic. He couldn't decipher words, but their tone lacked surprise or urgency.

For a moment inquisitive. Desultory. Were they in another garage? Was there a row of garages? Condos?

He heard shoes on gravel, the door rolling back down. It was not this garage at all. The car engine started. "No!" he shouted through the tape. "In here!" And Stona lost control of his body, twisting in spasms, erupting in one final explosion that would free him. His head pounded on the lid, pounded until he heard the metal chink of the hinges and latch, pounded until the blackness behind his eyelids grew deeper, until the blackness began to seep with color: sapphirine blue, the yellows and oranges of fire. Stona pounded his head on the wooden lid until he no longer felt the pain, until his head was numb as frozen fingers, until a moist purple cloud burst behind his eyelids.

In Stona's dream Nunny was springing off a diving board in her white bathing suit. She drifted like an angel, wings spread wide, through an amethyst cloud, and Stona was with her. The cool purple air brushed over their bodies, and he pressed his thumb into the hollow behind her anklebone, sliding his hands along her calf, massaging the doughy flesh, the sinewy muscle, massaging so deeply his own calves were soothed. "Chicken legs," he used to tease her, so skinny up to her knees. Her calves were not as tight now, but he loved them more than years ago.

Nunny rolled over to her back, wind filling her hair. Stona swam around her, scissoring his legs, stretching his arms over his head and reaching them out to his sides. His body was liquid.

Nunny's knees. A quarter-moon scar on her left kneecap as pink as the flesh inside of her, as if in healing, her body had not closed up over the wound, but had opened out to fill the wound, as if her more sensitive inner flesh blossomed to the surface. The scar was the flesh of her lips, the flesh of her labia.

Stona held the backs of Nunny's thighs. He held them tight and caressed his face on her inner thighs, nudging her penny-sized mole with his nose. With his fingertips he jiggled the loose flesh, he jiggled and tickled until he heard Nunny's laughter. She was embarrassed, but how could he convince her he loved her legs more each day? Her tight body at sixteen, when Stona and Nunny had started dating in high school, seemed unreal to him now, plastic as a department store mannequin. He tickled her until he was laughing too, and the sound of his laughter, the spasm in his belly, the smile stretching his face—they were, he sensed, a desperate and final joy. Over Nunny's white bathing suit he gently pressed the palm of his hand on her vagina, looking into her eyes, gripping his fingers over her pubic bone. Pressing, holding, cupping like that, and no words passed between them. Stona laid his head on Nunny's pelvis and slept.

Then Nunny was bathing Stona, rinsing away the buildup of life, like rinsing dead bugs off a windshield. She dripped cool water over his face with a sponge. She poured buckets of water over his chest, dousing his seething body. . . . And he was awake again, his eyes pinching. The box. He was urinating. He constricted his muscles, and a surge rushed through his bladder, stung his lower back and his swollen, tender kidneys. One nostril was blocked with mucus. He filled his lungs and blew. Then again, and the mucus bubbled on his cheek, and he breathed more easily.

But the pain in his kidneys was unbearable. He lifted his knees the two or three inches they'd go. He pressed them against the rope, but there was no relief. To bend his knees for one minute . . . for thirty seconds . . . he would trade his home. His kidneys felt on fire. Fingers of pain clawed at his pelvis. The pressure began to tear his bladder. A tiny, lengthening rip.

Stona let it go. He relaxed and let the urine flow. He let it stream into his pants, and something like pleasure unleashed from his groin.

Moving through the halls that last spring of high school had been like riding in his father's squad car: it felt like gliding on high-performance tires, a Police Interceptor motor pulling him along at an idle. In an instant, Theo could stomp on the pedal and blast wide open. The cruiser windows were rolled up, the police radio scratchy in his head, and the kids he passed all had something to hide, humping along or loitering at lockers, seeing him out of the corners of their eyes, straightening up and moving along. He heard things—"Probably art history," "Division A lacrosse," "Tri-Delt"— and he knew they were code for other things. He knew everything meant something else.

They talked about college as an "of course." They paraded the halls wearing university sweaters: Rutgers, Fairleigh Dickinson, Providence College. "Did you decide?" "Did you get in?" The guys talked about girls there'd be in college, and also vice versa. But Theo had made some discoveries of his own—about having a 392 Hemi-powered Plymouth Belvedere and some money in his pocket. About balling and hippie girls.

But it had always been Colleen he wanted. He held the car door open for her, which was the kind of thing she deserved and had a right to expect. She was that type of girl, good family, pretty hairstyle, nice clothes. Not a girl you go out with a couple towns over and push the car door open for at the curb so nobody sees, but one you're proud to bring home. Which he had many times. "Do I hear wedding bells?" Theo's mother said after supper the last time Colleen had eaten at the house.

Theo snapped a crisp twenty-dollar bill from his wallet and slid it under the ticket window. "Two, please." He saw that Colleen noticed the twenty. Always she noticed. He tucked the change into his wallet, pulling out a five and replacing it so the presidents' heads lined up the right way, and he held his wallet in his hand, weighty, chunky, smooth thick leather—a solid package, a serious wad. He and Colleen got in line for the movie. He sank the wallet in the back pocket of his jeans and pressed the edge of the tickets to his lips, whistling through them, which made a squeak and a hiss—

Colleen gave him the eye, and he froze. He crossed his arms and thought about all the things he was trying to stop doing, like wearing white socks and sticking his hands in the waist of his trousers and using Vitalis.

Sometimes he did things without knowing it.

He watched Colleen examining other guys in the lobby. Looking them up and down. Most of them wore sport shirts like Theo's, khakis or blue jeans like his, but their shoes . . . They wore penny loafers or sneakers. Theo's shoes were clunky black lace-ups. His father wore the same ones, ordered through the police supply catalogue. Class A dress shoe, style number A-42. Cop shoes.

When he looked at Colleen, he knew what he wanted. He wanted to motor upriver in the Chris-Craft with her to a notch of secluded beach at the mouth of a stream, where they'd anchor the boat in knee-deep water, and wade to the shore. He'd carve a well in the sand for her butt, build a mound under her knees, and slope a wedge for her back, shoulders, and head. She'd recline in her bikini reading a magazine in French with photos of high-society Europeans relaxing in their châteaus. Sitting beside her, the skin stretching over her pregnant belly golden in the sun, Theo would teach their first baby to make miniature sand castles with her tiny fists. Their little girl would grow up to be just like her mother. Their second baby would not be long coming, then the third and finally the fourth. Two girls and two boys. Theo would be devoted to their care.

The line started to move. Colleen stepped ahead. Theo had a recurring nightmare about losing her in a crowded, ornate lobby swarming with people speaking a foreign language. He caught up with her, but he couldn't get his mind off his shoes. They looked steel-toed, like gas station shoes.

In a flash he knew he'd never wear the shoes again. Which was how things happened for him—figuring them out in an instant. He would do anything for Colleen.

He reached forward with the movie tickets and the girl in a red vest and black bow tie stared at him with a snotty little smirk. Theo looked at his hand and saw that he'd torn the tickets into tiny pieces. A small pile of confetti in his palm.

Would you make the salad, dear?" Theo's mother said.

Rest probably *was* the best medicine for Mr. Brown. Theo was right about treating for shock, Colleen thought. They were keeping him warm, forcing fluids. Mr. Brown had three of their softest old duvets and two pillows. She'd cleaned and re-dressed his wound. She'd given him plenty of water and two multivitamins. Colleen was a believer in vitamins. She respected the body's capacity to heal itself.

But she felt sorry for Mr. Brown—the *not knowing*. He didn't know that they'd chosen him simply because, among the several Petrochem executives they'd staked out, he didn't use a driver, the houses on his street were set back in the trees, and he was punctual. He didn't know when he'd be released. It was awful that he'd have to be in the box so much longer than they'd originally planned. When Theo had determined that there wasn't enough time for the insurance company to get the money together by tonight, they hadn't returned to the locker to try for a third time to record a tape. They had decided to let him rest.

She set out the last of the forks and knives, chopsticks for Tiffany, and removed the pill bottles, magazines, and napkin holder from the lazy Susan. Colleen liked to make a nice table.

"The *salad*, Colleen dear."

"No problem at all." When she opened the fridge, she couldn't help crinkling up her nose. People didn't appreciate that plastics absorbed odors, which the inside of this same fridge had been absorbing since Colleen and Theo dated in high school. She snatched the bag of lettuce and slammed the door shut.

Iceberg lettuce. Could tonight be the very last time in her life she ate it?

"Nothing good as the smell of Dot's golumpki in the house," Malcolm announced, barely getting out the words before his breath left him. When he paused in the doorway, the dog quivered excitedly by his feet. Malcolm shuffled across the linoleum and leaned on the back of his chair.

"Can I get you a glass of something?" Colleen asked him, helping him down to his seat.

He waved her off, fidgeting with his inhaler, shaky hands rattling the mouthpiece against his teeth. It broke Colleen's heart to know that his mind was still sharp and his body still strong but his lungs were nearly useless. It wasn't fair. As she set a glass of ice water at his place, she laid her hand on the middle of his back.

He was certainly in worse shape than Mr. Brown, who had his beautiful home to return to on Sunday night. Malcolm was stuck in this house, financially unable to move to Florida or even across town, and too stubborn anyway. He fancied himself a fix-it man, but the place had gone terribly downhill. That same metal awning had stuck out over the front door for thirty years—red, white, and blue stripes of pressed metal, rusty at the scalloped edges. The flimsy aluminum storm door didn't close. The dog had left stains on the carpet. Lace doilies spread on end tables had yellowed around the ashtrays placed at their centers. Drapes hung heavy and smoky.

As she tore apart the head of lettuce, Colleen thought of the plantation shutters in their Hilton Head house—three-inch hardwood louvers painted the color of pearls. She was constantly opening and closing them to adjust the light. Plantation shutters were considered desirable, but they were expensive, and even some of the wealthier Hilton Head residents didn't spend the money. For Colleen, though, it was a quality-of-life choice: controlling the sunlight in your living environment. Soon, she'd have a home in a cool place and a home in a warm place. A home on the ocean and a home in the mountains. She was extremely sensitive to climate, color schemes, odors.

At six o'clock sharp Malcolm switched on the local newscast from Newark with the remote. Dot, her hands in oven mitts, laid the casserole dish in the center of the table. It was filled with a half dozen golumpki—cabbage stuffed with hamburger, rice, stewed tomatoes, and onion. There was a smaller dish with a vegetarian golumpki for Tiffany. Theo slipped quickly into his place beside his father, silent, eyes fixed to the TV.

"Now we'll get some details," his father said.

Theo stuck his fork into the casserole, scooped up a bite of golumpki stuffing, and blew on it. When he took the bite into his mouth, his teeth scraped on the tines. "Let's hope."

Colleen peeled a cucumber. The news lead-in began. The top story: Petrochem kidnapping in Asherton. There was a picture of Mr. Brown. He was wearing his glasses. He looked younger—a mannish face with healthy coloring, a warm smile. It was him. It was really happening. Colleen flushed. What had they done?

"I'll bet they don't have a lead," Theo said to Malcolm before Toshi Mikimoto began.

Colleen gripped Theo's shoulders from behind. The whole world knew.

She felt herself caving in. Theo reached around behind his chair with both hands and squeezed the backs of her thighs. Malcolm watched the newscast with a professional skepticism, analyzing as he listened; despite his old-fashioned stubbornness, he was an intelligent man. Dot set a plate stacked with slices of Roman Meal bread on the table, drained the peas, then stopped to watch, wiping her hands back and forth on her apron long after they were dry. Tiffany stood in the doorway, still wearing her Joey's Tacos name tag.

"Hey!" Theo snapped, and everyone looked as he took the vegetable peeler from Colleen's hand. Then they turned back to the TV, and Colleen saw the red mark she'd made on Theo's neck.

From the foot of Mr. Stona Brown's driveway, Chad Sturgeon appeared, live. Chad Sturgeon himself, interviewing a detective. It wasn't like seeing a shot of the state capital or the county courthouse. No, this place was *personally* familiar, the foot of the driveway demarcated with yellow tape, the view through the trees to the house, police cars and dozens of men in uniforms, dark suits, trench coats. Colleen and Theo had been there, they'd caused it, they were responsible for it all. They'd kidnapped a man at gunpoint from his home, and the world was reacting with horror. Colleen waited for Chad Sturgeon to say her name, and when he didn't, she felt so relieved, so grateful, it was as if the whole thing were over. Mr. Brown home and safe, the money theirs.

"Amateurish," the detective said, and Theo bristled. Colleen looked past Chad Sturgeon, through the trees, as he signed off somberly: "Where is Stona Brown?" And as the camera panned up the long driveway, across the wooded yard, Colleen squinted at the TV, trying to glimpse the front porch.

Theo gave Colleen's thighs another firm squeeze, then reached across his chest and took her hand in his. They were in this together. They were true partners again. They'd had their problems in the past, and she reminded herself now that the only way to steer clear of those same problems, the only way to save the family, was to do what they were doing. They had no choice.

Turning away from the report of a fire in Newark, Malcolm sucked at his teeth. "What's your take on it, Theo?"

Colleen finished making the salad.

"Milk, Tiffany?" her grandmother asked.

"Not tonight." Tiffany slipped into her chair, hooking a strand of dirty-blond hair behind her ear with twitchy fingers.

"Doesn't sound amateurish to me," Theo said. "I don't think they've got a single lead." There was an edge to Theo's voice, an anger that only a wife could hear.

"Sit down, Colleen," Dot said. "It's getting cold." Mr. Brown was going to be okay. He was resting. No one but Colleen and her husband knew.

"So they left the car running at the foot of the driveway," Malcolm said. "What do you make of that? If they'd taken his car with them, they would've increased their getaway time. Doesn't sound professional. You think?"

"Serve, Papa," Dot pleaded. Colleen would never call her husband Papa.

Malcolm nodded to Theo, who took up the serving spoon. "Hey," Theo pointed the spoon at his father. "Do they have any suspects? Do they have any leads? Doesn't seem so. Let the facts speak."

Theo handed his mother a plate with a golumpki and a spoonful of peas. "Looks good, Ma," he said.

"The guy probably kidnapped himself," Tiffany chimed in, "to get the money because he hates Petrochem."

Theo gave her a plate with her vegetarian golumpki. "A man like that doesn't need the money, dear," Colleen said, the sound of her own voice bringing her confidence back.

"Everybody needs the money," Tiffany countered. "The more you have, the more you want."

"You have a point," Malcolm said, taking his plate from Theo. "But if you're a group of professionals, why do you leave the car? Anybody knows you want to maximize your getaway time."

"I admit it seems that way on the surface, but if there wasn't a spare man to drive the car—"

"There you go. An organization has plenty of men."

"But they got away, didn't they?" Theo filled his mouth with hot golumpki, burned his tongue, kept talking. "So it's not the Irish Republican Army. But they knew what they were doing." Theo bit off half a slice of bread. "Looks like a good job to me. Well planned."

"You know, if Theo and I get lucky with this yacht club deal," Colleen blurted out, "we're planning a trip to Ireland next year. For all of us."

"What do you mean, if?" Theo said. "What do you mean, lucky?"

"That would be nice," Dot said, but then she looked at Malcolm, who hadn't touched his food, hadn't even picked up his fork, and her eyes went watery and red.

"I'll house-sit," Tiffany offered.

"Sweetheart, we'd all go. And your brother too."

Tiffany waved her chopsticks and rolled her eyes. "I'm sure the Young Republican will be much too busy campaigning for George Bush, and I will be"——with the chopsticks she peeled a single transparent leaf of cabbage from the outside of her golumpki, held it up to the light and looked through it——"*ocupada.*"

When Colleen thought of leaving Tiffany alone, she nearly shook with the vision of her daughter in the hospital in Vail down to eighty-seven pounds. "Brook'll be home for the summer in two weeks, so we'll ask him himself."

"Well, the FBI will be on it by tomorrow. I guarantee you that." Malcolm glanced sideways at his son.

"I hope they are. I seriously do."

Tiffany pushed away from the table. "Anybody want anything?" She got the soy sauce from the fridge. Piece by piece she'd disassembled the golumpki and spread it over her plate. But at least she was eating. Four bites, Colleen had observed. Colleen, herself, was too stressed out to eat.

Malcolm watched Tiffany shake soy sauce on her food, exaggerating his amazement. "Now I know you're only half Polish, but I didn't know your other half was Chinese."

"Does it freak you out, the way I eat?"

"Well, no. I wouldn't say that it does. Good to see you with an appetite. Start calling you China Belle." Malcolm's plate sat untouched. The newscast was on to weather: days clear and sunny, unseasonably hot; nights cool.

"Hey, Grampa," Tiffany said, "did you know that if you put a penny in Taco Bell hot sauce it comes out shiny?"

Malcolm laid his hand over Tiffany's and leaned closer to her. "Wouldn't you have to wipe it off with a napkin first?" he said, and the two of them cracked up. They had a private relationship that excluded Colleen.

Malcolm turned to Theo. "After supper, maybe we could sit down and go over a few things."

Dot looked from the TV to her husband.

"Tonight's not doable. I've got lots of work the next few days. A prospectus for the yacht club—financial forecasts, number crunching, that type of stuff . . ." He ran out of things to say.

"I'd rather not put it off too long," Malcolm said.

Dot's fork rattled on her plate.

"Fine. But I'm just too busy right now. You don't cakewalk into a deal like this. It takes work, time."

"Soon, though. Next few days?"

"Sure."

"Let's plan on the weekend then," Malcolm said. "Sunday morning."

Tiffany pushed away her plate, then reached down under the table. Colleen could hear the dog's vaccine tags clinking. "Excuse me a minute," Tiffany said, and as Colleen watched her daughter move out of the room, she thought of herself at that age—going steady with Theo, sitting at this same table with Mr. and Mrs.

Wolkoviak, eating golumpki. She'd never imagined that she'd still be living her life in this kitchen. The only way out, for all of them, she reminded herself over and over, was what they were doing. Financial stress had nearly destroyed her marriage in Vail, where Colleen had been on commission for a travel agent booking hotel rooms, and her income was spotty. Theo was on commission too, as a financial adviser, and he brought home even less. They had Hilton Head debts that weren't covered by the bankruptcy, plus Tiffany's hospital bills, then her therapy. How much did they owe? When they left Hilton Head, there was a ballpark figure; but since then, it was anybody's guess. Brook's tuition. The Ford Explorer. Credit card interest. They had twenty-three credit cards between them. Or twenty-six. Ten or fifteen had gone to collections, the rest were past due. They probably owed five or six hundred thousand.

But they were starting over again, and when she reminded herself that Mr. Brown was fine, that she'd done everything possible to care for him, she felt the excitement of that first year in Hilton Head. With Theo on the business side at "Insiders," and Colleen as the creative force, they had been building a dream together. Interior design was truly her first love. But then the bottom fell out on the business side, and they tried to start again in Vail. Within a year they were evicted from their apartment—a year in which their marriage was crumbling—and with their two children they drove thirty-nine hours straight from Vail to Ludlow, carrying the rubble of their marriage to Theo's dusty boyhood room.

"Is that true," Malcolm asked, "that Brook is working for the Republicans?"

"Brook's a bright young man," Theo said. "Hey, I *lost* a small business. I *know* how hard it is. This help-the-worker stuff was great. But then it goes to help the minorities, and where does it stop? A kid like Brook works hard, majors in business, but he's the dreaded white male. IRS cleaned *us* out. Twice. There won't be a job for Brook in three years."

And then Colleen found herself saying, "Excuse me a minute," stepping behind Theo, moving through the living room, its smell of ashtrays and the dog. She sensed it: her daughter's quiet choking. She was certain she could hear it now. The sounds Colleen had heard in Vail, and ignored, afraid to confront Tiffany until her only daughter nearly died. Afraid that anything she said would only make the problem worse. But now Colleen's lack of self-assertion was a remnant of her past. She'd kept a personal growth log for assertive behavior. She'd learned to say no without guilt. In a GoodLife workshop she'd been prepared for the responsibility that accompanies wealth, for the time when her statements and actions would be taken seriously, when Chad Sturgeon would, in fact, be reporting on Colleen Wolkoviak's influence in the world.

The bathroom door was closed. With one hand on the knob, and the other poised to knock, she stopped and listened. There wasn't a sound. Tiffany had eaten so little. Colleen would not barge in, she afforded her daughter that respect. She backed into the living room and sat on the arm of the sofa—silver-gray nubbed upholstery so rough it seemed the nubs were reinforced with shavings of steel—and she waited for Tiffany, to talk mother-to-daughter, but also woman-to-woman. Confronting your daughter about such an awkward and emotional matter required self-confidence. GoodLife had given her the raw materials, the inspiration, to attain personal power—power which had threatened her husband. She could hear him now arguing at the dinner table about welfare mothers with Cadillacs. There were a lot of reasons to leave Vail, but one of them was *not* Colleen's supposed breakdown. In fact, Colleen had been on the verge of the perfect GoodLife sales plan—going out into those living rooms with her whiteboard, her sample case, and her personal power. She had started something that would bring in the kind of money and prestige Theo was not comfortable with his wife attaining solo.

Colleen would give Tiffany one more minute. She picked at the arm of the sofa. She had made some mistakes with Tiffany, she knew. In Hilton Head she was consumed with their struggling furniture and interior design business, and she knew she'd been giving the kids less time than she should. Feeling guilty one day, she had bought Tiffany a pair of jeans on the spur of the moment. Tiffany jumped out of her shorts and pulled them on, but they were designer jeans, cut too slim for a twelve-year-old girl who still had some baby fat, so Tiffany couldn't get them snapped. As the two of them looked into the oval dressing mirror in Theo and Colleen's bedroom, Colleen had said, "You're too big for them." She hadn't said *fat*. She only meant the jeans were too small, that they'd have to exchange them, but her words were careless. She'd been so obsessed with the business, she'd forgotten the reason she wanted success— to provide a better life for her children. Tiffany ran out of Colleen's bedroom in tears and refused to speak to her about her body until three years later when she was in a therapy group for anorexics in Vail.

A year and a half from now Tiffany would be going off to college, and if she wasn't cured by then, she'd be without support. She'd be a wreck. It wasn't fair. She deserved a fresh start in college. She would study French, as Colleen had, art history and dance. Or maybe she'd study business and join Colleen in opening up parts of France for GoodLife. She wouldn't have to worry about money. She'd have the choice. Colleen and Theo were giving their children a cushion and a launch pad. Colleen and Theo Wolkoviak were earning their place among the great businesspeople in America. It was the Trumps, the Iacoccas, the Perots, Ted Turner and Jane Fonda, the GoodLife founders, Samuel Anderson and Kirk P. Barnes, who were the great Americans. How many people knew the name of the chief of brain surgery at NYU Medical Center? The name of last year's Nobel Prize winner in . . . in *anything*? We'd returned to the time when the businesspeople, the people who truly built America, were getting the respect they deserved.

Colleen knocked softly on the bathroom door, then rapped harder. Her daughter would have all the advantages of wealth and prestige. Perhaps she would attend Princeton. "Tiffany," she said as she turned the knob and pushed the door open. If Princeton accepted Brooke Shields, certainly they'd accept the only daughter of Colleen Wolkoviak. *Life was a contest*, GoodLife had taught her, *and you can't win if you don't enter.* Tiffany was drying her hands.

"I said I'm *in* here."

"Honey, you're not . . ."

Tiffany pushed by her and turned around at the door. "Growing hemp in here? No. I'm not growing hemp in the bathroom, Mom."

Why did her daughter put up roadblocks? "You know honey, those Gloria Vanderbilt jeans years ago," Colleen said with a rush of emotion. "It was all my fault."

Through the tangle of her hair, Tiffany looked at Colleen. "What are you talking about?"

"I bought the wrong size."

Tiffany rolled her eyes. "You should get out more," she said, as she turned and walked away.

Colleen sniffed at the air around the toilet. Inspected the bowl, the rim, but there was nothing suspicious. Out of habit, she sprayed some Glade. She sat down on the lid.

If she couldn't talk heart-to-heart with her daughter, how could she ever assume the role of a wealthy and important woman of society? Was it possible that she was not ready for the leap to prominence? She'd always dreamed of going to France, improving herself, and coming home to make a grand return—more sophisticated, richer, wiser. But it occurred to her now, as the mist of Potpourri Glade settled around her, that the improvement in her character had to be earned. She and Theo weren't earning—but taking. What if she *wasn't* prepared for the responsibility that accompanies wealth? What if she wasn't good enough?

Tiffany was at her place at the table. Dot was watching the health news. Colleen sat down and picked up her fork. "Very dicey, pulling off ransom collection," Malcolm was saying to Theo.

"I'm telling you, he kidnapped himself," Tiffany said. "Money, money, money."

Grease had drained from Colleen's uneaten golumpki and puddled around the rim of her plate. She would never eat ground beef again.

It was Colleen's fault that her daughter was so cynical, so unambitious, such a free spirit. Colleen had sent her daughter the message that she had to restrain her dreams. That's the message Colleen had gotten as a girl, and it wasn't until she understood the GoodLife philosophy that she gave herself permission to say, "I want at the very least a *pied-à-terre* in Paris." Accepting the responsibility of wealth involved repositioning herself in the world. Identifying her

own list of needs and desires and giving them priority. *A small list
makes a coward of the bravest person.* Her needs would never again take a
backseat to cost. It was about caring for herself, about rejecting the
ways women were trained to behave. *Action, attitude, atmosphere.*
Colleen prayed that what she believed in her most confident
moments was true: that she'd adequately accomplished the personal work—the growth stuff—and lack of money was all that
held her back.

Dot picked up her own plate and Theo's, set them in the sink.
Colleen forced a bite. Cold golumpki.

Her feelings did not require the approval of *any* man, especially
a rich man like Stona Brown with the resources to care for himself
quite extravagantly. But her nervousness and fear this morning
were indications that she was not prioritizing her own self-respect.
Instead, she was once again emphasizing the feelings and opinions of
others: this time, Mr. Stona Brown. She had a *right* to her own feelings.

Colleen set her plate on the counter beside the sink. She
walked around the table and picked up Tiffany's plate, the food dis-
sected as if she'd been searching for a jewel. Malcolm's dinner was
still untouched. Dot shook her head and scraped the food into the
trash.

"From a getting-caught standpoint, a man's got a better
chance walking into a bank with a mask and a note than trying to
collect ransom," Malcolm said. "Statistically."

"Christ Almighty." Theo was getting tense, edgy. "Think
about the amount you get in a stickup versus kidnapping this guy."
Colleen stopped behind his chair and gave his shoulders a solid
squeeze. She'd encourage him to go a few times a week for a massage

and sauna, and she'd do the same for herself. She'd get a private trainer too. And a nutritionist. They'd come right to your house and throw out food from your cupboards you shouldn't be eating.

Theo threw his napkin on the table; it was torn into shreds. "Plus the political statement."

"Political?" Malcolm said.

Theo looked at the TV and crossed his arms over his chest. "I don't know, but I doubt it's a coincidence. Look at Petrochem's environmental record. What do you bet they're environmental terrorists?"

Tiffany piped up. "I think Dad's right."

"Voila." Theo nodded at his father, pointing at Tiffany.

As Colleen finished clearing away dinner, Dot set out dishes of raspberry sherbet. "A cold glass of milk with your sherbet, Tiffany?" Dot tried again, but Tiffany declined; then Malcolm declined a can of Ensure. He bent over to untie his black patrolman's shoes. Then he slipped out his foot and pulled off his sock for the nightly ritual with the dog. He stuck his bare foot out to the side, toes spread, and the dog lapped his foot. Colleen stepped out of the way because sometimes the dog got so excited it puddled on the linoleum. "Daisy needs salt in her diet," Malcolm said. "Just like a human. Probably no salt in that dog food. Damn health kick." None of this would ever happen again.

Within a year, Theo would be running a yacht club and marina in Hilton Head. Summers, as he raced the sailboat and golfed, Colleen would be by his side. Cocktails at five sharp, three-thirty on weekends. Theo would be a man people knew, famous for his beach parties with heaps of clams and lobster on the grill, free-pouring wine. Late at night the bonfire would glow on the faces of powerful men—celebrities, businessmen, politicians, retreating for a few days from the limelight with their perfumed wives drinking cognac and scotch.

Colleen sucked the raspberry sherbet off the stainless-steel spoon in her mouth. The percolator bubbled up decaf behind her.

The rest of the year she'd spend on Ile St.-Louis in Paris, where she planned to buy a building. The penthouse would be her getaway and she'd rent out the lower flats, one of them cheaply to a deserving theater actor or a ballerina. How much could a building cost? Two million? Three? It didn't matter, it would pay for itself as an investment and even if it didn't, it was what she wanted, what she'd *always* wanted. Her own needs first.

Colleen would take her time, use her capital and prestige to set up her GoodLife business right. She hadn't investigated whether someone had opened up Paris, but even so, with Tiffany by her side, she would do it bigger and better. She would dine at Maxim's. She'd keep a yacht in Monte Carlo, and in no time would make the acquaintance of Caroline and Stephanie. At first the princesses would be wary of this American newcomer, but Colleen would not be pushy. She'd be *confident not arrogant, happy not giddy.* During her seasons in Paris, Colleen's deep character growth would catch up with her outward self-esteem, and then she would relax into the woman she truly was.

Her family could ride on the coattails of her class and cultivation. In Colleen's new circle, Malcolm and Dot would be forgiven for being old, and she would buy them presentable clothes, teach them how to order a meal. Tiffany's hippie clothes and stringy hair, the humiliation of her anorexia, would be forgotten. Years ago she'd convinced Theo to switch from beer to Cape Codders and G&Ts in the summer, and she'd convinced him never to work on a car in the driveway. She'd continue to make him more refined—step one would be to shave off that beard immediately after they collected the money. Theo was powerful and definitive, a take-charge man whose self-confidence she admired, and when he decided to grow the beard as a disguise she'd fantasized that it might lend him a debonair and refined sex appeal. There had been a man once with a mustache, in Vail, at her first GoodLife convention. A man as successful as Stona Brown—

Colleen prayed that Mr. Brown was okay. She prayed that the plan would proceed without another hitch. Because if some harm came to Mr. Brown at Theo's and Colleen's hands, she knew that she'd never . . . She was too old for another chance at her dreams. The Wolkoviaks' musty house and sour fridge were already in her past. Golumpki and kielbasa were in her past. The present did not exist.

As the dog licked Malcolm's feet, Theo was telling the inappropriate story for the hundredth time about when the dog was a puppy. It was back when he was a cop, and he had bought the dog for the kids. Whenever they'd been out and returned to the house, the dog would have made a bowel movement on the family room floor. And every time, Theo would smack the dog and stick her nose in it to train her not to go in the house. Now Theo was laughing, telling how finally when they returned home one evening, the dog ran over and all by herself stuck her nose in her pile of feces. "Butt in the air." Theo chuckled. "That little tail wagging, thinking she's finally learned the trick. That's about when we decided to give the little shit to you, Pop." Why does his father laugh with him when he's heard the story a hundred times? And why does Theo have to tell it at the table, at *dinner*? Never again would any of this ever happen.

A sharp pain in his forehead, clawing down the back of his neck, the sweltering darkness, Stona couldn't remember for a moment where he was. He'd slept, or fallen unconscious, but he was awake now, alive. He was still in the box.

It had to be long after one o'clock, and still he hadn't been released. He wondered if the ransom had been paid, and then he realized that, of course, it would be paid at night. That's why he had to wait all this time. But now it was almost over. He felt himself getting stronger as he figured this out, he felt his mind getting sharper. It would only be another hour, maybe two. He'd need assistance, but he would walk from this box to the ambulance, and he would stretch. Good God, he would stretch.

He had to occupy his mind for the short time that remained, so he continued his search for the kidnapper. From Rosenblatt's Men's Store he drove to the Asherton post office. He examined the wanted posters, but his mind was sluggish and couldn't call up a single face. He got in line and moved through the ropes, past the stand-up ad for stamp collectors, and as he looked at the postal workers behind the counter, his memory began to function. He knew none of their names, but he saw their faces. A Chinese man on the far left, a woman who always looked as if she'd just had a perm, a fat man with a white beard, and at the window on the far right . . . He couldn't place a face, but when he tried to picture his kidnapper at that station—his hair combed, the jacket and tie— it wasn't right. He left the post office confident the kidnapper wasn't there.

For the sake of thoroughness he drove to the Florham Park post office too. Then, he pulled into Henderson Garden Supply, but as he walked around the greenhouse, he felt the humid heat press on him, and his forehead and temples throbbed. He tried to see the faces, but he could only see the darkness of the box. Then he felt blood dripping down his face from his forehead. How many hours had he been in this coffin? How many hours in the goddamned heat? Surely it was evening, but this garage would not let the heat go. He'd always thought his hell would be the cold—standing naked in the ice with no place to sit, the wind slicing razor-sharp specks of frost into his skin. He always took an overcoat with him, or at least a light sweater, even in the middle of summer. His heart couldn't take a sudden chill.

And now he'd die in a swelter. The spit-soaked rag slithered down his throat. But he could not die, not like this. There were things he had to confess. "A criminal act," Nunny had actually called it, but damn it, he'd had no choice. The company was at stake. An indiscretion with a girl in New Haven forty years ago. A longing for an adolescent friend of Jane's.

His lower back wrenched up, and Stona tried to turn again, dropped his left shoulder and twisted his torso against the ropes, and his heart made a flabby thump like a water balloon bursting. Blood surged from the hole in his arm.

He'd never been able to bring himself—his righteousness and embarrassment—to confess any of it. He could not die without last rites or he would be damned.

He felt blood reach his calf and then his ankle. The blanket was soaked. Blindfolded, he felt the physical presence of the box closing in. Solid. He had to get hold of himself. He was not going to let himself die. He tried pretending he was in a sleeping bag, out camping, feverish with flu. Sleeping in a mummy bag, sweating miserably. There was no box. No box.

Stona's blood rose around his wrist, catching on his watchband and wedding ring, knuckles, hairs, creases of skin, until the abundance of the hot liquid building against its own meniscus broke its hold, and the fingers of blood crept higher.

The smell of the Bayram slaughter after Ramadan. The reek of blood and heat. The peculiar smell of blood-soaked fur. The smell of his urine.

The blood rose and rose, pooling around the peaks of his knees. His body was emptying. There wasn't enough left for his arrhythmic heart to pump through his arteries. His blood was submerging him, rising above his ears, creeping up to his face, over his jaw, his cheeks. He tasted blood in his mouth. When it gurgled at his nostrils, he buckled his spine and reached his head straining for air, and his forehead once again crashed against the lid. He banged and banged, pounding harder each time, his skin mashing open again. There had to be someone, someone who would hear. He banged his head until the muscles of his neck gave out, until a trickle of blood down his cheek made him realize that the blood sloshing in the box was no longer there. It had never been there.

And everything was quiet. Stona felt the vastness of the moon and stars, of driving great distances with windows open wide. Somehow, by God's good grace, a cool breath of night feathered into the box, caressing him, kissing him, whispering to him, *You're still with us. Still alive.*

Nunny awoke with a start. Something smelled sour. On a tray on the bed, on her china was a half-eaten sandwich: roast beef, lettuce, cucumber, and horseradish. Jane was asleep on the chaise lounge. The clock said one-thirty a.m. All the lights were on. Nunny stared at the telephone, still no call; then she rushed into the hallway and stopped at the top of the stairs, listening to the hushed grumble of men's voices, the scratch and static of a radio, the beep of a cellular phone. It could have been the children in the living room ten or fifteen years ago, staying up too late watching movies with friends. As she walked back through the bedroom door, her vision was clear straight ahead, but around the edges it was blurred, as if she were looking through the center of a wreath. There were sparkles she couldn't blink away.

She pulled an afghan over Jane, then sat down beside her at the foot of the chaise, praying that they had given Stona a blanket. Why hadn't they taken his overcoat? Neatly folded in thirds, the slope of his shoulders apparent in the coat, it had been left sitting on the front seat.

Jane's hair was still damp from the shower, and she smelled of Stona's shampoo and Nunny's vervain soap. Nunny leaned over her daughter and kissed her forehead. When she pulled away, Jane's arm unfolded from her chest, and her fist opened enough to reveal her two silver button earrings. Nunny took them from Jane's palm, and the hand relaxed and fell open like an infant's, and Nunny remembered the smell of her babies.

Victor had called from Seoul earlier in the evening. He'd been sweet. He was sure, he'd told Nunny, that his father was giving the kidnappers hell. He was waiting for a flight, but the airport was closed for at least a few hours because of a storm. High winds. He said that he loved her. His voice—how had she never noticed before?—sounded just like Stona's.

She felt cold, so she moved briskly about the room, eyeing the sandwich Jane had made her on the bed. She touched the phone on Stona's bedside table, pressing her fingertips to the receiver, willing it to ring. Stona would speak to her. "Fine," he'd say, tired but vigorous. "It's going to be fine." As Nunny stared at the phone, an ache crept up her forearm which she reached to massage, and in that moment, she leaned her face toward the phone, then kneeled down on the floor, touching the phone with the tip of her nose: she could smell Stona's breath coming off the ivory-colored plastic, and she could smell the sharp oiliness of his ear. Under the kneading pressure of her thumb, her forearm felt hard. And when she clenched her fist, Jane's earrings pressed sharply into her palm. She began to set the earrings on Stona's bedside table, but thought better of it; Jane could forget them there. Instead, she put them on herself. As she fidgeted the backs onto the posts, the ache spread through her arm. Then it struck her that the soreness had come from pinching the two stray hairs she'd picked from Stona's shoulder before he left the house, the two hairs she'd held through the questioning by Bradford Ross, then a young Asherton officer whom Ross quickly dismissed, then Chief Tomkins when Ross no less than ordered him to the house. Couldn't Nunny remember a detail she'd overlooked? Wasn't there a sound she hadn't considered? Hadn't she noticed someone recently watching the house? Hadn't there been an unusual phone call? A delivery? She closed her eyes, struggling to remember.

When Jane had arrived at the house, she'd gently taken the two hairs from Nunny and laid them in a tissue. Nunny touched the tissue now, safe in the pocket of her sweater. She rubbed her arm and looked across the bed at her daughter in sweatpants and her law school sweatshirt.

Suddenly, Nunny couldn't stand the horseradish smell another second and without thinking opened Stona's bedside table drawer and clattered the plate and the sandwich inside, then shoved the drawer closed. She stared at the table—his glasses should be lying there, folded while he slept. Instead, they were in an envelope marked *Evidence* at the Asherton police station. Jane sighed, stretched out her legs, then began to quietly snore. Nunny was afraid that nothing in their lives would be normal again.

She blew her nose. Her allergies were usually over by Memorial Day, but this year they were raging. She stroked Jane's hair—dark, thick, fast-growing hair—as she passed toward the door.

In the hallway was a table. In the top drawer was a flashlight, candles, matches, drink coasters from the Accademia gift shop. There were TWA playing cards and a book of poems by Gerard Manley Hopkins, its gold lettering mostly worn off the cracked leather binding. Touching the table—Queen Anne, bought from Derek Colby before he closed his shop in Litchfield—gliding her fingers over its surface, Nunny knew the placement of every single item in that drawer. She felt their familiar presence as she moved past.

Descending the stairs, she wondered, was Stona able to sleep? Was he cold? He fell apart without his seven hours. She'd never known another person who slept so soundly. Descending, but looking up at the stained-glass chandelier hanging over the stairs, made by a woman with a single name in Edgartown, the iron chain by a blacksmith, part Indian, with hair to his waist. Nunny descended into the veil of smoke—two smells really—the stale smoke that had been settling into the carpets and walls since morning, and the crisp, stimulating smell of cigarettes now burning. She crossed the hall carpet—a Persian, a gift to Nunny from a minister under the Shah—and listened to the men from the darkened archway. "Eight pounds four ounces. That's a bit of all right." "The wife packed me egg salad again." "You seen the new one with Tom Cruise?" The hiss of a soda can, the rustle of a newspaper folded back on itself. She slipped into the kitchen unnoticed, where the lights were harshly bright.

The house was new when they bought it in 1964, and this was the third kitchen. The bay window and Florida room were add-ons. It had been chilly this morning—yesterday morning—when she and Stona ate breakfast. "Is your overcoat in the car?" she'd asked. Since the heart attack he had to be so careful about getting a chill. She had stood with him on this spot, fixed his hankie and tie, plucked the two hairs from his shoulder, kissed him loose and slow, and said, "I love you," as they had every morning year after year. In the last few years, though, she'd thought many times of reaching her arms around his waist at the door, letting her lips and body slacken, and seducing him into retiring on the spot—flying off to Praiano and doing the breakfast dishes in a month or two when they returned.

Twenty hours ago, she'd let Stona step down through the veranda. She had let him go, even though she had seen the legs in pink pants pausing at the foot of the drive, noticed the oddness of their stride. She had perceived the wrongness. Standing on the verandah with a chill, she sensed now that Stona was cold as clearly as she sensed the cool air washing up from the foot of the drive, where a policeman's head was silhouetted in the reading light of his cruiser. The police car was parked where Stona had stopped his car for the paper, the spot where the car had sat all day while men with magnifying glasses and tweezers crawled under the dash and over the seats, apologetic men who had found nothing but a tire track and a chip of blue paint. The air washed up the drive and through the pines, sifting through the screen and her light cotton slacks, swirling like rushing water around her legs.

She stepped down into the garage, and her eyes quickly adjusted to the darkness as she navigated around her own car. Yellow-white light from the carriage lamps dropped like faint searchlights through the windows. She saw right away that Stona's car had been pulled too far forward. What was anybody thinking? There must have been six feet, enough room to lie down on the cement, between his rear bumper and the garage door. She moved between the cars. How would Stona get to his gardening tools with the car pulled up so tight? *Do people think?*

She opened Stona's car door, and when the domelight didn't go on, she felt a sudden chill. The investigators must have switched it off to save the battery and forgotten to switch it back on. Simply forgotten. Did she have to second-guess the police? Did she have to treat these men like children?

She found herself crawling across Stona's seat, reaching over the parking brake to his overcoat, which was folded not in thirds as it always was, but in half. They had searched the pockets, of course, for the possibility of a note from the kidnappers. Or a note from Stona to Nunny—the other possibility, suggested behind her back, that Stona had thrown her over for a mistress with whom he'd escaped to Provence or Bora-Bora. They intended to examine bank activity for a sizable cash withdrawal, see if country club dues were paid in advance, ask if he'd been seen with a woman. Or a man. Did they think she didn't hear the murmured conversations in her own house as she was preparing coffee and buckets of ice? Did Bradford Ross think that his hushed voice didn't carry? "I don't want any questioning of the wife about marital affairs for twenty-four hours." Did he think his voice didn't resonate with the voices of the other men through the walls and ceiling and rafters—carry to where Nunny sat doubled over on the toilet? *Did they think?* is what she wanted to know.

She fingered the lapel of Stona's overcoat. If only he'd been wearing it this morning—yesterday—he'd have it now. Nunny wanted to wrap herself in the black wool and curl up on the seat of his car until she heard the telephone ring and the men went to bring Stona home.

But kneeling on the seat, her hip bumping against the steering wheel as she moved, she sensed something was out of place. She flinched when she saw suddenly, in the corner of her eye, a phantomlike shape flare up in the windshield where steam from his travel mug had lapped the cold glass. As she looked more closely at the windshield and the distorted reflections of Stona's gardening tools, she settled into the seat as if to drive.

And here was the thing that was wrong. Stona was four inches taller than Nunny, but their legs were the same length, so they adjusted car seats the same. Now, though, she couldn't even reach the pedals because these police, who found nothing with all of their self-proclaimed expertise and expensive machines and therefore chose to insinuate about Nunny and Stona's love for each other, had pushed back Stona's seat and did not take the time—or have the *thought*—to correctly readjust it. She tried to slide the seat forward, pulling at the lever and rocking her body, but it was stuck. Meanwhile these police sat in her living room, eating junk food and smoking and talking about movies.

Nunny got on her knees on the floor of the garage, yanking on the lever and pounding the back of the seat, the bones of her knees grinding on the cold cement. Yes, she could put everything in order for Stona's return, she could clean up after these police, but they had to do their job and get him back. They had to do *something*—it was not Nunny's job to know what. And she fought against the seat until the lever pinched her palm, and a trickle of blood at her wrist squirmed down the underside of her arm and reached her elbow. She yanked the lever even harder and positioned herself to drive the seat forward with her shoulder.

Malcolm couldn't sleep, so he left Dot in their bed, went to the john and then downstairs. He wondered how the kidnappers expected to collect the ransom, tried to get his mind around why they'd leave the car, engine running, at the foot of the driveway. When he got to the kitchen, there was Theo, sitting at the table leaning over a map. "It's three o'clock in the morning," Malcolm said.

"You know me. Can't get enough of maps."

Malcolm lowered himself into his chair at the head of the table. It was a road map of North Jersey. "I didn't know that about you. Just like Dave Tomkins, though. Since he became chief, he's been restoring old Asherton maps that the department is—"

"Don't you sleep anymore?" Theo asked.

"Here and there. What about you? Nerves up?"

"*Colleeen's* up. I can't sleep because she can't sleep. She's up there reading GoodLife sales plans in bed."

"I meant to ask you about those pillows. If they were too musty, we could've——"

"No, they're fine. She's propped up like a princess, keeping me awake."

What was it about Theo and the truth? This afternoon Malcolm had seen him fling the pillows into his car and drive off to the yacht club.

With the remote Malcolm switched on the TV. "Reading up on GoodLife, is she?" Malcolm flipped through the channels. Theo studied the map. A year ago Colleen had sent case after case of GoodLife stuff from Vail. Degreaser, car wax, dog shampoo, carpet cleaner. Malcolm wrote out the checks to Colleen and sent most of the stuff to the church. "She's taking up with GoodLife again, is she?" Malcolm tried again.

Theo drummed his fingers on the table. "She's real serious about it, got the entrepreneur bug."

"It seems you both do."

"It's working for us too. You'll see." Theo winked, and Malcolm was reminded of the way things used to be—flat on their backs under the Belvedere, pulling a blown transmission and spending an afternoon together muscling in a rebuilt one.

Theo looked back to the map, but Malcolm wanted to keep it going. "Where would you start looking if you were Dave Tomkins? With the kidnapping, I mean."

"I don't know, Pop." Theo traced his finger through Bergen County.

"Tell you what. In the morning I'll give Dave a buzz to get his take on this matter of the professionalism."

Theo looked up from the map. "You know, I could care less what Dave Tomkins's take is. From the day I joined the force I've been hearing about Dave Tomkins. I was never the cop he was. Fine. I admit it. But—"

"I wouldn't . . ." Malcolm shook his head. It had never occurred to him that Theo might feel he had to live up to Dave. "I never—"

"But you might recall I'm not a cop anymore. I was discharged, for which I get a whopping thousand dollars a month."

It was either a disability retirement or fire Theo, and if he'd been fired for excessive force, he'd have never found another job. Malcolm had pleaded with him. He'd ordered him to resign, but Theo refused. He told his father, "You fire me, or you get me disability pay." The last suspension—Theo's gun contacting the face of a suspect's mother—had turned up the heat from the mayor. Dave Tomkins, Malcolm's deputy at the time, had advised him that Theo had to go.

"Believe me," Theo said. "Dave Tomkins could never pull off this deal I'm working on."

"Tell me the—" Malcolm's voice caught and he reached for his inhaler. In some departments five out of ten cops went on disability when they'd had enough of police work. A back injury from a fall, a wracked-up knee. Some departments thought it was fair compensation considering the low pay for policing. Malcolm never thought so. Neither did Dave Tomkins. Malcolm had never discussed Theo's disability discharge with Dave, and Dave had never asked.

"It looks promising, then?" Malcolm asked when his chest had cleared.

"Very."

"Let's hear about it."

Theo looked away.

"Which yacht club is it?" Malcolm said.

"I shouldn't . . ." Theo tugged on the ill-shaped beard at his chin. "Okay," he finally said. "It's down in Golden Bay. Golden Bay Yacht Club."

"Ritzy."

Theo slapped the edge of the table. "I know what you mean by that. You don't think I'm good enough for it. You don't think I can pull it off."

Malcolm shook his head. "I don't mean anything of the sort."

"You were good at what you did, and I'm sure Dave Tomkins is too. But it's a small-pond life. What I'm doing is on a grand scale. I admit I've had setbacks, but that's the nature of this career. A series of ventures. Donald Trump has failures every week. Do you think his father doubts him every time?"

Malcolm had stepped in it again. "I support—"

"I don't need your support, and I don't need your respect. I just need . . ." For the first time in days Theo was looking directly into his father's eyes. "I'm making this deal happen, and it's happening big."

Malcolm didn't know the words for what he wanted to say—to explain that there was no likening his love for Theo with his fondness for Dave Tomkins. Even if Malcolm had known Dave's life depended on it, he would never have signed a false disability for him, or for any man, except Theo. This was the love of a father for his son.

He stood. He clapped Theo on the shoulder and pulled open the fridge. From the shelf in the door, beside the same six cans of

Ensure that Dot had put there for Malcolm months ago, he grabbed two bottles of Heineken. He twisted off the caps and pounded them on the table.

"You can't drink that," Theo said; then he smiled. He put his arm around Malcolm's waist.

"I can celebrate my son's success any way I please. Doctors be damned." They clanked their bottles together, and in the quiet, honest stillness of the night, they drank.

I sn't it unique to think we could make loads of money for the reason being that we're better people?" In Vail, in their living room, Colleen had arrayed before Theo the products she'd bought at the GoodLife informational meeting that afternoon at the Sheraton in Denver. "But this is the GoodLife philosophy."

Theo examined the hefty bottle of car wash, the glossy picture on the label and the bright red cap, weighing it in his hand. "What makes you think this stuff's any good?"

"They're excellent products. Everyone knows that. But the point being most of your money comes from the plan, from the system you set up below you, and not from your own sales." On the coffee table—made from a huge old blacksmith's bellows they'd found antiquing down toward Durango—she'd placed the various products: the car wash and wax, complexion soap made from honey (a quarter the price of department stores), dish detergent, metal polish, toothpaste, mouthwash, and the classic GoodLife product, LiquidGold, the all-purpose cleanser that had made millions.

"Twenty wide and twenty deep is my initial plan. It comes out to four hundred people below me at a maximum take of twenty-one percent. Plus bonuses. Think about it. I've started the calculations, it's very complex. Let's just say, for a ballpark figure, easily six digits within twelve months."

Theo smirked, looking off to the side the way he did. Ready to suck the wind out of her sails. To shoot her down. But she wouldn't let him, not this time. She understood that her new income might emasculate him. The freedom it would afford her. The entrée into certain social circles. She would be patient with her husband. "GoodLife is about understanding your goals," she said, "then setting out to fulfill them. It's about helping you get in touch with your own desires, what's inside you. Otherwise, you spend your life striving for some dream that might not even be your own. Do I want to achieve Distinction Status in six months, or do I want to take more time building a wider front line so I reach Laurel a little farther down the road, but I roll through Prestige and Majesty Status like a tank? I honestly don't know. So part of the system is that through my upline and my sponsor, I'll get to know myself better as part of the business-building process. In that sense it's very gestalt."

After the presentation in Denver that afternoon Colleen had gone right up to the speaker and shaken his hand. "Mr. Thompson, I've understood some things today, and I have to thank you. They were inside me, and you've allowed me to see them. You've changed my life."

He had held her hand firmly and glanced at her name tag so quickly she barely noticed. He'd said, "Colleen, this kind of feedback is immensely gratifying to me. And please call me Mitch." He wore a linen suit of a color she'd never quite seen before, a pale yellow with a hint of gold much more vibrant than typical pastels. His shirt was raw silk, ecru, and his earth-toned tie was loosely knotted. His mustache was full but trimmed neatly above his lip. A gold watch on a heavy gold-linked bracelet hung loosely around his wrist; his tan was a true bronze with the evenness and rich orange glow that come from salons. This was a man who carried his wealth with class.

He touched her elbow as he spoke, cutting through the chaos around them, the other people clamoring for a word. "Where do you call home, Colleen?"

"We made the break from the East Coast rat race, so we're in Vail year-round."

"Now you're bragging," he said, still clasping her hand and cradling her elbow. As his smile broadened, his mustache stretched and hooked at the ends.

"It made sense for us at this time, financially. Like you were saying about realistic dreams and lifestyle visualization."

Mitch stopped smiling. His face grew serious, concerned eyes so blue she wondered if he wore tinted contacts. "Are you happy with the move?" She imagined his breath cool as the comfrey-scented mist she had for facials. She'd never been kissed by a man with a mustache.

"Extremely." She nodded too emphatically. She had to work on a more dignified and reserved facade. Thoughtfully—indicating to Mitch with her pursed lips that this was an understanding that had come to her as a result of their discourse and not something she'd said a hundred times—she told him, "We like it. It's a very homogeneous community. We're in just the one condo for now, but we're laying the groundwork for acquiring some exclusive properties."

"And I'll bet an extra hundred and forty G's a year would fill a few gaps in that groundwork."

"A truer word was never spoken."

"I have a feeling you're coming on board."

"Mitch," she said, "I think you're very well in touch with my feelings," and she saw the ever so subtle squint of one of his eyes saying, *Yes, in this world we each are committed to complex lives so far apart, but in the desert island fantasy—the chance meeting on a business trip in a Paris hotel lobby or in the tiny bathroom joining our private sleepers on the overnight train to Rome—you and I would put romance novels to shame.* She sensed him preparing to move on to one of the others hovering around, so she was first to say, "I won't monopolize you, although you could engage me all afternoon. Thanks again, really," and he squeezed her hand and elbow at once, and allowed his fingertips to brush the length of her forearm as they turned their separate ways.

She was confident not arrogant, happy not giddy. GoodLife had already made her a better person.

That night, after the long drive back to Vail, when everyone was finally in bed, Colleen took a slow steamy shower. She shampooed and conditioned and tried a new finishing rinse on trial offer from Bath Etc. She shaved her underarms and legs, and when she was finished, she turned the shower head to pulse, dropped her head forward, and let the hot water pummel her neck and shoulders. She was always sore there. When she saw photos of herself, she was surprised to see how her neck curved forward and her shoulders were rounded. Hot water was the only thing that relieved the ache.

She had played it so well with Mitch. With her hair up in a towel and her thick robe wrapped around her, she sat on the couch with her starter kit, the products she'd purchased, and her notes from Mitch's presentation. Theo and the kids were asleep—it was past one. The only sounds were the appliances doing their jobs, automatically.

As she went over her notes, she couldn't separate Mitch from his ideas, from his voice, his quotes, copied onto her page. She had never heard a speaker so inspiring. The simplicity of the plan was what most impressed her, and the guarantee of return. He'd drawn one big circle for her dreams and a small one for her salary. There were two choices: shrink her dreams to fit her salary, or grow her salary to fit her dreams. She'd written Mitch's quote below the bubbles: *This concept, if you will, is the foundation of GoodLife.*

Hadn't she ever been pecked on the cheek by a man with a mustache? She must have, but she couldn't think of one. It seemed like such a basic life experience. What else had she missed? She was copying Mitch's plan from her legal pad to four-by-six note cards as he'd instructed. His quotes could fill a little book, a size that would fit in the palm of your hand, hardcover with a ribbon to mark your page, and delicate line drawings of leaves and berries below each gem of wisdom. *You can't cash in your unproductive hours at the Pearly Gates. Upgrade your life, friends, and dreams. You have no use for negative people. Always be people-shopping.* Colleen could do the drawings for the book. Would he joint-venture the project with her? She needed a computer and modem.

Would his mustache tickle her lips and nose? Would it tickle her neck? She lightly brushed two fingers behind her ear, along her hairline, the nape of her neck—one of her most sensitive spots, which her husband had never managed to figure out. The spot, that brush of nerves, remained her own. A private entrance into her sensuality where her fingers could go when she was alone. Was she saving it? Was it a door promised to a stranger, a lover she hadn't yet encountered? Or was she too old for that? Forty-three and waiting for life to begin. She looked at the circle on her pink index card. Written inside the circle—she heard Mitch's voice saying the word—*DREAMS*. She noticed how small her circle actually was. *DREAMS* barely fit inside. The *M* and *S* were scrunched up on the right. Her dreams twenty years ago were as large as the brightly colored hot-air balloons that lifted tourists high up over Vail. Sailing, Nantucket, Paris. A passionate lover, well-bred children, and a circle of quality friends. She could click down the list, and to be really honest she'd have to scratch a black X beside each one. She had lived her life waiting for life to begin.

Did Mitch have hair on his chest? She'd always wished Theo did. Anything to break up the expanse of pale skin: her husband was not fat, but thick—white and shapeless.

Except for the blue eyes Mitch looked Mediterranean— hot-blooded when he wanted to be, a bit of the animal. He was a much smaller man than Theo, a man she could get her arms around, a man who knew how to move, she could tell. A man who could dance. His bronze body swaying over her, she'd comb her nails through the dark hair curling from his chest.

She wrote out the next index card—*counseling from your upline, supply from the company*—each in its own interconnected circle. Mitch had made it so clear, it was all part of helping others.

She hoped she hadn't been too obvious—staring at his lips, the way he spoke with such self-assurance. *We're talking a win-win situation here*, she read from the notes on her lap. *Duplicate yourself as Ray Kroc did. You must be a one hundred percent user.* They would easily make the shift to being an exclusively GoodLife household. She took a can of Hi-Glo in her hand and read the label: *a protective layer of silicone uniquely combined with the wood-conditioning richness of carnauba wax for all your fine furnishings.*

Pictured on the label was a beautiful antique end table, mahogany she thought, a collector's piece. At first she'd found the packaging of the GoodLife household products a tad industrial, not very homey, but she was coming to see this look as part of their appeal. The sturdy chunky bottles, always heavier than you expect because they're so concentrated. A sameness about them—like a collection. Espresso cups, Japanese dolls. Colleen was starting a collection of tiny silver spoons, each with a tiny medallion on its handle identifying the national park or monument it came from.

Did Mitch have anyone to show him around Denver, or was he cooped up in his hotel room with nothing but the TV? He might not know what to make of the West. All the open spaces, the hugeness of the mountains out here. Of course he wasn't left alone, she realized, shaking her head, scolding herself for her naïveté. He was out with the bigwigs—the new Majesty Status members up on the stage who had received their pins and certificates at an invitation-only black-tie brunch.

She had to change her whole outlook. It wasn't just a matter of understanding the commission and bonus systems and memorizing the stats and vitals of each product. She had to embrace GoodLife, meld with GoodLife, and change her negative way of thinking, her preconceptions about the meaning of business, career, money, and her whole life vision. She had to *become* GoodLife.

The only light on in the apartment was the halogen floor lamp beside her. She had dimmed it to create a more pensive atmosphere, and now she turned it lower, below pensive to romantic— the couch, the table, herself, and GoodLife in a private candlelight glow. She arranged the products in a semicircle on the coffee table. The pictures on their labels looked even richer in the dim light— the hood of a luxury automobile, an expensive kitchen counter, the mahogany table. All of these desirable images were part of the lifestyle vision she had to incorporate into her own.

Forty-three wasn't too old. *New friends and a new direction,* Mitch had said. She was still young at heart and had a superb figure. She reached inside her robe and smoothed her hand over her tummy— nearly as flat as the day she graduated from high school—her skin still moist from the shower. Her legs were firm and strong. That's where a lot of women went first. Colleen let her robe fall open below the belt knotted at her waist. She lifted one foot from the table, turned her leg out from the hip as dancers do, pointed, then flexed. Her legs were delectable—smooth, shiny, and freshly shaved. Had Mitch noticed her legs? She wished she'd worn a shorter skirt. She could get away with it. Her derriere had always been rather flat, but that was a look.

She dropped her head forward over her knees, stretching her back and legs, squeezing her calves. The towel came loose, falling off her head, and the cool wet tips of her hair tickled her legs. She reached to the table for the Satinique Pour Les Hommes Men's Hair Shampoo. The *homme* on the label had his arms raised to rinse his hair, his well-defined muscles glistening under the stream of water. She popped up the lid, and she knew the scent immediately. That was why she thought of comfrey as she spoke with Mitch. It was subliminal. Mitch used Satinique Pour Les Hommes.

Colleen held the bottle underneath her nose, and brushed the fingertips of her other hand from her ear to the nape of her neck, barely touching the moist skin below the line of cool wet hair. Mitch's mustache would follow his lips over this spot as they danced in his hotel suite. His mustache scratchy, his lips soft. Like pretzels and ice cream—salty-dry and creamy-sweet. Colleen loved opposites together.

Kissing his way lower down her neck, Mitch would push Colleen's gown off her shoulders, his hair in her face as he moved down her chest. She took another deep breath of comfrey and let the bottle slide to her lap, her other hand reaching inside her robe. She lifted an arm and stroked the skin from her underarm to the underside of her breast—Mitch would know just where to go, where to excite her.

She wondered about *his* derriere. Did he have the sculpted depressions on the outside of each cheek made for a woman's hands, holding, guiding? Colleen opened her eyes now and realized where she was, but her fingers kept moving. She flung an arm to the side—those efficient motions that come with sex—and turned the light lower.

Mitch moved down. Her left hand reached across her breasts, and her right hand scratched over her tummy, her finger tracing the rim of her belly button. She tugged loose the knot in her terry-cloth belt. The bristly hair of his mustache met her own bristly hair, and with her finger she parted her lips. *Mouillé* was the French word for wet, *chaud* for hot.

And she let her legs spread and opened her eyes to relax and push herself out of the eddy she was in, caught in a curve of the warm river where she turned in circles and didn't progress, couldn't build momentum. In a semicircle down by her feet stood the bottles of GoodLife products. She couldn't make out the labels in the darkness, just the shapes of the identical sturdy bottles, the soldiers of her front line. *A whole new you,* she heard Mitch say. *Dare to dream.*

And the sound of his voice, the inspiration of his words, sucked her into the swift current. It was unstoppable now, focused. She felt the direction. The river inside her was rushing, she rode the wild current.

She hadn't come in months. She hadn't wanted to. And she was at the edge now, holding it there, slowing her finger, digging her nails into Mitch's scalp, the weight of a man on top of her pressing on her chest. A tight knot loosened in her pelvis and the heat expanded within her and her body broke free of a heavy shell that had confined her. She rounded her back and squeezed: she squeezed her breast in her hand, and she snapped her hips and snapped out her legs, kicking over the GoodLife bottles on the table. And she squeezed her thighs together, squirting Satinique Pour Les Hommes from the bottle and filling the air with the smell of comfrey.

As the green bubbles of Satinique floated back to earth around her, she whispered to Mitch, "You made a mess, honey," and with the damp towel she wiped shampoo from her freshly shaved legs.

saturday

Stona awoke to the sound of a car, of tires crunching over gravel, stopping so near it might have pulled into the garage. This time, he awoke without surprise or disorientation. The box had become a given, a new phase of his life, eclipsing everything that had come before it. The car engine shut off and it kicked, kicked again, dieseling until it raced and cut out in a series of knocks. Shoes scraped the gravel, a car door slammed, then another. Stona's impulse was to call out, to struggle, to pound his head. But those moments, that phase of his life, had passed.

The temperature had dropped. He was drenched and chilled, but he breathed more easily.

Then the garage door rattled, but was it this door? Or was it the cruel rattling of the next door down? Or the next?

Light! The door rolled up, clattering. Light rushed into the garage, into the box, seeping under the tape to his eyes. He felt the fresh air rinsing over him. He smelled the early-morning dew. It was over. He lay still. Already he'd left the box. Already this was a horrifying incident in his past.

He sensed the presence of a man, someone obstructing the spray of light. He heard the sound of a padlock pulled taut on a hasp, the smooth clicks of a key. The hinges let out a slow squeak as the lid was laid open. There was breathing and feet scuffing the floor, but no voices, not a word. But then a smell, and Stona knew—Old Spice and Irish Spring. It was him. So Stona would be taken somewhere to be released. He did not try to speak.

The man began unlacing the ropes strung above Stona, pulling them through holes in the wood, the wood resonating, surrounding him with a deep-throated hum. Stona pushed up his knees, pushed them against the ropes until the ropes went slack. Then his knees were bent and the soothing spread through his back and hips. It was over.

"Oh, God!" Stona heard the voice of the woman.

"Quiet," the man ordered.

"Oh, no," she said.

The man grabbed Stona's jacket behind the shoulders. "Up." And he helped Stona to sit. His head spun with fever. He was nauseous. Pain expanded from his brow to his eyes and head. "Up," the man repeated, hoisting Stona to his feet. He wasn't sure if he was standing on his own or being held, but it didn't matter, he was being freed.

"Mr. Brown . . . Morning." He breathed the morning air. "How are you feeling today?" Birds were singing, and from far away came the beeping a truck makes in reverse. "Your face has more color, but what did you do to your head?" His body tingled as he stretched his back. "We have no intention of hurting you, so don't hurt yourself." Fresh air.

"I'm going to remove the tape so you can drink. But no talking." A drink. And suddenly his jaw was free, the fistful of cloth popped from his mouth. His jaw was moving, stretching his face. Deep dry breaths of complete and utter freedom rushed down his throat.

He smelled the woman's perfume, then water poured over his lower lip, over his tongue, soaking into his mouth. He swallowed, and felt the water spread in long fingers through the dry tissue in his chest. She pushed a plastic bottle between his lips and tipped water a swallow at a time. Cool water filled his mouth and dribbled down his chin, soaking through the front of his shirt.

He was being released at last. Had they cut the rest of the tape? Were his limbs free? Was he about to step out of the box and walk blindfolded to a car? Did they know to walk him slowly? He spoke: "My heart."

His mouth kept moving.

"Thirsty. Nunny. Please." The sound of his voice.

He tried to separate his wrists and ankles. He teetered, and the man caught him by the shoulder. They hadn't cut the tape. Stona felt revived by the water, he was ready to walk to the car. What were they waiting for?

There was some shuffling, some silent communication between the man and the woman. The man still gripped Stona's suit jacket at the collar. And then the garage door rattled shut, and the sunlight disappeared.

"What you need to say is simple," the man said. "What you need to say is, 'This is Stona Brown speaking, and I'm being held by the Rainbow Warriors for my crimes against the environment.

Please do as they ask. I am in good health, and I am receiving good treatment. Prepare immediately eighteen-point-five million dollars in used twenties for environmental crimes.' And that's all you need to say."

Stona smelled something metal. Scissors? He smelled the man's breath. He wondered what the man had said, and tried to remember. He tried to separate his ankles, then his wrists, but the man still hadn't cut the tape.

He swayed forward and his lips touched plastic. He tried to drink, but it wasn't the bottle of water. It smelled of metal and the palm of a hand.

"Okay, and . . . go," the man said.

Stona took a step, but his legs didn't move. He fell forward, and had no arms to reach out. The box cut into his thigh as he spun face-first toward the floor. His shoulder was yanked at the socket, spinning sideways, the pain slicing to the bone of his thigh. . . . Then he was standing again. Standing in the box rubbing his elbow against his ribs, determining that his arm had not been pulled from his body, counting fingertips—one through four—against his thumb. There were new kinds of pain.

"What you need to say is that we're the Rainbow Warriors, and we have you." The man was speaking to Stona. The sharp pain in Stona's leg seemed to stimulate his heart, clear his mind like a slap in the face. Stona heard the man's voice saying, "Mr. Brown . . . Morning." He remembered that voice: "Mr. Brown . . . Morning." He'd sounded as if he were correcting Stona. As if Stona had said, "Mr. Smith . . . Evening," and the man was pointing out his error. He remembered the man's face: the small eyes set far apart, the knobby nose, his hair pushed up with static, a beard without shape. He remembered the man biting his lower lip, the anger on his face after he shot Stona in the arm. "Mr. Brown . . . Morning." And now he could picture the man in a jacket and tie, short hair parted on the side, bristly but flopping against the part in a wind that was not cold. A pleasant morning breeze. "Mr. Brown . . . Morning." He imagined the face, heard the voice. What did Stona say in response? Where did it happen? When?

"I'm going to start the tape, and when I say 'go' you start talking."

"Cut the tape," Stona said.

"That's right. Talk into the tape. . . . And . . . go."

"Mr. Brown . . . Morning," Stona said, trying to remember. Bristly light brown hair blowing against itself. The hair flipping up and back into place. "Mr. Brown . . . Morning."

"Jesus Christ, try to concentrate." The man was shaking Stona by his sore shoulder. And now Stona's heart skipped a beat, and the pain in his thigh became hotter, and so did the bullet hole in his arm. "Water," the man called, snapped his fingers, then tightened his grip on Stona's shoulder. "Get with the program, Brown. You don't want to spend the rest of your life in this box." The rest of his life. The man's breath smelled like creamed corn.

The water was at his lips, but he couldn't drink. His stomach was sloshing with water. Then the cool water parted his hair at the crown of his head, looped behind his ears, cascaded down his neck.

"Okay, I'm gonna make this easy for you," the man said. "I'll stop the tape to tell you what to say, so you just repeat after me."

"Stop the tape," Stona said.

"Right," the man said. "Here we go. . . . This is Stona Brown." Stona smelled the metal at his lips. "Stona Brown," he said.

"Good. I'm being held by the Rainbow Warriors."

"I'm being held by the Rainbow Warriors."

"Try to speak more clearly."

"To speak more—"

"Oh, for Christ's sake."

"Christ's sake . . ." Then Stona collapsed, hiccuping, warm water rising from his throat, down his chin.

And he was on his back again, bound with tape in the open box.

For a long time the man made Stona speak.

Colleen reached toward his forehead, touched the alcohol-soaked square of gauze to the splatters of blood. Mr. Brown was standing on his own, stronger now, but they'd reduced him to a state of filth and suffering. On the underside of the box's lid a frightening blood smear stained the fresh wood red. A sour stench seeped from his body. What had they done?

"Clean it good," Theo told her.

She never thought it would be like this. She felt sick to her stomach. She had to get him cleaned up at least. She wiped at the dried blood and his head jerked away, like a dog she was trying to give a pill.

"And a fresh bandage on the arm."

She understood the comfort for a man, especially a man of the older generation, to be tended to by a woman: a meal prepared, a bath drawn, his back scrubbed with a loofah.

Colleen shifted closer, too close to the smell coming off him, the stink and swampy heat of the box. It was like the corner of a sub-way stairwell, the stench pinching her nose. She would never again enter a subway, never confront the demeaning filth, never be stripped of her dignity. She would come out of Saks and have one of the Town Cars be hers, forgetting which one. *Mrs. Wolkoviak,* the uniformed driver would call and help her with her shopping bags, holding open her door.

Mr. Brown's clothes were wet with perspiration. His face had more color than yesterday, but was still cakey, like putty. His cheeks were irritated with red blisters from the tape that had covered his mouth. His lips looked punched—dark blue from the cold water she'd poured over them.

She tried to ignore the smell, repeating to herself over and over: *This is a difficult yet necessary step toward the fulfillment of your goals. The coward has a litany of excuses.* She touched two fingertips to steady the back of his head. Blood had caked in his eyebrows and along the edge of the tape covering his eyes. From the opposite corner of the storage unit, Mr. Brown's weak and confused voice played over the cassette: ". . . Rainbow Warriors . . . treated well . . . fine." This was hard on Theo—things not going the way he wanted.

Mr. Brown rocked side to side on his feet as Colleen wiped and swabbed, the gauze catching on bits of scab and splinters of wood stuck in his skin. With her fingernails she plucked the splinters out, and Mr. Brown winced. In her most comforting voice Colleen reassured him: "There, there."

"Away!" he suddenly shouted, louder than she imagined possible from so frail a man. He tossed back his head, then lurched at Colleen. She threw open her arms as his body fell against her. His swollen lips, his nose and cheek, his sickly flesh, smeared over Colleen's face, his chin hooked her collarbone, then his full weight slumped into her arms. He twisted and pushed, thrashing his sweaty hair against Colleen's chest. "Bitch!" he shouted, and she fought against him, to save him from falling over the edge of the box and plunging to the concrete floor. "Help!" he yelled out, then Theo's arm wedged between them. But Mr. Brown slammed his head back into Theo's mouth, cracking against his jaw. Theo locked his arm under Mr. Brown's chin, slapped a hand over his face, and pulled him off.

Colleen trembled. She couldn't get a breath. She felt she might vomit. Theo was wringing Mr. Brown like a cloth—yanking his face to one side, twisting his body opposite, an arm squeezed under Mr. Brown's chin. ". . . fuck with me?" Grinding his teeth, Theo touched his clenched lips to Mr. Brown's ear. ". . . I own you."

Colleen backed away from the box, moving toward the band of light and fresh air coming under the garage door. She lowered herself to her hands and knees, and as she took deep breaths of the cool morning air, looking at the scraped and rusty hubcap of their Mercedes, the nausea passed.

Still kneeling, her face and chest, her arms and blouse covered in bodily filth, she turned back toward Theo. Her eyes readjusted to the dim light, and she saw the bottle of alcohol on its side in the middle of a puddle. She watched the liquid evaporate from the concrete as if time-lapsed, as if the world were on fast-forward. If she only could fast-forward over today and tomorrow, over the anxiety of collecting the ransom and releasing Mr. Brown to his wife. Fast-forward to the near future when Colleen would be bathed and perfumed and dining at a window table on the Place de la Concorde. Why were there always another couple days, transactions, relocations, restructurings standing between Colleen and her dreams?

Theo was still manhandling Mr. Brown, who stood helpless in

the box. Theo's mouth pressed against Mr. Brown's ear. ". . . teach you about respect."

"Careful——" Colleen heard herself say.

Theo looked up, his face surprised. His hand dropped from Mr. Brown's mouth, and he loosened the lock on Brown's neck. A trickle of blood dripped down Theo's lip.

Mr. Brown's wrists were locked in police handcuffs, his ankles were taped together, and tape spiraled up his legs, binding his hands and arms to his body. The left sleeves of his suit jacket and shirt were cut off at the elbow, revealing his bandaged arm. Colleen stared at him and remembered the high school wrestling meet when Theo had broken a boy's collarbone. The ref had heard the bone snap and seen the boy go limp, and so had the coaches, Theo's teammates, and every spectator in the bleachers. Everyone but Theo had heard the frightening crack. Through whistles and shouts, Theo kept wrestling, turning the boy on his back, pretzeling his leg and neck, pounding him into the mat, until the ref and the coach and Malcolm pulled Theo off. But Theo fought them too, his sweaty and shiny white arms slipping from their grip. His eyes searched the stands for Colleen, and his face looked as it did now— surprised and unsure, a little hurt, as if he'd been doing what he was told, doing the right thing, and then suddenly the rules had changed.

Colleen rose to her feet and moved toward Theo and Mr. Brown. She banged her shin on the edge of the plywood box, reaching for Theo's forearm at Mr. Brown's neck. "He'll be good now," she said. "Won't you, Mr. Brown?" When Theo had found Colleen's face in the bleachers, she saw his face relax. He quit struggling against the men, and he returned to his teammates lining the mat, looking back over his shoulder, his eyes darting between Colleen and his father and the ref, trying to figure out if he'd won.

Now, he looked into Colleen's face, and his hold on Mr. Brown loosened. "Sorry," Theo said. Colleen wasn't sure who he was talking to.

Theo held Mr. Brown as Colleen finished bandaging his forehead. Then she flicked her fingernail under a corner of the bandage on his arm. It came off easily, the adhesive tape nearly dissolved by his sweat. She poured water over the wound. The bullet had torn a path in his skin a few inches long. The flesh was wet and raw deep in the wound, curled open and grizzled along the edges.

She looked up at Theo and shook her head. He touched her shoulder, nodding. *It's fine,* he mouthed, and Colleen blotted the wound dry, sprayed it with Bactine, and applied a fresh bandage. Then she could hear—coming from inside Mr. Brown's trouser leg where his ankles were taped together—the puddling of urine. Poor man.

Theo yanked a length of tape from the roll, and the squawk startled Mr. Brown. Although blindfolded, he turned his head toward Theo as if to see him. He said, "No." He said, "Please." He said, "I promise—" And Theo slipped a knotted cloth between his lips, and slapped his mouth closed with tape.

A groan seeped from Mr. Brown's throat, not human at all, as if a small animal were cornered in his suit coat.

"Down," Theo said. "Drop." Mr. Brown began to shake. He twisted his narrow shoulders, the muffled scream grinding from his throat. Theo collared him, then chopped him behind the knees, collapsing him onto the comforter. Theo began to weave the rope back through the airholes, but when Mr. Brown heard the rope against the plywood, he kicked up in the air. Colleen reached for his wet ankles, pinning them to the comforter, not thinking why they were wet, not thinking of the smell, her face turned away. Theo pulled the rope tight over Mr. Brown's thrashing hips, his chest, then his shoulders. And this time Theo ran the rope through the airholes by his head, while Colleen pushed her hands and all her weight against Mr. Brown's face. They had to protect him from himself. The tendons in his neck strained through his slack skin. His Adam's apple rose and fell with muffled screams. She pushed on his face until Theo tightened the rope above his taped eyes and mouth, and when she let go, he bucked his head up, but the rope caught him. It worked. He wouldn't be able to bang the lid of the box. He wouldn't be able to hurt himself anymore.

Colleen threw open the storage locker door and fell against the car. Still, she could hear the animal noise coming from Mr. Brown's throat. Then Theo dropped the lid on the box and she listened carefully. . . . Thank God, the screaming was gone. The sun had risen higher. She had no idea how long they'd been with him.

The blood had dried on Theo's lip. He was a mess and so was she: their clothes damp and soiled from Mr. Brown's body, their hair in tangles. Mr. Brown's waste on her hands.

Back at the house Theo washed his hands and face while Colleen took a hot shower. Then they slipped quietly downstairs—he could hear his father poking around in the basement—and scooted out the front door. But not before his mother, who'd been sitting with Tiffany at the kitchen table, called to him. "Not now, Ma," he shouted, pulling the door shut. "We'll be right back."

Colleen drove. On Theo's lap was his gym bag, which held a garbage bag containing a roll of tape, surgical gloves, and a sealed nine-by-twelve envelope. They passed the tiny park where Theo used to bike ride as a kid, then patrol as a cop years later, and where he now observed three black males drinking from brown paper bags. The ball diamond was grown over, nearly unrecognizable. The mesh was torn out of the backstop. The chains on the swing set were broken.

There was no coming back for the neighborhood. The decline hadn't even leveled off, the town was sinking. Sacrificed. As they got closer to downtown, many of the yards had no landscaping or grass at all. There were beater cars without license plates, houses with broken windows. Dogs, kids, and women out front. Bikes with no wheels.

If Theo drove the wrong way, not four blocks from the house, black kids with their T-shirts hanging from a belt loop would wave their arms at him from the curb. Why else, Theo knew they were thinking, would a white man be driving in the area if not to buy drugs? This was the route that Theo used to walk to grade school.

As they swung onto Liberty Avenue, Ludlow's main drag, Theo tried to see what he remembered, not what he saw. It had been a great little one-street town—the soda fountain at Salmonson's Rexall where Theo, son of the deputy chief of police, got free refills on his Cokes; the hardware store where old Mr. Fulsom wore a smock with pockets full of treasures: chips of blue chalk, carpenter's pencils, rulers, balsa-wood gliders.

There'd been a Woolworth's, a butcher, a movie theater, a bank, and a newsstand. But now Route 22 blazed four tight lanes through the middle of town. Battered concrete Jersey barriers sat smack up against the buildings on what used to be the sidewalk.

When the sidewalks disappeared, along with the front entrances of stores, most of the merchants went out of business. Dave Mamulski's service station and the Portuguese bakery next door had been bulldozed and replaced by a sprawling Gas-N-Go complex. A respectable pub now had "Live Girls noon to 2 am." The liquor store, which had once carried a variety of Chiantis, kosher wines, vodkas, pipe tobaccos and cigars, now had a cage across the storefront, and the windows were papered with advertisements for "cheapest price" on fortified beer, half-pints of off-brand whiskey, Thunderbird, and generic cigarettes.

Traffic was heavy on 22. They'd be later than he'd scheduled, but Theo's plans were elastic, variables were accounted for.

"God, I want this to be over," Colleen said.

"Remember what you've told me. 'Keep your eyes on the dream, not on each difficult step of the journey.' "

"It's just, the plan wasn't for him to suffer like this."

"I suffered at Petrochem seven years, and how much suffering do you think that corporation causes? He'll be well taken care of in the hospital, I promise you that. And thank God it's him that got shot and not one of us. Tiffany's hospital tab is bad enough. We don't need more bills."

"You're sure he'll be okay?"

"The man will be stronger for the experience. Now, keep it pegged at fifty-five."

A Jag glided by them, British racing green, which was subtle but Theo would have white—much classier. Thank God Brown was recovering. Mostly he needed to rest. He'd had plenty of water this morning. By tomorrow he'd be even stronger. Theo had thought about rigging a watering system for Brown, but there was no way to keep him from shouting out unless his mouth was taped shut. In

Vail the mountain bikers carried water in a pouch on their backs with a hose running to the mouth. Fascinating concept. Talk about simple. And somebody was making millions off it. A man with an idea.

Theo had lots of ideas. Moneymakers. Like the machine that automatically tosses a ball for your dog. The dog learns to drop the ball in the receptor, then—*thup!*—off he goes chasing it. Back and forth, all day. Runs himself ragged! Just plug it in, forget throwing out your arm on a drool-soaked tennis ball.

In twenty-four hours he'd have the capital to see these ideas to fruition and at the same time turn the ransom money legit. Their lack of capital had caused "Insiders" of Hilton Head to fail, which had caused Colleen to lose faith in herself and in her husband. She had struck off on her own with GoodLife, but the stress had led to her breakdown in Vail. It had been a sad low in their marriage. She'd lost respect for Theo. Sitting in a cafe in Vail one afternoon, he'd told her about the automatic ball thrower, and she'd rolled her eyes. "For one," she'd said, "the dog wants the attention of his master, and for two, he likes his master's scent."

What the hell was *that*?

When they reached The Mall at Bishop Hill, Colleen let the high idle pull the car slowly along past Brooks Brothers, Bloomie's, Ralph Lauren, Saks. Theo took note of security guards and traffic flow. He'd been to bigger malls, but this was the most exclusive. The only better mall in the country was in Beverly Hills. The mall you saw in movies.

"East end," he told her. "Left by Neiman-Marcus." He'd discovered during his preparation that this was the only section of parking lot that was not monitored by security cameras. Dave Tomkins would be patting himself on the back when he seized the videotapes, but then mall security would break the news: no camera in the east lot. "These terrorists are good," Theo could hear Dave Tomkins saying to an FBI agent. "Real good."

"Down there." He pointed, and Colleen steered down the first row of parked cars. He unzipped the gym bag, careful to touch nothing else, and plucked the surgical gloves from inside the garbage bag. He stretched them over his hands—a talcumy rubbery smell—snapped them at his wrists. There was something sexual about them—some reminder of condoms, women's stockings, illicit sex. A stirring in his chest corkscrewed down his belly and stirred his prick.

He'd stepped into the zone.

"Do you see anyone?" Colleen asked.

"Negative. How about you?"

"There was the couple with the baby——"

"I've got them in the side-view. They're entering the mall. But good. . . . Good work."

He had the envelope and duct tape on his lap. He'd thought they'd have to cruise the rows a few times until people disappeared, but the area was empty, and the next pole was shielded by a Range Rover with tinted glass. "This one. Stop." Colleen swung close to the light pole, and while the car was still rolling, Theo was out the door. He pressed the envelope flat to the metal pole. He wound around once with the duct tape, then twice, backing into the car as he tore the tape from the roll, but the tips of the surgical gloves were stuck to it, stretching off the fingers as he tried to pull away. "Hurry!" Colleen shouted, but fuck!—the tips of the fingers were tearing off the gloves, his fingerprints etched in the talcum inside. The cops wouldn't even have to dust. Theo yanked his hands free, and the gloves dangled from the pole, twisted up in the tape. He peeled his shirt over his head, wrapped it around his hands, and jerked on the tape until it ripped. Clutching the roll and the shredded gloves, he fell back into the car seat. "Go!"

He swung in his legs and slammed the door. "That way," he said, pointing to the exit at the far end of the lot. His shirt was inside out, in a ball. He peeled off the mess of tape and turned on Colleen. "Goddamn surgical gloves!"

She looked straight ahead, leaning into the wheel when she drove, even after he'd told her repeatedly it was the wrong way to drive.

He said, "They were your bright fucking idea if I recall."

Theo had his shirt back on by the time they pulled up to the McDonald's drive-thru, and he was behind the wheel. One of the fine points that Theo understood—anything abnormal, like the woman driving and the man in the passenger seat, could invite a second look from a police officer. "What do you want?" he asked Colleen.

She shook her head.

"Two Big Macs, large fries, large Coke, and a medium diet Coke," he said into the microphone, thinking as he spoke that if he'd held the tape recorder farther from Brown instead of closer, it might have forced him to speak up, and he wouldn't have sounded so weak.

At the pickup window Theo looked in his wallet—two singles. Shit. "Col. You got some cash?" He tapped her arm, then turned out the window to the McDonald's girl—her beautiful big lips, her headset perched crooked in her hair.

With young tan fingers she folded and creased the white bag stuffed with food. On the tender underside of her forearms were little white dots, scars, Theo figured out in an instant, from hot oil splattering out of the fryer. He *did* love a girl in a uniform. "Shove in some extra napkins, will you?"

The girl's lips seemed swollen, so glossy and wet. They sprouted from the baby fat still soft in her cheeks, so when she spoke, when she said, "Your order, sir. Six forty-two, please," it was as if she hadn't learned yet how to move words around her luscious lips. It was a known fact that high school girls gave the best head. That they were turned on, even more than college girls, by older men, not real old but men Theo's age. Theo was not ashamed that he could discern at a glance if a woman gave good head, if she loved it enough to make it good: you could tell mostly in their lips— sucky swollen ones, of course, but also the slutty and narrow slack lips. A woman like Colleen whose lips were average and pretty gave passable head, but Theo always knew he was getting a favor.

Colleen laid two fives in his hand. Never again would Theo Wolkoviak ask his wife for money.

He parked behind the McDonald's, facing across the access road to the mall. From this distance, the envelope was a brown dot on the light pole. "Ready . . . aim . . ." he said to Colleen, waving a couple napkins at her as he got out of the car. "Fire." He clicked the door shut.

The pay phone was in the far corner of the parking lot. He picked up the receiver with a napkin, unconcerned that anyone might be watching, the kind of thing germ freaks did all the time.

He wished he hadn't come down so hard on Colleen about the gloves. They *had* seemed like a good idea. He rubbed a quarter clean, and with the napkin stretched over his fingertip punched in the number he'd committed to memory: The Mall at Bishop Hill, Office of Security.

The ringing was a beautiful sound. Finally, advancing toward the ransom. Phase two activated.

The second ring sparked in Theo's mind, and in that instant he saw the thing complete: the full and successful feeling of the money, a day and a half from now. Investigators speculating how the mini-storage concept evolved. Who were these environmental terrorists, and where would they strike next? But there wouldn't be another strike, and it would go down in the history books as one of the great unsolveds—Lindbergh, Kennedy, Sophia Loren's jewelry.

Someone picked up the phone. The hollowed-out sound of connection opening through the wires. A breath: "Security."

"East lot. On a light pole." Theo's voice lowered, scratching from his throat. "An envelope you'll want to deliver to the FBI. Do it now. Get yourself on the news." He slammed down the phone.

Fuck, he was high. It would be a miniseries, for sure, but who would play the elusive kidnapper? It might be a Scarlet Pimpernel kind of presentation, with a modern-day Leslie Howard—Tom Selleck or maybe Jim Rockford playing Theo.

Back in the car he bit into a Big Mac. "I don't want a soda," Colleen said.

"Just hold it, then. I don't care. Or we look suspicious, just one person eating." On talk shows the supposed experts would be stymied, the Petrochem flatfoots humiliated. "Former U.S. Army Intelligence Officer, Currently Head of Security for Petrochem," the caption would say under Bradford Ross's plastic face as he talked to

Bryant Gumbel: "We have the best information in the world, but finally we've come up empty. We are only thankful that Mr. Brown was returned unharmed."

Watching the pole. Watching the entrance to the mall. Watching for the white Chevy S10 pickups that security drove. Theo wrangled fries into his mouth, gulped down Coke, took another bite of Big Mac. On the inside of his shirt the gummy residue from the tape pulled at his skin.

In a few minutes a white pickup appeared from behind the mall with police lights on top, Street Hawks, Theo could tell from this distance. Did he know or *did he fucking know*? It took two security guards to consider the envelope and look over their shoulders, peering into the Range Rover. Then they cut the tape and took the envelope in their pickup and sped off—it was done. Total satisfaction spread through his chest. He was fulfilled, replete, ecstatic.

"Sorry for blowing up earlier," he said to Colleen now. "You did real good." He looked down at his lap to open the second Big Mac, which he easily had the hunger for, but he was surprised to see—surprised and disappointed— two empty Styrofoam boxes. He'd already eaten them both.

L ots of guys would have told you to cut plastic six mil or better, wrap *it* around the asbestos, and duct-tape the seams. But hell, when you could buy a five-pack of duct tape in sixty-yard rolls for $14.19 down at the Discount Hardware, why not seal the asbestos up tight?

His eyes moving between the rearview and side-view mirrors,

Malcolm backed into his driveway. Theo and Colleen had gone out great guns this morning before eight. His son was working hard on the yacht club deal. Malcolm could see now that Theo's heart was in this entrepreneurial work. Last night father and son had broken through ten years of misunderstanding. It was a heavy weight lifted from Malcolm's shoulders.

He stopped to catch his breath on the back steps, and damn, the steps were spongier every day. Could be the stringers were rotted, but he'd never know *that* until he cleared out the weeds. He'd call the kid down the block about coming over with his Toro.

"Hi, Grampa," Tiffany said in the kitchen. "*Qué pasa?*"

Daisy barked and ran circles around Malcolm's feet.

Dot sipped hot water from a teacup and turned a page of the newspaper.

Tiffany eyed the five rolls of duct tape that Malcolm dropped on the table. She peered up at him with that smirk so similar to Theo's. "You gonna open up a tape store?"

"Laugh all you want," he said. "At the price I paid I should've bought *ten* rolls. Course I feel like I'm stabbing old man Fulsom in the back every time I walk into Discount Hardware, but the truth is his prices always *were* high. Right to the end."

"Can I get you something?" Dot asked.

"People say they miss downtown, and I admit, I will too, on occasion. I used to take your father in the patrol car down to Salmonson's Rexall for a Coke float. But times change. A mall's convenient for people. And the discount stores. Volume is how they do it. Anymore, it's parking people want, especially as they get older."

"Oh, shush, Papa," Dot said. "You'll put Tiffany to sleep."

"I love Grampa's stories."

"Well, never mind that," Malcolm said. "I've got something

much more interesting. . . ." He pulled open the fridge. From the shelf in the door beside the cans of Ensure that Dot kept in there, even though he'd never drunk a one, he snatched the jar of dill pickles. As the fridge door swung shut, he noticed two cans of Ensure missing.

He set the pickles on the counter. "You'll see," he said to Tiffany, and opened the cellar door. In the recycling bin at the top of the cellar stairs were the beer bottles from last night and several assorted containers, but no empty Ensures. He thought maybe Tiffany had drunk them, and then he thought it best not to mention it.

Standing at the top of the stairs, Malcolm suddenly couldn't catch his breath—like he was reaching out for handfuls of air. Daisy sniffed his shoes, and he felt himself beginning to tip down the flight of stairs. He clutched the doorframe, fumbling for his inhaler.

Then Tiffany was beside him, her hand moving up and down his back. Dot was edging toward the phone. He avoided Dot's eye, neither one of them wanting to acknowledge the truth: she was always at the ready to call for an ambulance. Daisy was whining.

"Lie down," he tried to shout at the dog, but the words squeaked out. "I'm perfectly okay."

"Do you need something from the cellar?" Tiffany asked. "Let me."

"Under the stairs," he said. "On the shelf . . ." He took the deepest breath he could. "With the paint." And he had to pause again. "There's some broken extension cords." He'd be fine. "Bring the white one." His breath was back already.

Tiffany swooped effortless as a bird down the stairs. Malcolm cleared his throat. "Nothing," he said, and Dot sat in her chair. She pinched a long sharp crease at the fold in the newspaper.

"This one?" Tiffany was back, handing him a cord with the plastic outlet end smashed.

"Don't you gals go anywhere," he instructed them. "Mind if I use your bedroom, Tiffany?"

"*Mi casa, tu casa,* good-lookin'."

What had given him the idea was Tiffany's remark about a penny coming out shiny from Taco Bell hot sauce. It was the kind of trick he used to show Theo, which Theo had always been curious about. In the den, which for now was Tiffany's bedroom, he sat in his overstuffed chair, and with his pocketknife cut the busted outlet end off the extension cord and began stripping a few inches of insulation from the wires.

The cot Tiffany slept on was unmade—a couple stuffed animals, a heap of sheets, and Malcolm's old army blanket. There was too much life in that girl to stop and make a bed. Her clothes were stored in milk crates and two drawers he'd cleaned out below the glass doors of his gun case. Her school work was spread out on the floor. It was no way for a high school girl to be living. Damn it all, Theo was not providing.

Until Theo quit Petrochem he'd had his life in good order. Colleen was a truly beautiful girl, and a nice girl, excepting, God bless her, her occasional snobbishness. Malcolm was the first to say that Theo was lucky to catch her. Theo had earned a fine salary at Petrochem, more than Malcolm ever made. They owned a home, two reliable cars, and had plenty of money for ski vacations and trips to Florida.

They had two terrific children. Aside from his few problems on the force, and then the disability discharge, Theo had really done fine. If Malcolm could just live long enough to see Theo cinch this yacht club deal, he'd feel he could pass on without a worry.

The gun collection was something to add to the list of things to discuss with Theo. It was something he could keep, a tangible memory for Theo as he got older himself. Some of the guns were quite valuable. The .36 caliber Allen & Wheelock Navy Revolver with a German-silver-blade sight was over a hundred years old. The Harpers Ferry U.S. Rifle was a beautiful piece, engraved with a spread eagle. Unfortunately, it had been converted to percussion, which lowered its value.

It wouldn't take but half an hour to explain the finances to Theo, but he'd be patient and wait until tomorrow as they'd agreed. Theo just seemed at such loose ends as far as a career went. Fact was, though, when Malcolm was about Theo's age he too had been scattered. He'd felt a longing he was never able to satisfy. It was then that he'd sold those stocks that his own father never took the time to explain about. It was the biggest mistake of Malcolm's life.

But that was in the past. A man built a life up to a point, and then a man started to shut his life down, and that's where he was now: repair the back steps, seal up the asbestos in the cellar, settle with the boy down the block on taking care of the lawn. A matter of putting things in their place. Not so different from getting ready to go down to Florida for a few weeks, which he was proud to admit he'd done seven times with his wife: first-rate accommodations, meals out, Disney, Cape Canaveral, Busch Gardens, bus tours— they'd always done it up right. Which Dot deserved. She'd been a good mother and a good wife. She had lots of years left. Never smoked or touched a drop of liquor. He'd leave her with an adequate pension, Social Security, the CDs and IRAs. She'd be fine.

When he was ready, he called in Tiffany and Dot. "Close the curtains," he told Tiffany. "Close them up good."

Dot sat down at the foot of the cot. She eyed the big, whole dill pickle that Malcolm had set up on the coffee table with the hot wire stuck in one end and the cold wire stuck in the other. He wondered if she remembered.

"Nope, not dark enough," he said to Tiffany. "Throw your blanket up over the curtain rod."

Dot had always gone along with Malcolm. She wasn't contesting him his whole life like some other men's wives. She was easy, and when he thought about it, he'd say the word was . . .generous.

"And the door," he told Tiffany. She closed it and sat beside Dot, rested her head on Dot's shoulder.

The room was plenty dark. "Now, this doesn't take much by way of introduction, but it struck me as one of those mysteries of the universe that Malcolm Wolkoviak's granddaughter should be in on." Then he plugged in the cord, and after a second or two the pickle glowed. Brighter and greener than he'd remembered. It glowed like something from outer space. The three of them sat in silence, mesmerized for a moment, and then Tiffany started to laugh. She kissed Malcolm on the cheek, and now she was giggling. Dot started to chuckle, then Malcolm. He laughed so hard he felt tears in his eyes, and as the pickle glowed brighter he needed to take a puff of his inhaler to keep from dying on the spot.

S he'd insisted. "Mr. Brown needs nourishment," she'd said, showing Theo her purse full of Slim-Fast and Ensure that she'd taken from the house.

"It doesn't look right," Theo had said. "Us hanging around the locker too much."

"Take me there, or I can't go through with this." They argued but Theo relented and swerved across three lanes of traffic to exit. As they passed through the American Mini-Storage gate and rolled slowly by the office, Colleen scooched down in the passenger seat. Theo opened the storage unit door and sat Mr. Brown up in the end of the box. As soon as Theo peeled the tape off the man's mouth, Mr. Brown spit out the gag and pleaded, "Before it gets too hot again, please—" He twisted away from Theo's grasp, so Theo slapped the tape back on and said to Colleen, "See?"

She held her ground. Theo lashed Mr. Brown, sitting up, to the end of the box—immobile but able to drink. Then Theo tore off two lengths of tape and stuck them dangling off the lip of the box so she could cover his mouth in an instant if she had to.

She'd insisted. It was the right thing, so she focused on the self-reliance they were achieving as Theo dropped the metal door. She huddled on the roll of carpet pulled close to the box and switched on the flashlight. She shivered from the smell. Mr. Brown's wool suit still looked expensive. The collar of his white shirt was still rigid with starch, but was stained like the water-damaged ceiling above the dormer in Theo's bedroom. His bandages were still fresh. She reminded herself, as Theo stomped the metal door down tight, rattled the padlock through steel plates and locked Colleen inside, as he started the car and pelted the door with gravel spun from the tires . . . she reminded herself that this was her choice.

Mr. Brown groaned through the tape covering his mouth. "I want to give you a drink," Colleen said, "but you have to promise not to make a sound."

When she peeled back the tape, he whispered, "Too hot."

She lifted the can of Ensure to his lips, and a bead of sweat trickled down her underarm.

He swallowed half a can. Then, in a panic, he whispered, "That tin roof is already creaking. It's an oven in the sun."

"Shh," Colleen said, and as she held the water bottle to his lips, she tried to calm him down by telling him in hushed tones about discovering how to cool herself off when she was twelve years old in the thick heat of summer.

A girl could only spend so much time baking cookies. That summer thirty-three years ago, as the afternoon got hotter, she'd press the back of her hand to her forehead. "I must get out of this house," she'd mutter, and rotate the oven dial to off. She'd slip her hand inside a pot holder mitt, pull a sheet from the oven, and tip the oatmeal-raisin cookies onto a cooling rack. She'd untie her apron and hang it neatly on the hook beside her mother's.

She'd been baking in her mother's oven all summer. She'd loved to be in the kitchen ever since she'd outgrown her Playtag sink and stove set. She remembered the day she got them, her sixth birthday. After the party, she'd rousted her family from her room, closed the door, and started to organize. She went to work placing the four-inch bottle of Ivory liquid behind the tap, and beside it, the miniature box of Brillo. There was a foam sponge wrapped in plastic mesh, a rack with thimble-sized salt, pepper, and spice shakers, tiny cans of corn and peas, Campbell's soup and deviled ham, a box of Quaker Oats, two pork chops, and an entire little chicken with holes in the ends for the rotisserie. The appliances were plastic, as shiny as the appliances in her mother's kitchen, and it sounded the same when you slammed down the spatula because you'd burned the chops.

When she was organizing that first day and discovered the

timer at the back of the range, she reached up on her tiptoes and twisted the dial. She listened to it tick down the minutes, first wondering, then hoping, then praying to God, begging Him to make the timer actually ring. Every part of her focused on the ticking and the silver crown perched over *Playtag Princess.* Finally, the ticking sped up along with her heart and she spoke the words, "Please, God," and pressed her hands together as hard as she could. The ticks slowed, then trailed off to a quiet broken-sounding buzz, and Colleen saw that the range coils were just stickers and thought, *A sink without water is stupid stupid stupid.* She shoved herself away from the stove—that buzz still struggling from the timer. "I *hate* my new—!" And then it dinged: a sound as high and sweet as the bell rung by the altar boy at Mass. And Colleen knew that these new appliances would make her happy like nothing she'd ever had. She could smell her first chicken baking, she could hear the droplets of fat sizzling on the bottom of the stove. She knew she'd have quite a job of it cleaning up.

Now, she left the cookies to cool and wheeled her bike from the garage, past her mother, who was weeding the flower bed along the driveway. "Where now?" her mother said. "At this hour?"

"Mother, *please,*" Colleen said.

"Is that how you talk to the sisters at school? Can you afford your mother a little respect?"

"To the park. I find this house stifling in the *après-midi.*"

"Supper at five-thirty sharp. That means hands washed and at the table."

"*Oui, oui, ma bête,* but I do prefer my *dinner*"—Colleen emphasized the word like grinding out a cigarette in the dirt—"at a more civilized hour. Nine or ten perhaps."

"Lord help us."

"A bientôt."

There was a hill to climb, which was all the better: it made her even hotter and stickier. She leaned forward on the pedals, the soles of her tennis shoes bending under the pressure. Her bicycle was white, from Montgomery Ward, and she kept it spotlessly clean. She loved the bike. She loved the white basket hung from the handlebars, the pink and blue daisies stuck on the front. She loved the sporty chain guard and the thin graceful tires. But her favorite part was the metal plate with three words printed in gold letters on the rear fender: *Made in France.*

One day she would live in Paris, France. In movies she had seen the stone townhouses with wrought-iron balconies overlooking the wide, sculpture-lined boulevards. She would be proposed to on the quays of the Seine. She would eye an old lover on the grand staircase of the opera house. She would picnic on the grass beside the *Tour Eiffel.*

French was Colleen's best subject. In fact, she had straight A's, but she especially excelled in French. Sister Angeline gave her extra work and an hour of tutoring every Wednesday after school. When the other kids were still learning to count to one hundred, Colleen was saying, "I'm a little bored. Let's go to an expensive restaurant." When the others were memorizing the days of the week, Colleen was memorizing "high heels, stockings, dress, skirt, blouse, silk slip, diamond earrings, gold necklace, emerald brooch."

At night she lay in bed with her Larousse pocket dictionary, flipping through the pages for new words. This was how she'd discovered the nickname she used for her family—*ma bête,* my beast. And the same night she had come across *fou,* fool. At dinner the following day she told everyone, "Sister Angeline taught us a new expression. *Je suis fou.* I am full. Try it, *ma bête,*" she said to her mother. "Oh, that's very good. *C'est superb.*"

She reached the top of the hill and pedaled down Clark Street. Ahead she could see the Turnpike, the streaming flash of cars and trucks zipping across the overpass. She pedaled harder toward the arch of the bridge, squeezing the white hand-grips as she pumped into its shadow—into the cool and wet-smelling air. Cars zinged over her head with the sound of an arrow released from a bow. When she'd passed under the bridge, she leaned her bike against a phone pole, and began to climb the steep dirt bank to the highway. By now she was as hot as she got. Beads of sweat tickled her scalp, her arms glistened, and she tasted salty drops on her lips.

A loose rock rolled out from under her tennie, and she slid on her knees a few feet down the bank. She got back up in a cloud of dust, a light coating of grit on her skin. At the top of the bank she first gripped the lower cable, then the upper one—two cables that stretched from post to post all the way to New York City. As she pulled herself up, sweat was streaking down her face. She wiped it away with her forearm and planted her feet on the ledge of pavement; the ground beneath it had eroded away. She leaned her bare legs into the sun-heated cables. Where she stood, hidden by the side of the bridge, the cars and trucks coming across couldn't see her, so as they passed, they didn't swing wide around her but hugged close to the shoulder.

The first car whizzed by, throwing out a whoosh of air. Colleen could see the top of a truck rocking over the bridge and another behind it. The blast of hot wind smashed against her, and she held herself up by the cable; then as the truck passed, suction pulled her forward—only the cables against her legs kept her from being sucked into the lane. The wind from the second truck smashed her again; then again, she was sucked forward.

And this is what she did. Back and forth, the wind powerful and fresh and thrilling, the racket so loud she couldn't think, then the suction. And with every passing truck teasing herself: This time would it pull strongly enough to lift her tennies from the pavement and suck her over the cables and into the rush of speeding trucks?

They shanghaied Theo into the den. His mother was making Tiffany's bed. There was a weird, burnt vinegar smell in the air. "Close the door," Tiffany told Theo. "We don't want Grampa to hear."

"I don't have much time," he said. "I left your mother at the mall. I have to go get her." After he picked up Colleen from American Mini-Storage, they would make the phone call. "What can I do you for?" He clapped his hands.

"First, the birthday party for Grampa, don't forget. About five tomorrow. Just us. It's a surprise."

For Chrissake, was Theo's first thought, but then he calculated that it would actually work out fine—a little wind-down time before going out for the ransom. "Done," he said. "The whole fam-damily." It wasn't smart leaving Colleen there, but he couldn't have the mini-storage manager seeing the car in front of the locker hour after hour either. He'd tied Brown tight to the end of the box.

"Also I got tomorrow night off work because I'm going to a party with Erica which I've already discussed with Mom over a week ago."

"No problemo," Theo said. "Now, I verily must go—"

"Please," Dot said as he reached for the door.

Theo leaned his palm into his father's gun case. What was he going to do with those guns? Rusty old things his father had picked up at flea markets. When he got his parents into a condo, he'd have a cabinetmaker do a built-in, then he'd buy his father a couple really valuable pieces to inaugurate a new collection.

"Your father's emphysema seems to be getting worse," Dot said.

No, not this conversation now.

"He doesn't want to admit it, though." Dot centered the lace doily on the arm of Malcolm's overstuffed chair. "I'm afraid he might have an accident."

Theo wanted to make the phone call by four o'clock. They'd have listened to the tape by then, and the traffic wouldn't be so heavy that they'd risk stopping dead on the highway. He'd bought a clone phone off the street in a dope area of Newark. Some scum with a catcher picks up a serial number and phone number of a passing cell phone. Then he programs the clone phone with the intercepted codes, and voilà, you can call on the stolen account. The only way they could get caught would be for the cops to triangulate the signal while Theo was making a call, but as long as they kept moving and kept the call short, there wouldn't be a chance.

"What I'm thinking," Tiffany said, "is that Grampa should move down to this room for a couple months till he feels better."

"It's the stairs that are so hard for him," Dot added.

"And I'll sleep with Gramma," Tiffany said.

Theo's eyes darted to his watch. "Sounds like a plan." It was nearly one o'clock.

"Just a second, Dad." Tiffany twirled her hair around a finger. "We want *you* to suggest it to him."

His mother was stretching the doily, smoothing down its rippled edges. "He'll think we're just a couple women trying to boss him around. But he'll listen to you, Theo. Your father respects you."

M*r. Brown . . . Morning.* Stona played and replayed that voice through the crushing heat. He replayed it to remember who he was: Mr. Stona Brown; husband of Nunny; father of Victor and Jane; 34 Carnegie Lane; President, Petrochem International Division. *Mr. Brown . . . Morning.* The voice with an undertone of reproval. Correcting Stona: *No, you're still alive.*

The woman had been with him earlier in the day before the worst of the heat. Maybe she'd done a decent job of first aid, enough to forestall an infection. But what about nerve damage, muscle damage? Christ, he'd lose half his effectiveness with a lame arm. All of it, if he was an amputee. What would the goddamn Saudis think of him?

Mr. Brown . . . Morning. The first time he'd heard that voice had been years before. He had thought later in the day about the reproving tone. He'd thought about it where? In his office? Could he see the Remington bronze in the window? The map of the Middle East?

In his mind he took a drive around the grounds of Petrochem, and already his head was clearing. The lawns were lush blankets of golf course grass. Hedges were meticulously manicured. Berms topped with flower beds lined the oil-black road, a clean bright yellow line painted down the middle. It was calming. Many times Stona had thought, bring the Congress through here and then ask them about privatization of public works. Was there a public park as beautifully kept as this? Look at the state of our roads, the Garden State Parkway and I-95 were riddled with potholes. If they were privatized with the possibility of competing roadways and you let the consumer vote with his dollar, you'd see well-maintained macadam that got you there without rattling apart your car.

Consider mass transit. Anyone who had ever stepped into an office building knew that public buses were . . . Example: A man with a legal practice on the thirtieth floor of an office building pitches in with the other tenants in the building to purchase an elevator for clients. The clients effectively pay an elevator "fare" in the portion of the legal bill contributing to their attorney's overhead. Question: How is a city bus system anything more than a horizontal elevator? I.e., in its fundaments, the world can be seen as one big office building.

And don't stop with the elevator. Take the security guard at the front door. The tenants of that building found it in their interest to hire him. Why was policing a government function? The judiciary could be privatized and the . . . Stona had driven to his parking spot, where he inspected the faces of anyone arriving as early as he, but then he remembered something he'd missed.

He backed out and decided to drive the long way around, out behind Complex A, to the front gate. Petrochem security was unparalleled. You could be sure that when the kidnappers were caught, it would not be Asherton police or the FBI who were to be credited. Petrochem hired the best in the world: the cream of the FBI, CIA, Army Intelligence. Stona enjoyed the long view across the lawn to the mini-refinery, the duck pond overrun at the moment with Canada geese resting on their trip north. He looped back out the main gate and squeaked a U-turn. He braked, then rolled toward the guard booth where half a dozen men in uniform monitored video screens, manned phones, and drank coffee. Stona came on them slowly and quietly, and looked at their faces: two black men, a third who left a few years ago, the gray-haired man—Vince? Or Vinny? There were many of them over the years, but they were not the kidnapper, because they wore dark blue uniforms, white shirts, red ties. He looked deeper in the guardhouse, past the uniformed men who usually checked Stona's company ID and waved him in, and he saw a man in a suit who was the supervisor for a year or so, for the year before Stona's most recent promotion. It was unusual, but on some mornings the supervisor would examine Stona's ID, taking Stona's card in his hand and reading it closely . . . his fleshy face pockmarked, his blue eyes set far apart.

"Mr. Brown . . . Morning," he said, as if he were contradicting Stona's misstatement of fact.

Stona was afraid, as if someone were suddenly there in the dark, someone with him in the box. He gasped through his blocked-up nostrils, sucked air through the tape covering his mouth until something buckled, his windpipe crimping.

Mr. Brown . . . Morning.

It was him.

W hen his father died, Malcolm kept the savings bonds and the stocks just as Papa had asked. He preserved the meager inheritance in a firebox inside a footlocker of the old man's memories—military uniform, postcards, football awards, immigration papers, documents written on brittle paper with a fountain pen.

In the spring of 1961 Papa had been gone two years; Mama

three. Theo was a strapping fifteen-year-old with nothing but life ahead. Malcolm had made deputy chief and the force was expanding beneath him, more men and responsibility each year. Dot was growing more beautiful with middle age: her blond hair had turned the color of walnut shells, her angular figure had softened, there was a peacefulness about her face. Malcolm could not have asked for more.

But then, in the middle of the night, a Tuesday he remembered, three-fifteen a.m., he'd woken up hungry, famished, the mouth of a lion opening inside him. The kind of irrepressible hunger produced by the smell of coffee and bacon on a Sunday morning. He slipped out of bed, pulled on his robe, went downstairs, and stood in front of the open fridge. He never cooked for himself, never even made a snack. Dot made breakfast, sent him off to the station with a bag lunch, had supper on the table at five-thirty sharp, and popped the corn or dished out the sherbet in the evening, depending on what Malcolm had a taste for.

That night, he'd poked around until he settled on Sunday's pork roast, a jar of mayo, and half a head of lettuce sliced sharply down the middle. He made a sandwich and ate it standing at the counter. And then another. Then two hunks of angel food cake and most of a box of Ritz crackers washed down with half a bottle of milk. He set the percolator brewing and spent the hours before dawn on the breezeway, drinking coffee and looking out at the side yard.

Dot appeared just before dawn, hastily wrapped in her yellow ruffled dressing gown, all her curlers but one aligned in regimented rows, worry on her face.

"I was hungry," Malcolm said.

"Didn't you get plenty of supper?"

He reassured his wife and coaxed her back to bed, where she stayed until the alarm went off, but he knew she didn't sleep.

In the kitchen he refilled his cup and went back out on the breezeway. The light had shifted from the blue-gray of the stars and moon to the damp white light of morning. He couldn't see the sun; it was still too early and the wrong direction anyway, but that precise moment of the shift from night to morning had passed, and he'd missed it. Countless mornings out fishing or sitting on the breezeway, he had watched—watched with the scrutiny of a stakeout. But he'd always been baiting his hook, inside for a pee, or closing his eyes for a minute's rest, and when he looked, the moment had passed: it was the next day.

Malcolm wolfed down food all that day: the kielbasa and hard roll Dot had sent him with, a plate of ravioli and meatballs at Guido's, Ring-Dings and candy bars from the machine. He ate more steak and potatoes at supper than Theo did, and before bed he had two bowls of raspberry sherbet with chocolate sauce and a tall glass of milk. By then he thought he'd capped the hunger. Worn out from lack of sleep the night before, he was in bed by ten.

Dot came in later, and left the door ajar to undress in the light from the hall. Malcolm watched his wife of twenty-two years dip her head, the light falling over the feathers of hair on the nape of her neck. She lifted the strand of pearls around her hair then, trying to be quiet, lowered them slowly onto her bureau, each pearl clicking on the varnished pine. She slipped the large white buttons of her housedress through their slits—first at her collar, then between her breasts, over her navel, her crotch—and she stepped out of the flowered cotton dress and draped it silently over the chair.

"Pssst."

Her bare shoulder glowed in the light. "You must be exhausted," she whispered.

"Come here," he said.

She came to his side of the bed, and he sat up, slipping his legs over the edge and locking them around the back of hers.

"Malcolm. Where's your PJs? You never sleep in the nude—" He buried his nose in her chest and inhaled the moist salty air beneath her brassiere and slip. "Malcolm."

He didn't speak. He pushed the straps off her shoulders and peeled her slip down below her bosom. Without unfastening it, he tugged her brassiere down around her belly. Her breasts dropped full and rich. He lifted a breast in each hand, felt their weight, their sloshiness. Desperately famished, he filled his mouth with her flesh and sucked until a taste from inside her body passed through her skin.

This was what he wanted. He was forty-five years old, his wife was forty-two. In their years together he had never melded with her. It was as if they'd never seen each other's bodies, as if they'd made love with a sheet between them, as if he'd never tasted her saliva. This was what he wanted: to turn her body inside out.

He pushed her arms over her head and pressed his nose into her armpit, filled his nostrils, his head, his lungs, then he took the warm bristly flesh into his mouth. He pulled her onto the bed and moved over every part of her body in ways he'd never imagined, led by his nose and his tongue. When she pulled his mouth in tighter between her legs, when she arched up and forced his front teeth into her pelvic bone, he was surprised to feel her fingernails digging into his scalp: he had forgotten this was his wife. And at that moment he knew it would always seem there was a sheet between them. She climaxed with a rush she told him later she'd never known.

For a few minutes he let her rest, then he settled into her, shuddering before he eased off and pretended to sleep. The hunger that had gripped him less than twenty-four hours earlier hollowed him out even more. When he heard the familiar rhythm of her sleep, he went downstairs again. He leaned into the edge of the refrigerator door, peering through the cold light at the neat Tupperware containers, a white bowl stained purple with pickled beets, a plate of cold pierogies, the jars and tubs so familiar. Then he ate.

At dawn he opened the old footlocker downcellar and brought the firebox upstairs, carrying it in front of his body as if it were a crown. On the breezeway he sat down with it on his lap, and in the early- morning light withdrew the fattest envelope. The fattest, but least valuable. It was about five thousand dollars in stock from the typewriter company Papa worked for in Poughkeepsie, given to him as bonuses throughout his years as a repairman. In the two years since Papa's death the stocks had increased in value by only a matter of pennies.

By day's end Malcolm had sold the stock and bought the boat: a 1941 Chris-Craft barrel-stern runabout with triple cockpits, 380 horsepower twin Liberty V-12's, mahogany hull, brass rails, and leather seats. It was a collector's piece. He had a spring kit and hitch put on the station wagon and drove home with the soon-to-be-christened *Theo's Joy*.

The boat would be good for the boy. He'd learn to take care of a thing of value and develop a hobby. Theo played sports in school but always third-string. He came on the field in the final ten minutes of the game only when Ludlow was way behind or way ahead, when the game was as good as over. Theo wasn't passionate about sports the way some of the other boys were. He sat on the bench, a little pudgy in his uniform, kicking up dirt with his cleats.

The boat was the single extravagance of Malcolm's life, the one time he threw good sense aside.

It was only two years after Theo swamped the boat that the stock shot up like a rocket. Malcolm knew all about IBM now, but back then nobody did. Worst of it was Malcolm suspected his father knew something about what might happen with the company, but instead of telling Malcolm, he just said, *Hold on to these,* and then he died. He never took the time to explain himself. Which was a mistake Malcolm would not repeat with Theo. There was nothing of that kind of value—when they came due Malcolm had put Papa's savings bonds into Woolworth's, which he thought would always be as stable as the U.S. dollar. But that had gone to hell. He'd make sure Theo knew exactly about the IRAs and the CDs. The house was fully paid and so was Malcolm's fifth of the fishing cabin. You couldn't spell out these things too clearly. If Papa had just *told* him.

For at least ten years, Malcolm would take the newspaper into the living room or out to the breezeway while Dot was washing up the supper dishes and calculate how much his stock would have been worth. It was his penance, like keeping the boat where he was forced to look at it day in and day out. He followed the value of IBM until finally, when he would have been a millionaire the second time over, he stopped.

The air blowing through the kitchen window was warm. At least it was warm. Thirty-one hours had passed without a ransom demand, without assurance of Stona's safety. Nunny pressed on the band-aid across her palm, the cut from trying to move Stona's car seat forward. The dull pain was a comfort, *any* sensation was a relief.

At her kitchen table she sat with Dave Tomkins, Bradford Ross, and Special Agent Tony Jackson from the FBI. "The Federal Bureau of Investigation is not officially involved at this point in time," Jackson told her. "As soon as there's a ransom demand, we'll be batting for you with our best people. However, in order to minimize playing catch-up later, I'm here now to keep up to speed and, of course, in consideration of your husband's position and as a personal favor to Brad."

"Thank you," Bradford Ross said. "Dave and I appreciate your two cents." He nodded to Jackson with an absurd graciousness.

Could they get to the point? They all knew what this conversation was about. Thirty-one hours without a ransom note, and they wondered why. But in no way did they wonder with the passion and intensity and despair that Nunny did. A note should have come within hours. Was it so complicated? Apprehending an innocent defenseless man, demanding money, setting him free ... Nunny's breath caught like a hiccup—she prayed he wasn't bound with rope, she prayed there was no gun.

"There are a couple avenues I need to pursue with you, Mrs. Brown, just so we know we're covering all our bases." It was all too predictable. She just wanted to get it over with. *Have you and your husband experienced any discord recently? Do you have reason to believe he might be unhappy with his life? Do you have reason to believe he might be romantically involved with another woman?* Thirty-one hours of anguish had coiled up along Nunny's spine. She was poised to snap like a whip.

"Mrs. Brown," Jackson began. "First, and let me say again, at this point we just need to rule out some possibilities, so I apologize that I have to ask you about a certain affiliation ..." He paused. So they had someone specific already in mind. Who would it be? A secretary who called in sick today? One of the women from the golf circle? Ted Johnson's widow? Or Ted's daughter? "Your affiliation some years ago with the group Struggle for Justice."

Tony Jackson's eyebrows, like his double-breasted dark blue suit, were too perfectly neat. Along the lower ridge of his eye socket was an arc of whiskers his razor had missed. He was a black man. Nunny leaned closer to him and began counting the hairs ringing the underside of his left eye, until she was able to hear what he'd actually said and not what, in her confusion and craziness from lack of sleep, she'd thought she heard.

"When was the last time you had any contact with persons formerly affiliated with Struggle for Justice?" Although she was looking across her kitchen table into the small eyes of Tony Jackson, she noticed a heavy and sweet male odor to her right, seeping through Bradford Ross's clean white shirt. It was the smell of waiting for Stona outside the men's locker room—of freshly showered and scented men and men coming off the racquetball court.

Tony Jackson was still talking. ". . . Samuel Blackman, Kenneth Parsons, Mohammed Nichols, James Smith a.k.a. Matuma Kunjufu, Sandra Volek . . ." The horror of her present was snaking back to the horror of her past. She prayed that Special Agent Tony Jackson would not unearth the volatile container sunk in the ground for almost twenty-five years, that he would not compound the pain of her husband's kidnapping. As an image of the legs in pink pants flared up from Nunny's memory, ". . . Timothy J. Thompson . . ." he said, and the name ripped through her like an explosion.

"Timothy Thompson is dead, Mr. Jackson. And the answer is no. I've neither seen nor spoken with anyone from Struggle for Justice since November twelfth 1968. Furthermore, my husband and I have known a love"—she tightened her jaw as she spoke to smooth her quavering voice, staring hard into Jackson's small eyes—"a love and commitment that most people do not even consider a possibility. No, we had not been arguing recently. No, there is no chance he was seeing another woman. And *no*, Mr. Jackson"—she wanted to cleave him in two with her words—"my husband was not inclined toward homosexuality." She turned to Bradford Ross. "It seems to me you have a job to do."

Nunny stormed away from the table, shivering as she caught a glimpse of herself in the mirror by the door to the verandah. She watched her fingers reach up to touch Jane's silver earrings. A uniformed police officer pushed through the door from the dining room, nearly knocking into her. And as she stepped by him, she heard Chief Tomkins's voice: "Mrs. Brown." Still moving away, she turned her head and torso back, as someone running from the police might glance behind to see if they were gaining. "Mrs. Brown." Chief Tomkins was standing behind her now. "There's been contact." Nunny lunged for the phone.

But there was no one on the line, just a dial tone. It wasn't a call but a tape, a minicassette. Nunny was sitting at the dining room table, waiting for the tape player to be set up and the stenographer to be seated. Why were these men so . . . not just slow, but deliberate and self-important in their every movement? Jane, standing behind her mother, massaged Nunny's shoulders, the base of her neck. On the table lay a large Ziploc bag bulging with ribbons of duct tape and a manila envelope sliced open. Through the clear plastic of another bag marked *Evidence,* Nunny touched the embossed letters of her husband's name—STONA C. BROWN—stamped on his American Express card.

"Are we ready?" Chief Tomkins said, and the group of men— Bradford Ross and Tony Jackson, the insurance man, a Petrochem lawyer, two detectives from the Asherton police, the stenographer—all murmured in the affirmative.

There was silence. "This is Stona Brown—" It was Stona's voice, but as she'd heard him only once—during his three and a half days in ICU after the myocardial infarction. She could see Stona's barely moving lips, cracked and swollen and gleaming with smears of petroleum jelly, a clear tube up his nose, his face without blood. She could smell disinfectant, medicated creams for the skin, and wilted floral arrangements in a hospital room kept too warm.

Jane began to cry. Her fingers dug into Nunny's shoulders, and Nunny placed her hand over Jane's. She felt the warmth of Jane's face beside her own, but when a succession of blips and chopped-off utterances spit from the tape—as if it had been poorly edited or mangled—Jane erupted with a sob and ran into her father's study.

Nunny did not take her eyes from the red spindles spinning in the tape player. She heard each word—"Rainbow Warriors . . . Environmental crimes . . . Eighteen-point-five million dollars . . . I'm being held . . . Good health . . . Fine . . . I'm being held . . ." She heard the words, but she was listening for the strength of Stona's heartbeat. She could hear his voice growing weaker with each phrase. Listening more closely, she heard the beep of hospital monitors, the gush of a respirator, and the seventeen drips per minute of heparin and lidocaine into the saline and dextrose solution that flowed into Stona's cephalic vein. She heard mixed-up dreamy murmurings as he drifted off after an injection of morphine. And when she listened more closely still, she heard the white-noise emptiness of a life from which Stona had passed.

Nunny pressed at the Band-Aid on her palm. Good God, he was kidnapped because of Oakville.

Then the voice of the kidnapper spoke on the tape. "I represent the Rainbow Warriors." It was the voice of a man. A voice stronger than she thought this mini tape and tape player were capable of reproducing. In contrast to Stona's voice . . . They had to get him home.

"Mr. Brown is a prisoner in the war for the environment." He was an American, not an Arab or Hispanic as everyone had supposed. A white man. From New Jersey or Long Island. He sounded to Nunny like *any* man. The butcher behind the meat counter at Shop Rite, the clerk hulking a bag of loam to her trunk at the garden center, the Mercedes service manager suggesting they rotate the tires, the painters this spring, the roofers last summer. "Mr. Brown will be tried for crimes against the environment, and he will face near-certain execution." The words were insane, the voice was not. Not a lunatic, but any man. Like any of the men in this room.

The red spindles turned for some time without further sound. Blood rushed through the tiny veins in Nunny's eyes. She looked up at the men around the table, the men leaning into chair backs, the men standing in the archway to the living room. She was suddenly cold.

Tony Jackson spoke first. "Is it your husband on the tape, Mrs. Brown?"

She said that it was, nodding.

"Is it your husband with absolute and complete certainty?"

They would never find him. It was these men against other men. Deals, postures, arguments. Offers, intimidations, self-inflation.

"I'm certain," she said flatly. And as she listened to the empty sound coming from the tape, for the first time she became afraid he might never come home.

H e would never be the same. His mind had crossed a line. What would he say to Nunny when he lay with her in clean paja-mas on their bed, the window open wide, night air filtering through the baffles of pinecones and washing over them? Would he ever be able to explain that he was not the person whose tie she straight-ened, whose lips she kissed yesterday morning? He no longer had the strength to steer his mind away from a past that was now con-suming him.

Marjorie was emblazoned across his mind in the frilly cursive script of her name tag. She had worked in one of the Jewish-owned shoe stores in New Haven. For many years he couldn't remember her name. But then, from time to time, it would bubble up in his consciousness, and he would remember that her breath smelled like the meat of a pear, and her hair was as thick and red as a fox's coat. Her skin made Stona think of skim milk—very white, but with a bluishness beneath the surface. Freckles formed the shadow of a mask around her eyes. Her lips stretched into an embarrassed smile when Stona teased her, revealing tiny crooked teeth. Her ears were the size of an infant's. He would remember her, then quickly forget.

Does every man's first partner have the body of Aphrodite? Marjorie did, and like a goddess she kept it veiled. He'd had no idea what was hidden under her heavy sweaters, coats, and knee-length skirts.

It was all the worse because he'd never told Nunny, nor confessed to a priest. What if he died without last rites? He'd committed a mortal sin every time he received Communion—too cowardly to speak the truth in confession. Was the box Stona's punishment?

It had been a dare, his initiation into Cloak and Dagger his junior year at Yale. He had impressed her with a borrowed Oldsmobile. He had taken her to the Boar's Head Inn for dinner, slipped the waiter a dollar to make her Manhattans doubles and keep her wineglass full. Later, with great fanfare, he produced a bottle of champagne from an ice chest in the trunk, and he listened to the girlish slurring of Marjorie's accent as they sat watching the moon come up over Long Island Sound. When the moon was high enough to shine in the windshield, he said, "I love you," and he realized she was asleep.

It was over in seconds: the tickle of her bristly hair on Stona's virgin prick was nearly enough to bring him off. Before he'd fully penetrated, his load of sperm emptied inside her. She hadn't been aroused enough to wake.

The act was duly witnessed by Cloak and Dagger brothers on stakeout in another car.

The following Sunday as Stona passed out bulletins at Mass on campus, a white-gloved hand touched his own. How had she found him? She didn't know his surname. He'd been so careful.

"It was a certain *life* I saw in you," she said, in a coffee shop after Mass.

"But you?" Stona said. "You're Catholic?"

"Yes."

"And you work at Goldschmidt's?"

"Why not?"

"I just assumed—"

"My parish is St. Andrew's." She bit from her doughnut and held it in her mouth as she sipped coffee, then chewed it all together and swallowed. A smirch of powdered sugar remained on her upper lip. "I could see beneath your Yalie skin a sort of love for humanity that told me you were Catholic," she said, and for the first time since he'd picked her out as the girl for his initiation into Cloak and Dagger, Stona found—coming from his insulated world of tennis, sailing, and cotillion in Greenwich—something exotic about her accent. To Stona, it was the sound of urban tenements with bedsheets, work clothes, and sleeveless ribbed undershirts pinned to lines sagging over the street. Stona conjured up big-bosomed mothers of eight leaning out windows calling to their children playing in the alley. God's people.

"Queens," she said later. "We're all the same there. Irish, Jewish, Italians. It's the Goldschmidts' cousin got me the job up here, and the room. Maybe I'll go back. I don't really know. Trying to plan a future."

After this Sunday in the coffee shop, he took her to dinner again. And one more time. For a few weeks it went on like this, and in those weeks, looking at himself from the outside, he had to pat himself on the back—driving with the gang up the country roads to Vassar one weekend, a formal dance, Nunny so splendid in a dress from Peck and Peck, a Rose Parlor reception, then two nights later under the harsh lights of a diner in North Haven having a plate of meat loaf with Marjorie. She was awkward with a knife and fork, and somewhere on her lips she always had a chip of bread crust or crumble of chocolate cake—a floating beauty mark—which Stona would let be for a few minutes; then he'd reach across the white-and-silver-speckled table with a paper napkin pulled tightly over his finger and dab at her mouth.

"Such a dear," she'd say, sounding like she was telling her mother *about* Stona, rather than speaking *to* him.

Stona knew exactly what he was doing. "You must see our summer cottage. Down on the Sound in Clinton." "You'd love France, the way you go at food." "We'd be a great pair, traveling together, seeing a bit of the world." Implying. Planting expectations. Saying, "My mother keeps roses, you'd love her," and meaning, *Trust me now and spread your legs.*

He poked at any excuse to get up to her room, and he could see she resisted, knowing it was inappropriate. Then one night as he walked her home, they passed St. Andrew's and she said, "I can see the spire from my window. It's comforting to see the cross, always there against the sky." Stona tried again, and finally, "It's a mess," she said. "If you promise to ignore the room and just look at my view, well, okay, for just a minute."

They stood in her dark room, their knees leaning into the edge of her bed. A streetlamp cast her furniture all brown and gray, and exactly as she'd described, over the roof of Gottesfeld Curtains and Drapes the cross of St. Andrew's stood facing her room—black against the dusty blue evening sky.

"Brilliant," Stona said, and he shifted his weight to one leg so their hips touched, imperceptible as breath.

"I sometimes lie here with the blind open wide and look at it as I say my prayers."

He touched the small of her back, then pulled his hand away, his palm sweaty, hovering in the dip of her spine.

"The bells ring for Mass. And for weddings, of course. It's a wonderful sound."

Now he pressed his hand to her back and eased himself closer, pulling her shoulder to his chest. "And how do you imagine your wedding?" he said. The lie was sincere and genuine, so when she turned to him, her lips were already parted—the smell of pears— and their bodies collapsed to her bed, embraced, her lips feverishly hot on his own.

It was the first time Stona knew physical passion. She was wrapped around him, he tasted saliva, sweat, skin. He smelled perfume and soap. Her breath on his ear. The ruffles of her white blouse, her cardigan, the straps and cups of her brassiere were rumpled around her waist. He kissed her white freckled shoulders. Her body, her breasts, sprouted from the muss of clothing like a flower, like Venus, like Primavera—springtime itself blooming before him. Her breasts were the creation of adolescent fantasies, so full, so inflated, they looked tender to the touch. A gold cross on a gold chain hung in the deep cleavage. He took each in a gentle hand and put his mouth to her nipples.

Bound in the box, lying in his sweat, his urine, Stona felt disgustingly aroused. After he returned to his dorm room that night, creeping so as not to wake his roommate, he slipped under the covers and with a handkerchief on his belly he stroked himself and tried to fantasize about Nunny, but compared to Marjorie's body, Nunny's was like the white tennies she wore—sleek and trim, narrow and conservative, practical, dainty, with nothing extra. A figure that would look good even after babies. Trim and neat in tennis dresses and swimsuits, poolside at the club.

How he loved Nunny. Was it possible to love one woman absolutely, and at the same time lust after another? Why was it a sin? With his roommate sleeping a few feet away, he had pictured Marjorie straddling him, brushing one nipple, then the other over his lips, and his tongue shot out to flick at the darkness as he thumped onto his chest.

The following night he took her out again, and again they climbed the creaky stairs to her room, and again in the dusty light of the streetlamp Stona kissed her breasts, her nipples, her gold cross, saying a sort of prayer that he wouldn't have to go home to his handkerchief again tonight.

She held his head steady against her breasts. "On our first date, Stona, that wonderful evening forty-three days ago——" adding quickly, "I think," embarrassed by her precision. "I'd wanted to ask you, you know, darling, when I woke up the next morning, well, there was a mess. And I'd had too much to drink, which I never do, I'd never had champagne until then. I wasn't going to tell you that. But what I'm saying is I don't remember, I mean I truly don't remember if something happened between us. I was so sick in the morning from all I drank, but as I said, there seemed to be a mess . . ." And Stona's gaze did not waver from her eyes, gentlemanly and sincere. "I'm terribly ashamed I might have let my passions take ahold of me because even that night I knew from the way you helped me with my coat and touched my hand when you explained about which fork to use first, I knew we were a real pair and we'd fall in love as we have." And Stona let his gaze soften, which he knew meant, *Yes, it's true*—the sin of silence. Or did he love her? His head was swimming through the stickiness of lust. And still, like watching a baby sleep, Stona gazed into her eyes, which now filled with tears. "I wouldn't normally bring up such awkwardness, only I'm more than two weeks late, you know, on my monthly, and another week or so I might want to see the doctor if you could yourself remember if I acted badly that night."

Cloak and Dagger made the arrangements. "We take care of these things"—a senior boy who had seemed so savvy to Stona at twenty, his feet up on a cherry desk between stacks of books. "Harold will give you an address. Take cash."

Stona told Marjorie, "I want to marry you," and he touched her cheek, "but two years until I have my degree." He said, "My career. Our family. Proper timing." He fabricated scenarios of his father cutting him off. He said, "Do this now, for me, for *us,* and we'll be blessed with many children in years to come."

Then, in the evening, on a street that bordered an unsafe neighborhood, Stona led Marjorie to the address he was given. It was a doctor's office. It was after hours. They knocked on the door, then followed the doctor down the hall to the waiting room, where the shades were drawn and the lights were out. Stona was holding Marjorie's hand. An aquarium in the corner gave off blue light. The only other light came through the partly open door leading into the examination room. Stona squeezed her hand, then let go to pull the money out of his pocket. Marjorie bent down and stared into the aquarium to avoid looking at the doctor. "Angelfish," the doctor said. Blue light wrapped around her face. "They're fascinating," the doctor said. Stona put the money in his hand. "Aren't they."

Stona hugged her, bracing her. She was strong, thank God. They'd made a decision, and she wasn't falling to pieces. She turned and followed the doctor into the next room, and just before the doctor closed the door, she turned back to Stona, mouthing, *I love you.* She asked with her eyes one more time if he was sure this was the only way, and Stona nodded, *Yes,* until the last moment convincing her.

Then, looking through the frosted window in the examination room door at the blurred shapes of Marjorie and the doctor, he tried to convince himself. He was twenty, a student. He was in love with Nunny. They'd already picked names for their children. His parents would be devastated. He could see Marjorie lie back, her figure so splotchy through the frosted glass she seemed to sink into the table. The doctor wheeled over a tray; then neither of them seemed to move—dark and blurred, motionless. Stona was inviting a mortal sin into his heart, forcing it into Marjorie's. He turned from the window and looked at the angelfish. How could he ever bring himself to confess it? How could he ever wipe this away?

He sat down in a chair, then stood back up.

He heard a car gunning down the street, he heard the aquarium bubbling. He leaned down into the blue light and looked closely at the fish behind the glass. They were not swimming, just hovering in the water. How could he tell Marjorie that he wasn't going to marry her in two years? How could he live with himself? His nose touched the aquarium glass. The fish floated, their long fins gently ruffling, their gills pulsing, flaring. . . . Then Marjorie screamed. She continued to scream as Stona bounded down the hall, crashed out the door, and sprinted up the street.

That scream was the last he knew of her.

S low down," Theo told Colleen. "One click slower than the flow." They were moving north on Route 17, moderately heavy traffic, center lane. On his lap Theo held the cell phone and the Petrochem home directory, his thumb stuck in the B's. Traffic tended to slow just beyond the water towers, but at this hour, beyond there they were golden. If there was an accident or anything unexpected, they could turn off at dozens of access roads and mall parking lots in Paramus.

They passed over 208. "Okay," he told her. "Drive carefully, and don't make a sound."

"You don't understand," Colleen said. "It's like an oven in the sun."

"You sound just like him."

"He said he had a bad heart. If we could keep him somewhere else—"

"You talked to him?"

"No. I just said that maybe we could—"

"You chatted? You were just supposed to feed him."

"He had a heart attack three years—"

"Of course he's going to say that. You've *never* known when you were being lied to."

Theo dialed the number. He'd given them his voice on the tape, and now he was giving it to them again. It wasn't supposed to be that way. All of the communication was supposed to be in Brown's voice. Damn Stona Brown for screwing things up.

On the second ring, it was answered. "Special Agent Jackson."

Theo let a pause work on the Fed. Some dead air to collapse in on the man. The staticky connection, the cheap phone, disguised Theo's voice plenty. "What's your first name?"

"Tony Jackson. Who is this calling?"'

Did Theo know the man? He thought hard. He thought names. He thought his father's friends, Petrochem security. "Tony the tiger." He didn't know him. "Are you a tiger?"

Colleen gave Theo a look. There was so much she did not understand about men.

"What is the business of this call?" Jackson demanded.

In a high-pitched, child's voice Theo whispered, "Roar." He said, "I see. You're Tony Junior."

"This phone is reserved for official business of the FBI. If you have none, disconnect immediately, or you'll be arrested for interfering in an investigation."

"Put your dick away, Jackson. This is how it works. The money goes in Eddie Bauer laundry bags. No beepers, no dye packs, no tracking devices, no consecutive bills. We find anything, Brown's a corpse. You'll be called later with further instructions."

"Hold on! I need proof you have him."

"Are you calling me a liar?"

"We've had seven calls."

"I said, are you calling me a liar?"

"We'll only pay if there's proof."

"I represent the Rainbow Warriors, and we sent you a cassette which by now you've heard."

There was a pause and Theo could picture the group of men, Dave Tomkins and Bradford Ross among them, exchanging glances from under their headphones. They had the kidnapper on the phone. Every one of them, Theo included, felt the slightest pulse of an erection.

But then Jackson said, "The wife couldn't confirm his voice. We need substantive proof."

Theo's stomach dropped. They were bluffing. They had to be. Of course she'd know her husband's voice. Or was Brown in worse shape than Theo had figured? Maybe Colleen was right? No. They were trying to rattle him. They were stalling, trying to lure him into showing himself. He *hated* to be fucked with. Grinding his teeth, he said, "We'd planned to release him tonight. But you can tell your boss and tell Brown's wife that because of your games, we're keeping him an extra day. Tomorrow night. That's what your bluff has cost you. And Jackson, you cocksucker. If you lie to me again, I'll kill the son of a bitch." He snapped the phone closed.

"What's going on?"

"Don't screw up now. Left lane."

"I can drive the car. Tell me what they said."

"They're just trying to rattle my cage."

"What did they say?"

"For Christ's sake. They said they'll have the money whenever we're ready."

Colleen took the left at Saddle River as planned into a new subdevelopment. "I think we should let him go," she said. "Call it off."

Theo stared out the window at the brand-new houses with high porticos in front, brass and glass chandeliers hanging over the doors. "Are you really so afraid of success?"

"They don't recognize his voice, do they? They don't even believe we have him."

"It's incredible to me that you'd want to sabotage our dreams when we're so close."

"We have a man who needs to go to the hospital. He could die, Theo."

"This has nothing to do with Brown, Colleen. Does it seem odd to you that just as everything was picking up in Vail and you were all ready to start selling GoodLife, you had a nervous breakdown? And in Hilton Head—"

"I'm talking about being responsible for a man's life who we've got wrapped like a mummy in a sweltering box—" She was shouting now.

"No! You *think* that's what you're talking about, but in fact, you're afraid that instead of blaming me for keeping us from the big money, you're going to have to—"

"Enough!" she screamed, and the sudden silence reverberated inside the car. She stopped short at a red light, then turned back onto Route 17. They passed a Sizzler, the smell of steak filled the car, and Colleen said quietly, "If Mr. Brown dies, our lives will be ruined."

"Why don't you tell me what they'd be doing for him in a hospital."

Colleen had nothing to say.

"Tell me, Doctor. What would they do in the hospital for a man in mild shock grazed by a bullet? Explain it to me. I want to know. Seriously."

Her lips wrinkled. She squeezed the wheel too tight, her age showing in her hands.

"Talk to me. I'm waiting to be instructed by the expert." They passed the Tool Bonanza and three independent furniture stores in a row, all selling the same low-end crap. What a fool idea "Insiders" was. The world had enough furniture stores.

"You're afraid to make your mark is what it is," Theo said. "We're a heartbeat away from firing a shot heard round the world, and you can't handle it."

Colleen was silent.

But it was more than that, Theo knew. She was doubting him. She didn't believe that he could get the world to sit up and listen. He'd grabbed an important, powerful man, and when Theo made his demand, they ignored him. That's how she saw it—Theo still at the bottom of the food chain, a man taking orders; nothing had changed. That was his wife's low opinion of him.

Kmart, used cars, fur coats, Levitt's. A billboard for 1-800-LIMO-RIDE. Another for the Channel 7 news team. Chad Sturgeon, Colleen's heartthrob, loomed over the roadway beside the weather girl. Traffic was clear. He had an idea. If he made another call, they could still turn off on 280 toward the Holland Tunnel and loop back on the Turnpike. Colleen watched him punch the numbers into the phone. Theo Wolkoviak could make things happen. Theo Wolkoviak could make Chad Sturgeon and Special Agent Tony Jackson and anyone else he wanted jump through hoops.

"Jackson, this is how it works," Theo said, looking at Colleen. "Tonight before the local news, I want Stona Brown's wife on Channel Seven. I want her to say that her husband is being held by the Rainbow Warriors for his crimes against the environment. I want her to say that she understands he's fine and will be returned unharmed when conditions are met. I want her to say that the environmental criminal Stona Brown is being detained an extra day because of FBI uncooperation. Is that clear, Jackson?"

"I heard you," he said.

"I asked if it was clear."

"Clear," he said, "but I can't promise——"

"Jackson. It happens or Stona Brown is executed, and your career hits the skids." Theo opened the Petrochem directory to the name of a vice president they'd considered nabbing before they found out he had a driver. "And if you force us to kill him, our next target will be Michael Graham, 22 Crescent Drive, Florham Park, then Alden Holcomb . . . You get my meaning? Like dominos they will fall until our demands are met. They will *not* be abducted but treated as soldiers in a war."

He closed the phone, directed Colleen east. He would not let Jackson humiliate him. He would not have Colleen doubting his capability, implying that he was responsible for the few glitches so far.

He squeezed Colleen's knee. "What have I told you? 'You don't get a good price from a busy man, you get a good price from a hungry man.' We're making this Jackson very hungry. Dave Tomkins and Bradford Ross too." They drove in silence, the traffic increasing, past diners, warehouses, gas stations, and row after row of little postwar shit boxes. Colleen damn well better know that Theo called the shots.

The New York City skyline stabbed up on the horizon, and they swung south on the Turnpike.

Nunny was sitting in Stona's desk chair, listening to the loud ticking of his ship's clock, when Jackson knocked on the study door. "Yes," she said, and she watched him come in. He was in his mid-forties, about the same age Timothy Thompson would have been. She prayed that he knew what he was doing.

He was carrying his briefcase, popped open, under an arm. As he sat opposite Nunny in the university chair, setting the briefcase on the floor, he said, "Try to be as natural as possible. We want the wife of Stona Brown, sitting in her home. Personalize."

Nunny could tell that he cared. He wanted, truly wanted in his heart, to find her husband. From inside his briefcase a phone rang. He snapped up the lid and slipped out the phone. "Jackson," he said.

But could she trust him?

"What's the DPC?" Jackson demanded. She sensed his authority.

Did they know about Oakville already?

"Get it done," he said, then flipped the phone closed and dropped it on a stack of file folders in his briefcase.

"Personalize," Nunny said.

"Precisely." His phone rang again. He held up his hand apologetically as he reached down to answer it.

He talked about overtime. He said, "Imperative." He said, "I need two hundred men running down stolen cars and rentals," rising from the university chair. "Probably a van, dark blue," moving toward the door. "And I need a hundred more running former Petrochem employees," stepping into the hall. The racket of the police and the television crews in the living room rushed into the study, and Jackson's voice trailed off. Nunny gripped the leather arm of Stona's desk chair. She let her head turn sideways, and breathed the sweet oily smell of his scalp.

Jane slipped into the study and pushed the door shut. "They want you in the wing chair. Next to the fireplace." Jane was wearing a clean white shirt—a man's-style shirt, but her own. "They're setting up lights. Bradford Ross and Chief Tomkins are talking to the reporters. They told them you won't answer any questions."

Her fiancé, Joe, was here now too. Upstairs or out back in the Florida room. He'd brought Jane fresh clothes, and he'd put a little confidence back in her. Jane had always been a bit vulnerable—quick to hide behind her mother's dress, quick to cry from an unfriendly dog or a forward stranger. But she'd do fine with Joe.

"I brought you a cup of tea."

"How's Joe?" Nunny said.

"He'll be here all night." Jane handed her mother the tea. "Victor called. He's on a flight out of Seoul in four hours."

She wanted Victor here when Stona arrived home. She wanted Jane to be sure about Joe.

"Trust is the main thing," Nunny said, sipping the warm milky tea. "In a relationship."

"I do, Mother. I trust him completely."

"Your husband should bring out your best." And Stona did. She'd lived a fulfilling life because of him.

As Nunny touched the warm lip of the mug to her chin, her eye was caught by her own name: typed on a light blue label, stuck to the tab of a file folder in Tony Jackson's briefcase. She set the mug on Stona's desk and slipped off the seat of his chair. Kneeling, she fingered the edge of the folder. *Why are they compiling notes on me when they have so much work to do? How will a file on me help them to find Stona?* She hated how they mistook thoroughness for competence. She hated how the precision in their speech and actions masqueraded as real thought.

When she opened the folder, she did not see a page of scattered notes from Jackson's interviews with Nunny, his impressions of her state of mind. She did not see a list of follow-up based on information Nunny provided. What Nunny saw brought a heated rush first to her face and eyes and then through her entire body: a glossy black-and-white photograph of Nunny and another woman, wearing wool sweaters and marching arm in arm, holding placards in a line of people on a chilly November afternoon in Newark. *Freedom, Power, Justice.* The flat November sunlight lit Nunny's face brightly. Her face—the face of a thirty-five-year-old mother of two small children with a lovely home and a devoted husband, the face of a woman who was in the final moments of believing that she could define her own life—was circled in red.

She pinched the corner of the photo and drew it aside. When she saw the photo beneath it, her breath left her. She stared at the image of herself, her hands pressed to the sides of Timothy Thompson's head, his body ripped in two by a bomb. After the explosion, Nunny had rushed to what remained of the man—his torso, head, and arms. His legs were in the photo too, blown across the sidewalk against the chain-link fence. His legs hung on the fence, twitching, seeming to run away. He had been wearing pink pants.

At the edge of the photo the fence ran into the side of St. Mary's. Handwritten in black ink over the church steps was the date and the time: 4:01 p.m. She remembered feeling the heat pouring out of Timothy Thompson's body on that cool fall day. She'd thought of turning him upside down to keep his organs from spilling out. But in a matter of seconds she knew that all she could do was hold his head until he died. She lied to him for the last moments of his life. *Fine. You'll be fine.* She still remembered his gurgling breath, the wiriness of his Afro, his face turning yellow. She held him and kept him from looking across the sidewalk at his own legs as the church bells struck four times, calmly, like any other afternoon. The indifference of those bells had led to Nunny's crisis of faith, which lasted for years. And she saw now that just as calmly, routinely, an FBI agent had snapped the photo.

"Mother." Jane was shocked. "It's you."

"My God."

"What is this? Where?"

"This young man was innocent. He couldn't have known he was carrying a bomb in that duffel bag. We were a peaceful group."

"But what were you doing?"

"I got involved working for civil rights through the church. It was only a few months. But Newark was crazy then. The anger, the race riots. Groups were infiltrated by more violent groups. You never knew who was telling you the truth. Half the people blamed the Panthers, the other half blamed the FBI."

"Who is this man?"

"It's too long ago, Jane. We all believed that God wanted us to work for grand change." Nunny stared at the pictures, stared at her own face twenty-three years ago. "Your father was immersed in his work at the time. He'd come into himself. You and Victor had started school, and I'd started to wonder what defined me. I was a wife, a mother, and the keeper of a nice house full of nice things. But it had been too easy, and I hadn't made my own mark. I felt disconnected. But in the years after the bombing, I came to understand that life is about starting at home, doing your best for your family. From there it spreads bigger. You can't just go out into the world and change it, Jane. It changes on its own from the cumulative effect of the good work we do at home."

Jackson burst through the study door, and from his expression Nunny knew he'd remembered the file in his open briefcase. With the cell phone in his pocket, making his suit jacket hang unevenly, he stopped behind the chair, slowly laying his hands on its polished wooden back. From where she and Jane kneeled on the floor, the two photos at their knees, Nunny looked up at Jackson. She stared at him without self-consciousness, as if searching a photograph for subtle shading, obscured images and intentions. She stared without regard for his discomfort, without the slightest inclination to look away. She stared without any concern for Jackson at all.

"A yellow and brown Chanel scarf. Your father gave it to me. Find it. Please." Nunny sat at her dressing table in her slip. She raised one arm, then the other, and sniffed—that wasn't it, but she rolled on more antiperspirant anyway. She brushed her hair, looking into the mirror at the dark, splotchy exhaustion of her face. It was the face of a woman who falls asleep in front of the late movie, then drags herself to bed and lies awake, the face of an old woman who is alone.

Maybe it was her mouth, a taste like a rotting tooth. She brushed her teeth, scouring the bristles over her tongue, gazing out the bathroom door at Stona's side of the bed, remembering how he loved to lie there watching her cool down at her vanity after a bath.

The taste of mint was fresh in her mouth as she powdered the dark circles under her eyes, the mottled skin on her cheeks. But at the foot of the bed, stepping into the dress that Jane had laid out, the bad smell that had been following her around returned. A faint smell of rotting apples, or worse. She smelled it in the skin of her arm. She tasted it on the back of her tongue.

"They have a chef in for special occasions rather than going out," Jane was saying, but Nunny hadn't been listening. Her daughter was telling her about the engagement dinner with Joe's parents, trying to distract Nunny, but it was futile because Nunny could move in only one direction: she was spearing deeper inside a quiet panic. Nunny knotted the scarf. "There was a very large porcelain pot at center table, a pot shaped like a bull, arranged with fallen leaves, just a very few flowers, and some stalks of wild grasses. If I'd done it, it would have been vulgar, but really it was delightful." Only her loyalty to Stona kept her from losing control. She had to be calm. She had to do this broadcast. Her sheer will had to bring him home.

From the foot of the stairs she could see the bright lights of the television crew beaming through the living room doorway, lighting up

Jackson and a TV man, a young man, a boy just out of college, needing a haircut. Jackson tapped his watch at Nunny, and she held up a finger, slipping into Stona's study; Jackson's briefcase, the files, were gone.

She opened Stona's stereo cabinet. The five black components were marked with tiny white labels: *On/Off, CD, Tape, Din. Rm., Liv. Rm., Patio, All Spkrs.*, and on and on, dozens of labels that Stona had made for Nunny's benefit. He loved his gadgets. He loved labels and lists. He loved to file.

There was a rap on the study door. "Mrs. Brown," Jackson called. "It's time." She remembered when Stona had splurged on this stereo. He spent an entire weekend running wires along baseboards, drilling sloppy holes through plaster. He rehung the Hudson River School painting in the living room when a hole that was meant to lead a speaker wire to the bookshelves came out in the middle of the wall.

She found the CD. "Please, Mrs. Brown. One minute." Jackson's voice modulated between a plea and command. She pushed several buttons thinking of Stona's Cross pen in his hand printing the tiny labels, his fingertips smoothing them onto the stereo face. Then she was moving through the hallway with Jackson hurrying in front of her, as if he could pull her along more quickly with the energy of his pace—but she'd done something wrong, she couldn't hear the music, the song that was their song. There was no time to go back and do it right. If he was watching, he'd see the scarf that would let him know she'd forgiven him for Oakville. After his heart attack, when he returned to work, he'd given her the scarf without explanation, and she'd accepted it without comment, though they both knew what it meant. She'd never worn it.

"Put a lid on it!" Jackson ordered, and the fifteen agents and policemen in the dining room immediately went silent. Nunny turned the corner into the living room, squinting in the hot lights, where reporters kept their conversations going as they eyed her. The shaggy-haired boy with a clipboard and headset led her over black cables snaking over the Bokhara they'd had shipped from Turkey, around the candlestand tipped against the couch. The boy led her into the lights shining on the yellow wing chair, and he said, "Just speak in a normal conversational voice. We'll count you down from five, in about ninety seconds."

So Jackson had lied about one minute left, and she considered dashing back to the study to get the song playing right. But as sudden as a stab, a phantom pain seized her breast. She slid sideways in the chair as if she could move away from the hovering pain, and she thought of the woman in Oakville. Two young women sat cross-legged with cue cards in front of her, below the cameras. The din of the roomful of reporters trickled off. Not a mumble or whisper from any of them, so silent she could hear the song now, piped through the tiny speakers beside their wedding portrait on the bookshelf. It had worked after all. A man sitting on the arm of the couch slowly stood up and straightened the upholstered arm cover. Another gingerly removed his steel camera case from the Federalist table and set it silently on the floor. They all stood straight as reprimanded children, not a sound from the twenty or more reporters packed into the back end of the room, staring at Nunny in the yellow wing chair. She had never known reporters to show any deference, she had known them only as aggressive and righteous. As the pain spread across her chest and into her throat, she could hear the song she and Stona would play when saying good-bye between weekends in college. She could hear the spinning of cameras, the hum of lights, and as she gazed at the silent roomful of reporters,

she hated them deeply for the tragedy that their solemn consideration implied.

C olleen was chopping green onions for the salad when Mrs.
Stona Brown's face came on the screen. She put down the
knife. The handle rattled on the cutting board. The woman was
nothing like Colleen had imagined, not as young-looking or tall,
not flashy. She wasn't a woman at the head table of a charity banquet, a woman introducing Paloma Picasso or Barbara Bush at a
fund-raiser for the Guggenheim. She was an exhausted woman in
an ordinary dress, silk scarf, and coffee-colored blazer sitting in a
Colonial chair desperately following Theo's instructions.

Her voice was quavering yet stern. "We love you, Stona," she
said. "If you can hear me, be assured that we're doing everything to
get you home. We have no reason at this time to doubt that you're
being held by a group called the Rainbow Warriors."

"Ha!" Theo said. "Told you, Pop. It *is* environmental."

"Crucial!" Tiffany said, and Colleen moved closer to the television.

"That poor woman," Dot said.

Cameras flashed in Mrs. Brown's face, foam-covered micro-
phones bobbed above her head. She paused for a moment, seeming
confused about what to say next: her face froze. She looked
haunted. Her eyes were set deep in dark tender wells. Her pro-
nounced cheekbones seemed brittle. Then, her pursed lips began to
move again, but the rest of her face remained lifeless. Music was
playing softly in the background.

"That's 'I'll Be Seeing You,'" Dot said.

"The delay in your return caused by investigators is most regrettable," Mrs. Brown continued.

Theo pointed at the TV. "Somebody's making things happen there."

"Very peculiar," Malcolm said.

And then it was over. Colleen sighed, relieved. Dot drained a pot of pasta shells through the colander, and steam rose into her face.

But the lead-in to the local news began immediately. The top story was the kidnapping. Again the picture of Mr. Brown, hardly recognizable as the man Colleen had cared for. Another mention of Rainbow Warriors. Undisclosed ransom amount. They cut back to the Brown home, to Chad Sturgeon in the living room. Reporters and men with the hulky roughness of police were milling around in the background. The Colonial chair was empty, glaring bright with spotlights.

"There's Dave Tomkins," Malcolm said.

Dot raised her head to the TV. "He's lost some weight."

Colleen looked at Theo, who she knew was searching the screen for someone besides Dave Tomkins who might know him. For Bradford Ross or someone else from Petrochem.

"A bizarre and paradoxical tale," Chad Sturgeon said. "A staunch protector of the environment within the Petrochem top echelon abducted, according to kidnappers, for his environmental crimes."

"Protector, my butt," Tiffany said.

"For now, it remains to be seen just who these Rainbow Warriors are. Back to you, Toshi."

Tiffany thrust her fists over her head. Colleen wished she'd shave her underarms. "Let the revolution begin!"

"Don't talk like that," Colleen told her. "This is a tragedy. Did you see that poor woman's face?" She was not aloof and glitzy. She actually seemed a lot like Colleen.

"It's just awful," Dot said, setting a plate of food in front of Malcolm, then handing him his fork. "It's with the eggplant. How you like it," she said.

"You convinced, Pop? Rather professional outfit, seems to me."

"It's got a ring to it," Tiffany said. "Ecoterrorists."

"Please," Colleen said. "They're not terrorists. It's horrifying what they've done."

"I'm truly not sure," Malcolm finally said. "From the outside, it's hard to know who's playing who. I grant you, they wouldn't put the wife on TV unless they took this seriously."

"Erica says this is what the hemp movement needs. Radical action. If just one out of ten people start growing, we'll clog the courts. George Washington and Thomas Jefferson both had hemp plantations. Total radicals—ponytails, buckle shoes."

"If a lunatic escapes from the nuthouse and holds a gun to a hostage's throat," Malcolm said, "you give him some ground. Doesn't make him professional."

"No way, Grampa," Tiffany said. "This is for real. Tree spiking was only the start. We've been waiting. This is the revolution."

"We?" Colleen asked.

Theo tapped his father's arm. "The girl's an honor student."

Not much of a school was all Colleen could think. The first dime they spent of this money would be a check to a prep school for next year.

"Knock out the big corporations. One by one," Tiffany said. Colleen was thankful her own parents hadn't lived to see Ludlow decay. It wasn't right to be raising Tiffany in the middle of a slum.

"I'll just pour you half for now," Dot said, "but help yourself." She set the milk carton next to Tiffany's glass. "Good for those gorgeous teeth." A blurry photo of a little girl—*Have you seen me?*—was on one side of the carton.

"But if they've got their victim," Malcolm said, "what do they gain by making the wife go on TV? Seems impulsive. Irrational. Like maybe something got botched——"

"For Christ's sake," Theo said.

Impulsive, irrational. Botched. Colleen shivered from the facts of what they'd done. A man, their prisoner, in a coffin.

Malcolm set his elbows on the table. "They want their money as fast and quiet as possible. They don't gain——"

"It's for the publicity," Tiffany interrupted. "To make people think about the environment."

A smile stretched across Theo's face, and he tipped his head to his daughter. "The girl's going to college all right."

"So you think the environmental thing's for real. Don't think it might be a diversion?"

Theo nodded. "I believe it, Pop. I really do."

"This is a great moment in history," Tiffany said.

"Stop it!" Colleen spoke too sharply.

Tiffany pouted. She poked at her shells with the chopsticks.

"It's awful what's happened to this man, and you're discussing whether it's a good plan and whether it's some noble act, but somewhere there's an innocent man tied up——"

"Easy, Colleen." Theo cut her off. "Chill."

Malcolm looked at Colleen in a way that made her feel guilty.

"Innocent, my butt." Tiffany rolled her eyes and the tips of the chopsticks. "Mr. Petrochem is probably having the time of his life right now. Chill, Mom."

"I'm sure Mr. Brown is totally copacetic," Theo said.

"I bet they're feeding him vegetarian food," Tiffany continued, "that's not coated with the pesticides his own company churns out. Which by the way, hemp grows chemical-free which is another reason Petrochem hates it, and hemp won't deplete the soil either. I bet they give him soy milk and he loves it."

"Ooh," Dot broke in. "I meant to say, the manager at Food Warehouse told me they don't carry the soy milk. He said they used to sell tofu but nobody bought it."

"Thanks, Gramma. Erica says you have to go to Asherton to get it. No worries."

Colleen had to check on Mr. Brown. The afternoon had been terribly warm. She'd left the mini-storage before the worst of it. She could only imagine. This morning he'd seemed much better, but by the time she left—even after water and half a can of Ensure—he was less coherent. Regardless of what Theo said, Mr. Brown needed care. "I have that meeting tonight," she said to Theo.

He looked at her blankly.

"The yacht club wives," she said. "You don't have to go."

"Neither do you."

She shook her head.

"We could blow the whole deal if we hang around there too much. Looks weird. Too eager."

"You're wrong," she told him.

"We'll talk about this later."

"Yep," Tiffany said. "The guy's probably getting waited on by earth-pigs with Birkenstocks and big boobs. I mean, they're not my style, but politically I'm in solidarity."

Colleen stared Theo down.

"My experience," Malcolm said, touching Tiffany's hand, "has been that people involved in a crime like this don't have much regard for human life at all. They might seem like us on the surface, but inside they don't feel things. Not like the rest of us."

Colleen's fist squeezed tight around the handle of her fork. "I'm going as soon as we eat." She feared for what had become of her husband.

"Let's just drop it," Theo said.

"Somebody's got to fight the system." Tiffany spun the milk carton around, clicked her chopsticks beneath the picture on its side. "A little girl gets kidnapped, she gets her face here. But when the corporate presidents and the politicians and judges aren't safe, that's revolution. It's treason against the capitalist order. If the kidnappers get caught, I promise you they'll fry."

"Shut up, Tiffany," Theo snapped.

"Martyrs," she said. "Toast."

A drop of water tapped on the tape covering Stona's left eye. He spoke in his throat. *Forgive me, Father, for I have sinned.*

He could see Nunny's face across the table at Marcelle's, Nunny's face lit by a candle from below. One bite gone from her crème brûlée. Her spoon was cast improbably at the edge of the table, a brown and yellow stain across the white tablecloth. So wrong that Robert asked if everything was satisfactory. Stona drained his port, signaled for another, waved Robert away.

It had been a great relief for Stona to hear the news about

Oakville. He'd called Marcelle's for a table, then called Nunny. When they ordered dessert, she'd said, "You haven't looked so light in weeks."

"That mean stomach of mine. It's been vicious." He hadn't been sleeping either. The knot in his neck had been drawing tighter. "But it's over." And he lifted his glass of port.

"Ting," Nunny said, raising her empty hand. Like so many times before, she had no idea what they were celebrating. She never wanted to know. She thought he spent too much time on his work as it was, and she didn't want it spilling into every moment of their lives.

"I've been thinking of a watch for Jane's graduation," Nunny said. "A nice one. A gold one."

"Damage control is half my job these days."

"I know it is, dear. A young woman should have a gold watch. What do you think?" Years ago, Stona ran the dinner table like a business meeting. He'd point at Jane: *You. How was school?* Then at Victor: *You win at soccer?* So Nunny had made a rule, and Stona agreed, that he would not speak for the first thirty minutes he was home in the evening. He needed to unwind.

"This one was eating us up." At the time, Stona had wanted to tell Nunny about Oakville—just to get it out—so he ran roughshod over the discussion of Jane's gift. Nunny yielded, exhaling back in her chair, striking a momentarily patient smile, her spoon poised over her dessert. She had always been supportive, she just tried to keep things in perspective—for him and for their family—which Stona respected. She was waiting, he knew, for him to unload, then she'd steer them right back to a gift for Jane's college graduation.

Stona began to tell his wife about a by-product discharged

from thirteen of their plants in the chemical division producing a solvent used in extruded plastics. "A woman with nothing better to do with her time decided to wage a campaign about tiny traces of by-product in the water table near the Oakville plant in Ohio where she lives. Claimed there were health risks. The local news loved it."

"And what did your own people find?" Nunny asked. "Was there a health risk?"

"Well, the short answer is no. But, yeah. Possibly. I'm not saying I'd move *us* there, but nothing has been scientifically proven. Completely inconclusive. We contracted a disposal outfit to get rid of the stuff. For what they bid, it's hard to know how they're processing it, but sometimes it's better not to ask. Our asses are covered is what matters. But we couldn't afford to have production interrupted for an investigation. The legal department and the lobbyists can keep us going for—"

"What *are* the supposed health risks?" Nunny was losing patience. She broke through the burnt sugar on her crème brûlée with the spoon.

"Nothing was proven at all. The point is within seven years we'll have moved the plants overseas, by which time it's not an issue. India's taking two larger plants with open arms. That consolidates five. Venezuela might take one, Bangladesh and Turkey. Until then we've *got* to keep the plants up. But this woman organized herself a local environmental group, and then started contacting people living near other plants. Thirteen plants in the U.S. I know you hate percentages, but *significant* in the chemical division, enough to depress stocks a good year. And we had enough suits pending on this woman to bankrupt King Faisal, but she's got no assets. Nothing to lose. She can only gain. President of her own environmental group. She's thinking Love Canal, checks probably pouring in. And

then in some truly bizarre publicity stunt she has herself pho-
tographed stark naked from the waist up and the media goes nuts.
So she——"

"Are you saying the chemicals gave her——"

"No, no. Not at all. You misunderstand. The *point* is it's not
clear how litigation should deal with people who have no assets.
Should they have the same prerogatives? If you can only win at the
game, if you're staking nothing, it's hardly fair to the other side. She
had to be discredited. But the real coup was getting the EPA on our
side. I spoke with their two investigators a few weeks ago and told
them I understood it would be unethical for Petrochem to hire
them at this juncture, but when the investigation was complete,
we'd hire them over to our own environmental department for
double their salaries. And today, the court papers were withdrawn.
Case closed. But never mind. Let's talk about Jane's watch."

"She had breast cancer?" Nunny stiffened.

"It was totally unrelated. Horrible for her, of course, for anyone. Nunny, I'm not saying it's not horrible. I'm just saying it's not
our fault." Stona looked across the restaurant, then back at his wife.
"I think a gold watch is a great idea."

Stona had seen Nunny close her lips around the spoonful of
crème brûlée, then remove the spoon from her mouth with the
custard still on it. He saw her move strangely sideways, as if she
started to stand, then changed her mind. She dragged the spoon
across the tablecloth, smearing the brown and yellow custard; then
she dropped the spoon as if it burned her.

Stona saw all of this, yet he persisted. He was high from tawny
port and relief. He wanted to convince Nunny that he'd done the
right thing. He was bragging, a man who gets things done. So he
kept talking about the rise in Petrochem stock that day instead of

the plummet they'd feared for over a month. "Don't think the community was behind this woman. They understand jobs and property values, people paying mortgages, car payments. It's not good for anyone if a plant closes for the wrong reasons because a woman with no assets——"

"You said she had to be discredited?" Nunny asked, speaking slowly.

Robert removed Nunny's spoon and set a clean one beside her dish. He placed a napkin over the smear on the tablecloth. Stona ordered another port, finished off the glass he had with a full swallow.

"The largest employer in a community requires . . ."

Her face was frozen in a way he'd never seen before. Her eyeballs darted around looking for something to settle on, but her chin and mouth were fixed. She sat oddly propped in her chair, like a stuffed version of herself, diagonally slumped.

"What did you do to her?"

He'd known it was wrong. *My God, I have made mistakes, and I understand that this box is my punishment, and now I am begging forgiveness. I beg for a chance to live the rest of my life as I should.*

"Nothing," Stona had said. "Our people infiltrate meetings. Dig up a little dirt. It's intelligence work, standard procedure. It's the only way to level the playing field. But none of this matters now that the regulators are on our team. That's the *point.*"

Nunny was examining Stona's face.

"For Christ's sake. Don't be so naive," he said. "Do you know in most countries . . . Christ. In Italy Petrochem foots the bill for the entire electoral process. *La bustarella?* The little envelope? You're out of your league here."

What did she think they were running? A soup kitchen.

Stona's job allowed Nunny to be a full-time volunteer. Her work with the church, the Children's Fund, and the Hamlin Foundation. Who bankrolled her life while she was slopping out chili at St. Thomas? They'd never spoken this to each other, but wasn't that the understanding? Didn't they both know the truth of it? They were a couple, a unit. Stona's compromises—the difficult and complex repercussions of some of his decisions, some of Petrochem's policies—were balanced out by Nunny's good work. And his compromises were slight, because even when a plant was built closer than people would like to a neighborhood, it brought huge numbers of good-paying jobs that families could count on. A small sacrifice brought product and prosperity to all. Sacrifices were sometimes *imposed* on people, he knew that, but then there was Nunny's charitable work. . . . On a balance sheet, as a couple, they were way ahead.

Nunny touched her breast. "My loyalty to you is supreme," she finally said. "You know that, don't you? You could commit murder and my loyalty would endure, but . . ." She searched for the words, and had she not searched for them and spoken them so precisely, they would have been unremarkable. But as she carefully enunciated each syllable, he became furious. She said: "You disappoint me."

In the middle of that night Stona woke up cold, smelling the damp cucumber fragrance. He slid his hand across the taut chilly sheet on Nunny's side of the bed. He opened his eyes and saw, in a rectangle of light, the blurry shape of his wife sitting at her vanity, elbows propped on the counter, head in her hands. Silently, he patted the nightstand for his glasses. She was naked. She lifted her head. Her nose honked when she blew it. She was crying. She'd taken a bath with cucumber bath salts. He knew the routine: she'd dried off with two towels, placed a third fresh towel over the upholstered vanity stool, opened the door to the bedroom to let out the steam, and sat down until she cooled off.

In that moment he was bored with the predictability of his wife. He resented that her distress was his fault. As he watched the light shining off edgy rivulets of water dripping from her hair and zigzagging down her skin, he hated her steadiness, her predictability, her righteousness and naive morality. *And what did your people find? Was there a health risk?* As if it were that simple. As if *anything* were that simple. He hated her for expecting he'd never disappoint her. He hated her for her allergies, for thirty-five years of her red runny nose, her sinus headaches, her goddamned honking, and her pockets full of wet tissues. He hated her skinny legs and bony shoulders, the fleshy shelf of her stomach. He hated her one deflated breast, all loose skin and a nipple knuckling toward the floor. He hated the tight-lipped scar, expressionless and stern, sealed up over her heart. He hated that the skin there was tighter, younger-seeming than the wrinkled breast that remained.

In that moment he decided that before he was too old he would have a young woman with plump breasts and voluptuous hips. There *was* a woman once, many years before, and he fell back to sleep remembering the warmth that rose from her doughy cleavage. But when he awoke, with Nunny sleeping beside him again, he had a terrible chill in his heart that did not pass through the course of his day. At home in the evening he lugged his briefcase inside, took off his coat, opened the fridge for tonic and a lime, and the chill squeezed tighter around his chest, squeezed like a vise until his heart stopped beating.

Through his time in the ICU and his thirty-seven days of recovery, and through the past three years, Oakville was never mentioned again.

Lord, believe me, Stona prayed. *If I am given the chance to live again outside the box, I will change my life. I understand that Nunny was right. There is always a "right" decision. I thank you Lord for this punishment, for the chance to set my morals straight.*

Stona looked back. He reevaluated his life moment by moment. The few indiscretions early in his marriage. He'd never crossed the line, but his lust had been powerful, and if the situations had turned just so, he knew he could not have refused. He would've cheated on Nunny. There were his taxes in the early years, before they were on their feet. There was the real estate deal in Pennsylvania. There were scores of decisions he'd made in the course of his career that had harmed the lives of innocent people for the good of the company.

He'd hit rock bottom with Oakville, and he understood his actions had been wrong. More, he was ashamed that he'd glossed right over the Oakville woman's breast cancer with Nunny sitting across the table, patiently listening. He'd been thinking only of his need to unload on Nunny, his need to brag. How could he have done that to her? He was ashamed of the thoughts he'd had that night watching Nunny after her bath. But they hadn't been true thoughts, even at the time. It had been his own anger at himself, his defensiveness, that made him lash out at Nunny. He hadn't meant any of it. When his heart attack came the next day, he'd blamed it on the stress of the previous month, and on Nunny's reaction. But as he recovered, he came to understand that the heart attack was punishment, for which he was thankful. He had resolved to love Nunny more each day. And he truly had.

If you release me from this box, dear Lord, I will be Your faithful servant. I'll leave my job and devote the rest of my life to Nunny and her good works. Forgive me, Father, for I have sinned. And Stona flipped methodically through his entire life, asking forgiveness for every compromise he'd ever made.

B rown had cash. Yesterday morning when Theo went through the man's wallet for the American Express card, he'd seen plenty of green. Theo was no pickpocket, he didn't want to take it, but things had changed.

"The gym bag's in the trunk," he said to Colleen after he'd hauled Brown to his feet. When Colleen ducked out under the door, Theo wriggled his fingers under bands of tape down into warm wet pockets. He snatched the cash from Brown's wallet and a wad of bills on a money clip. The money was in his own pocket by the time Colleen reappeared with a bottle of water.

It was already dusk, only fifteen minutes before American Mini-Storage closed for the night. Theo tugged the tape away from Brown's mouth, and Brown spit out the gag.

"No talking," Theo told him, and Brown's head fell forward.

Colleen took Brown's chin in her fingers and raised it up. "How are you feeling?"

"Please—"

Theo gave her a look. He was holding the man up by a band of duct tape between his shoulder blades. Theo slowly released him, then stepped back with his hands up to catch him in case. Brown stood on his own, and Theo raised his eyebrows at Colleen. *Am I right? Do I know?* Colleen could handle it from here. This was *her* idea.

Theo squatted down by the door to keep an eye out. He slipped the cash from his pocket. Five fifties, damp but new. He licked his thumb and tried to pinch out a sixth without any luck. The wad in the money clip was all ones. There must have been twenty or twenty-five one-dollar bills. He clipped the fifties in with the singles, and held the thick pack of cash in his hand, looked at the size of it in his palm, and . . . damn, it was a Petrochem money clip. The same cheap metal clips the company gave everybody one year for Christmas. Theo had been so pissed off he threw his away. It had already become clear to Theo by that Christmas that he was going nowhere fast at Petrochem. His boss had told him he'd be promoted quickly from his job supervising the uniformed men. Theo had wanted to get involved in intelligence work for Petrochem, collecting data on customers and environmental groups, investigative work, employee profiles. He'd pictured himself under cover—spreading disinformation in the markets, delivering payoffs to Arabs, influencing small-time politicians. But it became clear to Theo that the *real* work was done by the top ranks of Petrochem security—former Army Intelligence, CIA, and FBI men. A small-town cop like Theo would never bust through to the top. Theo had confronted his boss about the promised promotion at the Christmas party, and he'd told Theo: "Keep up the fine work. We like you where you are." Then they were all given a little cardboard jewelry box containing a fifty-cent money clip engraved with the Petrochem logo.

"Time," Theo said. Colleen was giving Brown a Slim-Fast. They didn't need the security guard coming by to tell them to leave. Theo rose. "C'mon," he said. "Bedtime."

Brown looked a lot better. A drink and a breather did him

good. As Theo ripped off a fresh length of duct tape, he thought back to the months of downsizing at Petrochem that he'd spent swooping into offices with a man from personnel, a company lawyer, and a uniformed man to fire people. Personnel read a statement, then Theo immediately walked the person to the parking lot. All summer, he went in on Saturdays to escort people into the building to pack up framed snapshots of their kids, group shots of co-workers and cartoons tacked up on bulletin boards, potted plants, *World's Greatest Dad* pencil cups. They were people who'd spent their whole careers at Petrochem, and the company was worried they'd sabotage computers or steal confidential information—as if a woman in building operations was just waiting for the day to set her plan in action peddling Petrochem secrets.

When his boss gave Theo the assignment, he'd said, "Since you're bored with your present duties, I've got something you might like. Lots of Saturday overtime too." He'd referred obliquely to Theo's suspensions from the police force. He'd said they needed somebody who wasn't afraid to use a strong arm. Theo hated the man. He hated them all, right up to Bradford Ross.

Theo placed fresh tape over Brown's mouth, and as they got him back in the box, he watched Colleen's eyes for a sign that she was bailing out.

Sitting in the car, nearly dark outside, she said, "I think we should let him go."

The security guard walked toward them, swinging a flashlight. Theo thought about calling her bluff. What if he said, *Okay, you win.* What would she do then? Get the guard to help take Brown to the hospital? Did she think he didn't see through her?

"Good night, folks," the guard said, passing by the car.

Theo waved.

"Everything that's gone wrong in our lives you blame on somebody else," Colleen said.

His wife did not believe in him.

Theo and Colleen had gone to the yacht club, and Tiffany was working late at Joey's Tacos, so Malcolm left the bathroom door ajar and didn't bother to switch on the light. But then he heard the kids coming up the stairs, and he leaned forward on the toilet to swing the door shut. ". . . you've got to believe this is going to work," he heard Theo say. Then Colleen's voice—"I'm afraid"— rising on a swell of tears. "I need you to trust me," Theo told her. It made Malcolm feel all the worse for Theo. Colleen was not supporting him in the yacht club venture. "I'll be right in," Theo said, and Malcolm heard Colleen weeping as she went down the hall to their room.

He switched on the light and reached for his toothbrush. From his bedroom, Malcolm heard the familiar scratch of his police radio. It was the Tactical Frequency out of Asherton—Tac Frequency One—established for the kidnapping. Theo *was* curious about the case. It must be that their discussions over dinner, which reminded Malcolm of exciting days on the force, reminded Theo of failure. All his life when Theo confronted failure, he sank his hands in his pockets and walked away. But of course he was interested, even Colleen was. She'd seemed emotional during the news. It was seeing the wife that got to her, no doubt.

Malcolm cleaned his teeth and swallowed his pills. He washed the back of his neck and behind his ears with a facecloth. Already he felt, as they say about the dying, more at peace. He wished Theo had objected twenty years ago to being measured against Dave Tomkins. Malcolm had been kicking himself all day. The important thing was they understood each other now. He wrung out the facecloth, and hanging it on the rod by the door, he could still hear the Tac Frequency coming from his room.

He dried his face and hands, and when he opened the bathroom door, he plowed right into Theo.

"Pop!" Theo jumped back. "I thought you were down on the breezeway."

"No, just getting ready for bed. Thought I'd turn in early."

Theo made a move to get by, but Malcolm sidestepped to hold him there for a few words. "Anything new? On the kidnapping, I mean?"

Theo raised his eyebrows, opened his palms.

"I've been thinking about the type of group that would carry this out—"

"You know, it's fun to shoot the bull over dinner," Theo interrupted, "but I've got too many things going on with the yacht club right now." He looked away as he spoke. "How are you feeling, anyway, Pop? Breathing good?"

"Just one spell today. Pretty good, though."

"That's good." Theo made another move to get by.

"I just thought if you wanted to listen in on the Tac Frequency, we could—"

"I don't have time, is what I'm telling you. Or the interest." He didn't say it harshly. "I haven't listened to a police radio since the day I left the force."

Something inside Malcolm collapsed.

"You look tired, Pop. Get some sleep, and we'll talk tomorrow. I'll tell you about the boat I'm gonna buy you." Then Theo spread his arms as wide as the hall. He reached around his father's back and squeezed. "It's nice to be back in town," Theo said, "to be close again. It's tough, though. Trying to start over. Lots of anxiety."

Malcolm's arms hung at his sides. His son hadn't hugged him in years.

He watched Theo shut the door to his old bedroom; then he turned and went into his. He looked at the scanner on his dresser, reached toward it, then stopped. He stared at it, hoping he'd misheard, hoping it had been the television or a CB from a parked car. He would show his confidence in Theo and his new business. His son needed him, especially since Colleen's support was lacking. Malcolm never could have achieved the success he did without Dot. Maybe he'd drive down to Golden Bay Yacht Club. He could see the layout, take his son to lunch.

He hesitated a moment longer, then touched his palm to the top of the radio. It was warm. Damn.

He loved his son. If only he'd started sooner making sure Theo knew it. If only Theo trusted him.

The smell of baby powder reminds me of the first time your father and I made love."

"Mother," Jane protested.

"You're a woman, Jane. There are people younger than you downstairs trying to get him home."

"I know but—"

"Don't try to tell me you and Joe haven't made love." Steam was drifting out the bathroom door as Jane spread baby powder on Nunny's back where they sat on the bed. "It was a different time when your father and I were young. Courtship and hand holding. He asked my father's permission before he proposed. It wouldn't have occurred to either of us in a million years that we might have sex before we were married. Sex came *after* love, it was doubly true for Catholics. On our wedding night at the Harborside Manor, with the windows swung open to the Sound, we were just a couple kids discovering something new together." She breathed in deeply, then exhaled, feeling the comfort of Stona's weight settling on top of her. "The smell of baby powder and low tide."

Jane helped Nunny into her robe. "Joe and I want to have a big traditional wedding like you and Daddy. We want a couple hundred at least and the reception in Thatcher Garden. We want to ride away in a horse and carriage. All the men are going to be in tails, and Joe's going to wear a top hat."

The rotting smell was there again. It seemed stronger to Nunny, more foul, as Jane talked on, trying to distract her mother.

She thought of what she'd said to Jane about love enduring. But loyalty and commitment could endure even after love had faded. Nothing about Oakville had changed Nunny's commitment and loyalty to Stona. The stakes were too high. She'd never do anything to shatter the family, because without it she had nothing. But could she say that she loved him the same after Oakville, after her respect for him was marred? A relationship, she wanted to tell Jane, grew and grew until you reached the other person's limits. You could move around within that boundary, but you couldn't go beyond. That was the disappointment.

That night when they'd returned from Marcelle's, Stona had

retreated into his study to call a plant manager in Saudi, which he often did late at night to catch them at the beginning of their day. Nunny followed him in, and as he sat in his desk chair she said, "I need to know how you really feel about Oakville. I need some sense of how this fits into your principles."

"What you need," Stona said as he dialed the phone, "is to realize how naive you are about what pays for this house and your trips to Italy and your clothes and your parties and your volunteer—"

"Do you—" she began, furious, but Stona held up his hand to cut her off.

"Good morning, Mark," he said into the phone. "How's that Arab Ben-Gay working?" Nunny stood in the doorway with her arms folded across her chest and listened to Stona chat with Mark Mansfield in Saudi about family and sore tennis muscles and production numbers and next week's meeting. She stood there after he'd swung around his chair and turned his back on her, his voice jovial and easy. Tears streamed down her face as she thought of the great relief with which he'd told her about the outcome of Oakville, the pride in his voice, the celebratory air of the dinner.

He'd talked with Mark for some time before Nunny gave up and went to bed. She needed to know how he could reconcile the decision that allowed Oakville with the way he lived the rest of his life. She didn't want to ask him rhetorically. She wanted to hear his answer, she wanted desperately to be convinced. Because if she couldn't be convinced, she didn't know her husband. The man *she* knew cared more for his children than for himself. He made large annual contributions to at least half a dozen charities. Without a thought he wrote off a check to Father Ryan for the full amount of repaving the church parking lot. He always had a roll of ones in his left front pocket to tip for the slightest service.

When Stona finally came to bed, it was late and she decided to let the conversation wait until the next day. But she couldn't sleep, so she got up an hour later and took a bath. Afterwards, when she was sitting at her dressing table cooling off, she heard Stona fumbling for his glasses on the bedside table. As she sat, patting drops of water from her neck and shoulders, Nunny could feel him watching her, and she knew that he was remembering how much he loved her. She knew that Stona was looking at her nakedness feeling the same desire he'd felt at the Harborside Manor on their wedding night. And knowing that he was quietly loving her from the bed in the middle of the night, she became less concerned somehow with his morality. He was gazing at her, loving her, and for the moment, that was all that mattered.

The next day was his heart attack.

Now she imagined Stona locked in a room like a jail cell, inadequate sanitation, no sheets on the bed, no blankets at night. She prayed that they let him watch her plea on the television; see the scarf, hear the song, her voice. He used to call her from Argentina or Saudi or Cleveland and tell her, "I get so damn scattered I don't know what I'm thinking anymore, pulled so many ways, but when I hear your voice, everything in me lines right back up in order. I remember who I am, what I'm doing." As Nunny thought of him, she knew that the awful stench was her own decay, her own questioning of their love in the midst of his suffering. It was her black heart, that wondered if their love would have endured a full confrontation over Oakville, the despicable part of her that saw the bright side of his being abducted.

Out of her love for him she had to do anything to get him back. But if she told Jackson that the kidnappers could be from Oakville, if she told him what Stona had done there . . . Her loyalty prevented it.

She was nodding off to sleep, and her thoughts hovered beyond her control, as in dreams. Was it true that she was working harder to remain in love with him? Was it true that the fear and anguish that shuddered through her with the understanding that he might not return was tinged with relief? They seemed to love each other more each day, but had the surface sweetened to cover a sour core? It was as if Stona had resolved to love her more after Oakville, a decision from the head rather than the heart. Another decision after a day at the office full of decisions.

All he ever cared about was his career. No one gets as far as he had without unbridled ambition. She'd wanted him to retire early so she could have him for herself. She'd wanted him to show her that for the remaining years of their lives he would give to her the attention he'd given for thirty-five years to his career. She'd wanted to be secure in his priorities. She'd wanted to be sure she knew him.

Stona, it was your job you lived for, your job that took you away from your family week after week, around the world to strike deals, it was your job that tested you in Oakville—the test you failed—and it's your job that's taken you away from me now. You poor man. Are you cold? I pray you're not cold. You bastard.

s u n d a y

"It's morning, Mr. Brown," the woman said. "You're going home today."

She slowly peeled back the tape from his eyes, and he saw manicured nails, long slender fingers. A relief. A bit of pleasure. A reminder of the world outside. He thought of his grip, of working more seriously on his golf game. He thought of stretching his back and shoulders at the tee. Spiking long strides over the green. It was a bit of joy—delicate young woman's hands touching his face.

He was sitting up in the box. The light in the garage was dim. The woman, wearing a black mask like an executioner's hood, squatted beside him, a lantern next to her on the floor. He was not blind, as he'd feared, closing one eye to check his vision, then the other. He wanted his vision to clear, but this was perhaps as clear as it got. He wasn't sure, he was never without his glasses. He even put them on when he got up in the night for a pee.

She folded the tape over on itself, holding it by the corners with the tips of her long fingers, handling it as if it were infected. She dropped it in a garbage bag beside her, then peeled back the bandage on his forehead. "Does that feel better?" she asked.

Stona didn't respond. In business he'd learned long ago that when you screw somebody, don't pretend to be nice. Screw him hard, and let him rebuild with dignity intact.

He leaned his head back into the cradle of her hand, and she poured cold water over his forehead. Then something split open inside him and bubbled beneath his ribs; he was afraid a heart attack was coming on, so he tried to breathe precisely and deeply. As he exhaled, the cramp in his heart didn't worsen, but the fluttering expanded to his belly. He was crying.

The woman, still supporting his head, wiped his eyes with a handkerchief that smelled of her perfume. She wiped away the gluey residue of duct tape from his brow and cheeks. She held his head against her body and drew the handkerchief over his lips and ears, down his neck and under his collar. Tears washed through his eyes.

"I miss her," he choked.

She held his head firmly against her chest.

"I don't want to die—"

"You're going to be fine, Mr. Brown."

"How much longer?"

"Sooner the better for all concerned."

"When?"

"Tonight."

"No!" He shook his head free of her grasp. He could not survive another afternoon in the box. Did she understand the heat? His
heart? "It'll kill me," he said. "Don't lock me inside. I'll die. Sitting
up like this makes all the difference." He said, "I can breathe." He
said, "Haven't I been punished enough?" The woman's hand covered his mouth, and pandemonium rang in his ears.

The woman was beside him. He was still sitting up, tied around his
waist to the end of the box, wrists and ankles still bound. The heat
had built while he slept. The metal roof creaked. The woman had
peeled her gray coveralls off her shoulders, down to her waist. She
wore a pale yellow, sleeveless tennis shirt with a small round collar
and buttons open at her breastbone. He could see a residue of white
powdery antiperspirant ringing her underarms.

"Water," he said. Her hands were more beautiful than she
deserved.

He drank. A bead of sweat traveled down her inner arm. "Take
everything . . . that I have." It took him a long while to get out the
words. "If you try to get ransom, they'll catch you." His voice was
gaining strength. "If you let me go now, I'll give you everything I've
got. It's not eighteen million, but it's plenty. I just want to retire. I've
made some decisions. Spend my life with my wife and my kids and
their families. I barely know my son. . . . I'll liquidate everything and
give you the cash. It'll only take a couple days. And then you won't
be caught. It's better for you."

With heavy eyes he pleaded with the woman. Could he hold
on to his sanity? He'd been letting it out slowly, like a kite, letting
more and more line slip through his hands. Letting his mind float

out on the wind, on a thin string, fluttering far above the box. But as the kite drifted nearly out of sight, the line sagging, Stona was afraid to let it out another turn, afraid the line would spin off the spool and wiggle away beyond his reach.

"I hated my wife once. Hated her for being so good. So righteous."

"I've hated my husband before."

"Hated her for being right."

"I know," the woman whispered. "I know that feeling. I've been there."

"I know I was wrong. I see it now. I saw it already, only I never told her."

"You'll tell her tonight."

"Make sure she knows. Tell her, please. The tanker specs, the Burnheart sell-off, the Pakistan deal, the woman in Oakville. Make sure she knows I'm sorry."

"Sounds like water under the bridge. Can't beat yourself up over it." She patted his forehead with the handkerchief. "Spilled milk."

"Say you'll tell her."

"You can tell her yourself very soon, Mr. Brown."

"With the other thing."

"Yes?"

"It was lust. And perverse."

"Shhh."

"Watching Jane's friend skinny-dipping. Just thirteen years old, and I was aroused."

"Shush now."

"A priest. I must—"

"Just breathe."

"Father Ryan at St. Thomas. You can trust him."

"Deep breaths."

"I'll make sure he won't tell a soul."

"You know we can't."

"There's more. I was just a college kid. My whole future . . ." He looked at the woman. "Forgive me, Father, for I have sinned—" Stona began, then he slipped beneath a black rubbery sheet that suddenly appeared in the box. There was a wobbly sound like mucking through mud in a pair of rubbers. He slipped beneath where his skin couldn't breathe. He'd read once that a child died one Halloween because her skin was painted head to toe with silver paint. Her pores were plugged. She suffocated. It was a costume of a fish.

"Mr. Brown? Are you okay? Mr. Brown?"

He couldn't get enough air. The burpy sound of flopping rubbers grew louder, and Stona fought the seasick sway that rocked his head toward sleep. For the first time he realized that sleep could mean death. He gulped at the thickening air. He would not die. He would not be damned for taking his sin to the grave. With his eyes forced open he watched the woman—her black mask, her blue-green eyes, the points of her collarbone, the jumpsuit peeled to her waist. With her delicate, long fingers she picked at a tiny tear in the crotch of the jumpsuit. She pulled at a thread, and the thread kept coming, and she pulled and pulled, the jagged thread unraveling. The seam split open wide, and the woman's sex opened, fleshy and syrupy, and a fish no larger than Stona's hand slithered out of her and slapped on the concrete floor, followed by a bucketful of seawater. He watched the fish, flapping on the concrete. Its eyes stared open, gills reaching for breath.

Theo lay back, sprawled out with his head propped up on one arm of the couch, his stocking feet sticking over the other. He could hear his father outside, poking and banging at the back steps—still talking about replacing them. Theo counted out the wad of Brown's one-dollar bills—seventeen singles on the damn Petrochem clip. He wiped the clip carefully with his shirt—a souvenir. He had put the fifties in his wallet. Theo felt like a scumbag taking the money, but they needed the added security for tonight. Actually, he suspected that Colleen was always sitting on a couple hundred bucks.

"*Ay! Dios mío!* It's a scorcher." Tiffany came in from her room, pulling something from a paper bag. "Look what I got for Grampa."

Theo slipped the ones in his front pocket. "That's one of the nicest long wooden abstract-type sculpture widgets I've ever seen."

"It's a foot roller. A massager."

"Definitely Grampa's sort of deal," Theo said. "Just what he was hoping to get, I'm sure. You pegged it."

"He's more open-minded than most people in this house."

"I bet he'll go in on the hemp farm with you too."

As Tiffany rolled her foot over the massager, Colleen came down the stairs. "Things to do, my lovely wife," Theo said. He had taped a note underneath the shelf in a phone booth in Metuchen this morning while Colleen was with Brown, then he'd untarped the boat and let the outboard idle for a few minutes. He'd pawned their wedding rings for that boat two weeks ago, and told his mother he was having them cleaned when she'd noticed. He'd probably get the rings out of hock as keepsakes, but the new ring he planned to slip back onto Colleen's finger . . . Theo would make her weep.

"Sweetheart," Colleen said to Tiffany. "Did you have lunch?"

"There's seventy million nerve endings in the bottom of the foot," Tiffany said, "each and every one of which is directly connected to every single organ and muscle in your body. Including the lungs. Stimulates blood flow. I'm going to start Grampa on a more holistic approach."

Theo wondered if Jackson had picked up on the significance of eighteen and a half million—the largest environmental fine ever paid by a U.S. corporation. Was it Union Carbide? Theo couldn't remember for sure.

"We're gonna do Grampa's party from five to eight," Tiffany was saying, "and then—"

"Gala fête!" Theo said. He had to get Colleen back on board.

"—and then we'll pick up Erica. Just as long as we're there by—"

"Problemo," Theo said. "Mucho."

"Mom, you promised." Tiffany's face went instantly red.

"Don't point at your mother like that," Theo said. "We have a very important dinner meeting tonight at the yacht club."

But Colleen piped up: "Maybe we can work something out."

All he'd wanted was some time to go over the rest of the day in his head—to visualize, like downhill skiers—and already he had a situation. "Erica's parents will have to—"

"No!" Tiffany shouted, and then Theo's father shuffled into the room. "Hey, birthday boy." Tiffany quickly stuffed the massager back in the bag, and a smile broke over her face. Theo couldn't help noticing she was a lot sweeter to her grandfather than to him.

"Colleen, you should get dressed so we can go," Theo said.

"I had a good look under the steps," Malcolm said, "and for the time being I could rig the stringers with some plywood scraps from that locker you built. Did you notice if I had any treated two-by-four in the shed? I could use about twelve inches—" He started coughing.

"Colleen, *you* could use about twelve inches, eh?" Theo kidded.

Colleen turned to Tiffany. "Maybe we can work out a ride for you and Erica."

Malcolm was hacking.

"*You* could use about twelve inch—"

"Say it again, Dad, maybe it'll be funny." And Tiffany jumped up to rub her hand on Malcolm's back and help him into a chair. "Mom," she said. "*How* are you going to work it out?"

Theo watched Colleen slowly losing her shit. They did not need extra hassles today. She was tugging at a wet strand of hair. Christ, she wasn't even dressed. "Maybe we should skip it tonight," she said to Theo. "Call it off completely."

"So we can drive Erica to a party? Am I surrounded by insane people?"

"I know you're busy," Malcolm said, when his breathing had quieted to a gentle wheeze, "but what time this afternoon were you thinking we might discuss the finances?"

Colleen was nodding to Theo, a little pre—nervous breakdown suggestion that they skip the eighteen and a half million so that Theo could devote the evening to competing for good-father and good-son awards. Her hands were shaking: a warm-up to tears.

"Pop," Theo announced. "Here's how it'll happen. Today I cinch the yacht club deal. Tomorrow you and I will discuss finances at exactly one p.m. over lunch. In fact, we will *do* lunch. You and me, father-and-son, then maybe take in a ball game or something. We'll look at the back steps when we get home and you can order me around and teach me how to saw a board the right way and how to measure accurately, and I'll lick it up big-time. One o'clock. Don't be late."

Theo stretched out more royally on the couch. "Tiffany." He pointed at her. "Give me the phone." She handed it to him, and he set the classic black phone, heavy as a bowling ball, on his chest. He dialed the number he knew from a billboard: 1-800-LIMO-RIDE. It took him a minute to dial—harder than hell to find the number that went with the letter—which detracted from the gallantry, but he could see in the corner of his eye that Colleen was coming around. She was believing again in Theo's ability to set things right.

"I'll need a stretch limo this evening," Theo said when they answered.

"No, Dad. That's so embarrassing," Tiffany said as he was giving the address. "So elitist."

Theo rolled his eyes at his wife.

"Tiffany, don't be a spoilsport," Colleen said. She was back with Theo now. "Most girls aren't so lucky."

"It'll be cash," Theo said, and hung up. Then he flicked the five fifties from his wallet and slapped them into Tiffany's palm. "Knock yourself out." He held out the phone for her to take it away.

"Anything else?" Theo asked. "Everybody good and wonderful?" Colleen was smiling. "Any more world crises to solve? Because if that's it, I'd like my beautiful wife to don some clothes, and I'd like a few minutes of peace to think through the huge afternoon that awaits me."

Theo locked his fingers behind his head. He closed his eyes and listened as they all left the room. There was the call to Jackson, ordering *him* to carry the ransom. There was renting another van to drop Brown off tonight by Samaritan Hospital in Newark. There was packing his gym bag with the Halloween mask, the time schedule and phone numbers, the dummy microphone and headset.

Colleen was back on board. She'd seen the assuredness with which Theo could make things happen, and she was behind him again. The plan was perfect. President Bush had promised "the mother of all parties" this Memorial Day to celebrate the victory in the Gulf. Theo and Colleen had their own personal celebration in mind.

Of course he's there. He's my son. . . . Theo Wolkoviak. . . . Yes. Call me when you locate him." Malcolm was trying to find out when Theo's meetings with the yacht club owner would be finished so he could surprise his son at Golden Bay and buy him a glass of something to celebrate. But the foolish girl at the switchboard didn't know a thing.

Although it was hot, Malcolm took the afternoon paper on to the breezeway. He wasn't sitting ten minutes when Dave Tomkins rapped on the screen door.

"Son of a gun," Malcolm said, scrambling out of his chair to meet him.

"Captain, you look well."

"Bullshit," Malcolm said, and he and Dave shook hands. Malcolm felt exhilarated by the young man's strength.

"Happy birthday."

"Stop that," Malcolm said, but Dave handed him a gift wrapped in blue paper.

"We've seen you on the news," Dot called as she came out from the kitchen.

"Well, young lady," Dave said. He stepped by Malcolm to kiss Dot on the cheek. Malcolm was sorry to let go of his hand.

They sat on the breezeway, drank the iced tea that Dot set out for them, and talked shop. "Three hundred fifty agents." Malcolm shook his head. "I hardly believe it."

"There's never been a case like it that I know. Feds from seven states, not to mention all that's come up from Washington. One of the FBI's best men in charge—Tony Jackson. Real top-notch."

"And you're in there like one of them."

"You taught me all I know."

"Nonsense. You were a better deputy than I deserved."

Dave tugged up his trouser legs and sat back deeper in the chair. Good to see a man in uniform. Asherton police chief. Malcolm was real proud. "I'm doing the grunt work," Dave said. "We're trying to track the vehicle. Me and two hundred federal agents. And still we've got next to nothing." Dave finished his tea. "Then there's another hundred agents working with Petrochem security running checks on former employees. They're through the L's or M's as of noon today." Dave shook his head. Malcolm could see he was tired. "Enough of that. How's Theo and Colleen getting settled?"

Malcolm wanted to talk more about the kidnapping. He wanted to hash out all the details of the investigation. It made his blood pump again. But he knew Dave would be reluctant to talk specifics—even to his old boss. Dave was by-the-book, just as Malcolm had taught him.

"Theo's got a big deal going with Golden Bay Yacht Club. He picked up an expertise in Hilton Head. I intend to drive down there and see the spread this afternoon. Today's when they sign on the dotted line, and I'd like to be there to congratulate him. Takes brass balls to do this entrepreneurial-type business."

"It's not for me." Dave clinked the ice around in his glass.

It was a good thing, Malcolm thought, a little sadly, that Theo wasn't home for Dave's visit. The focus today had to stay on Theo and Colleen, without any old grudges muddying the water.

"Well, I oughta get going."

"Another glass—?" Malcolm heard the phone and held up a finger. Dot called to him. "Just give me a minute," he told Dave, "then I'll walk you out."

In the living room he gripped the telephone table for balance before picking up the phone. A woman identifying herself as the assistant to the president of Golden Bay Yacht Club said there must be some mistake, there was no Theo Wolkoviak meeting with the president today. No, she had never heard of a Theo Wolkoviak, but this was a private club that did not discuss its business affairs. When Malcolm insisted, raising his voice, she repeated that she was very certain, she had never heard Theo's name.

Dave was already standing in the side yard, the grass as tall as his boot tops. He was looking at the burnt-up mower, abandoned at the end of the path of cut grass. Malcolm eased down the stairs. The humidity would kill him.

"Don't get me wrong," he said to Dave, looking down the yard at the old boat. "I have complete confidence in Theo when it comes to business. He's a risk taker, and the business world demands that."

They took a few steps toward the driveway, then stopped. Dave faced him squarely.

"I just hope the boy isn't getting scammed. Have you heard much about this yacht club? Golden Bay? Are they on the up-and-up?"

"As far as I know, they're reputable."

Malcolm wiped the back of his neck. Neither man moved.

Finally Dave said, "I know the chief at Golden Bay PD. I'll call him to put your mind at ease, then later in the week——" Dave leaned toward Malcolm, touched his arm, lowered his voice. "We expect something tonight on the kidnapping, so I'm real tight. But don't worry, I'll look into it."

Malcolm breathed more easily as they walked past the concrete ducks. The one that Malcolm had stood up was leaning over crooked. Dave bent down and worked the duck into the soft ground for a moment until it was straight.

"I can't get my mind around it," Malcolm said. "The two of them have been going full-bore on this deal for weeks, especially in the last few days."

Dave was still down on a knee. He had taken a gentleman's five-foot tape from his pocket and was measuring the width of the rut that Theo had put in the soft dirt beside the driveway with the van. "Ha." Dave shook his head. "I've been looking at too many tread molds the last couple days." He got to his feet. "That's a Goodyear Regatta, P2-15-75-15. Half-ton vans and pickups. Same one we're tracking. Unfortunately, it's about the most common tire in the nation."

"That's just from Theo." Malcolm smoothed out the rut with his foot as he spoke. "He spends two days building a plywood locker for life jackets, then rents a van and scrapes it all to hell with this shoddy——" Malcolm didn't need to be talking Theo down. He shook his head. "Maybe Golden Bay wants no part of Theo."

"Don't you get worked up, Malcolm. I'll check it out."

As they walked toward the Asherton cruiser, Malcolm rested his hand on Dave's shoulder for support. He was wheezing. "I just don't want the boy at the bottom when I die."

Dave reached his arm around Malcolm's waist, and held him until he used his inhaler and his breath returned. "Captain," Dave said. "More than any man I know, you give a damn."

Malcolm loved Dave more for what he didn't say: *You're not dying.*

Malcolm's eyes were watery. "Hell," he said and slapped Dave good and hard on the back to lighten the mood. "If this yacht club *is* putting one over on Theo, we'll seize the box and . . ." Malcolm couldn't help but chuckle. "It's the right size for my casket."

Dave opened the door to his cruiser. They shook hands, squeezing like that for a time; then Dave slid into the car. "I'll call the chief down Golden Bay right away," Dave said. "Happy birthday again, Captain."

Then the dispatcher came on over Dave's radio. If Malcolm heard right, they'd found the van.

Dave gave Malcolm the thumbs-up and sped off.

For a third day, pressure expanded with the building afternoon heat. Drips from the lid of the box snapped against Stona's drenched clothes. So he left the box, and drove in a convertible through the cool night, to the ransom and release. Nunny was beside him, Jane and Victor wrestling in the backseat. A family trip with young children—an air of festivity, time away from the office, paternal responsibility. A black road with a bright yellow line led them through a wooded area that Stona had never seen before. Dusk settled.

They got out of the car and walked among large trees; Stona didn't know what kind of trees though his wife and children were looking at him, waiting for him to tell them the name. He saw their church and led them inside. He walked down the aisle on the well-worn carpet, breathed the church air that is like no other, air sweet with incense, candle wax and black carbon, wood too heavily varnished, sanctity. He smelled sweaty palms passing over scroll-top pews, coins and cash in the basket, the inky missalette. He smelled body and blood.

The good Father Ryan raised his palms to God and bowed his head. Jane's gloved hand slipped from the crook of Stona's arm. He turned to her adoring eyes beaming through her veil, cascades of white silk all around her, and as he let her go, he choked on his tears.

Then they were in the car again, dropping the kids at the cottage where they would stay. Victor and Jane piled out, but on the backseat there remained a tiny baby no bigger than a fish you'd throw back, flopping like a fish on the seat. It saddened Stona that Victor looked at the ground when he shook his father's hand.

Wind scooped under Stona's and Nunny's clothes as the convertible sped deeper into the woods, tearing at their clothes until seams split and buttons popped, and they were sailing in their underwear through the night. They neared a farm, and in the splash of headlights he saw chickens pecking at the side of the road, and suddenly one of the chickens darted in front of the car, scrambling one way then the other—too late for Stona to react. One quick thump in the wheel well.

On the front seat, in the hot lapping wind, he sank his hands into Nunny's bunched-up abdomen, deliciously soft and expansive, seersucker puckers in her skin. He stroked the dark brown hairs caterpillaring up to her oblong sulky navel. He pressed his hands to her ribs as if he were going to lift her over his head and release her into the sky. Sliding up her body, he reached behind the padding in her bra and pressed his hand flat on the scar. He pressed until he felt the beating of her heart, until he felt her phantom pain, creeping like a spirit through his palm, spreading up his arm to his shoulder and into his own heart. Then suddenly, the pain radiated out like an exploding star. And in the box the solid weight of the heat slammed down on top of him.

A butcher's hands, callused rough as pumice, tore deftly under his ribs and throttled his heart. In the cold strong hands his heart was a nasty old rooster trying to beat free with powerful wings, ripping the hands' thick skin, flinging torn shreds of flesh with its beak until its own blood flowed with the blood of the hands. A wing was broken and snapped off. Ribs popped. The chambers and passageways of Stona's heart collapsed. A hand gripped the rooster's neck, strangled, and snapped.

He touched Nunny's cheeks with his fingers. She was standing beside the car now in front of the villa on the cliffs of Praiano, waving as he drove away. The brush of her lips remained on his own as he craned his neck uncomfortably back to watch her getting smaller. The fish flapped its tail against the backseat—he was taking it with him—and Stona turned ahead and squeezed the loose wheel, speeding down the road into the woods, his headlights casting bright ovals on the curving pavement and on the thick trunks of maple trees crowding the sides of the narrowing road, the curve bending sharper, the accelerator pressing flat to the floor, the tires slipping on the shoulder as the lights cut black.

He would come home, they promised, this evening. But Nunny couldn't make it that long. It seemed she was forgetting how to breathe. She was losing control of her hands, and where was Jane? She'd said she was going for a walk with Joe, a little fresh air. Nunny would like to go for a walk, but there was work to be done, the house to clean before Stona came home. He liked a clean, orderly house, and Joe had taken Jane out for a stroll, for a breath of fresh air, and the kitchen alone would take half a day to clean.

Three brimming ashtrays were stacked on the cutting board. The bottle of Absolut Citron, Joe's favorite, was standing on the counter. So as well as some fresh air, Joe had needed an afternoon drink. *Don't bother to put it away, Joe. Stona will do it when he gets home. Can he fix you another? Don't get up.* Stona liked things put in their place, stowed, the sailor in him. It was his house. Was it too much to ask?

And why wasn't Victor here yet? He'd flown from Seoul to Hong Kong. From there, he was taking an evening flight. It seemed like he should've gotten here hours ago. He was always working, just like his father.

The lid had been screwed on the mayonnaise jar in such a way that mayonnaise on the rim had oozed down the sides. She tightened the lid and rinsed off the jar, and the phone rang, startling her. The jar slipped from her fingers and splatted in the enameled sink. She charged through the door, but Jackson turned away from her.

Bradford Ross shook his head. "No," Jackson said into the phone. His voice lowered. "I want every man off the Robbins case. Top priority."

As Jackson was hanging up, Dave Tomkins came in the front door and made a beeline for Bradford Ross. Did Brad remember a certain man who had worked for Petrochem security in the eighties? Brad said he wasn't sure, but he'd have the man's file and photo sent over immediately.

The water was running in the sink, milky mayonnaise swirling around the shards of glass. The top of the jar, yellow label and lid intact, sat at an angle in the heap of mayonnaise. Nunny began to pluck out the broken glass, but she didn't have time for this. There were too many other things to do. The sheets had to be changed. Fresh towels in the bathrooms. Stona could not come home to a house on its head.

At the foot of the stairs she saw Joe's coat over the newel post, and maybe Joe would like to move in today. Maybe Joe would like the master bedroom until Stona came home. Maybe Joe would like to take over as the man of the house. Shallow Joe, she thought, as she climbed the stairs. Only the third time they'd met him, he'd engaged Stona on the topic of the Church's definition of sin as if he were interested in Stona's insight. Stona and Nunny had taken him and Jane to brunch after Mass. And the minute Stona had made himself vulnerable—it was a casual talk over Belgian waffles with kiwi—Joe attacked Stona point by point. Snide lawyer. Glib. Arrogant. "Horseshit," Joe had said repeatedly, at brunch at the club after church. "Horseshit," to the parents of the girl he wanted to marry.

Today was the first Sunday in many years that Nunny had missed Mass.

She slammed through the door to the bedroom, and the smell hit her like a wall. She darted around sniffing, first in the bathroom, then in the hamper. She yanked out all the dresser drawers. She sniffed under the bed and under Stona's nightstand, then she slid open the drawer, and the smell burst out—roast beef and horse-radish on her wedding china, two days rotting in the heat—the smell of a dead animal. As Nunny stumbled toward the bathroom, vomit overflowed her cupped hands.

Theo looked at his watch as he shoved the key in the padlock: 4:55. In five hours they'd have the money, in six they'd let Brown go. The feeling in Theo's body was like pissing in the sun off the edge of a cliff.

He rolled up the door, and they were clobbered by the smell and the heat.

Neither of them entered the storage unit. "He must've shit," Theo said. "Poor guy." Theo rolled the door open wide to let in some air. "I told you not to give him that Ensure." He looked up and down the row of lockers. No one was in sight.

"Stay here in case someone turns down the row," he told Colleen. The Mercedes blocked a view into the unit unless someone walked right up.

Theo filtered shallow breaths through his nose, twisting the padlock off the box. He turned his head away and flipped open the lid. The stench burst out, and he barely caught a glimpse of Stona Brown, as he jumped back out the doorway for a breath.

"How's he look?" Colleen asked.

"A little pale." Had Brown woken every time they'd opened the box? "But good. Better actually." One time, he thought Brown hadn't stirred until Theo tore the tape off his mouth. There'd definitely been that once.

Colleen popped the trunk of the car for the spring water and bandages. With his sleeve over his face, Theo took a few steps back into the unit. In the box, beneath the weave of rope, the man lay perfectly still.

Theo scratched his neck. Sweat seeped from under his beard. He couldn't wait to shave the damn thing off.

What if . . . was all he could think. *What fucking if?* It wasn't Theo's fault, for one. He stepped closer to the box and looked down at Brown's colorless cheeks and hands. The Mercedes trunk slammed shut. He squatted and began to work the knot where the rope came through the airhole. He felt sick. They would not be robbed of success again. Colleen tiptoed toward him, as if walking that way would lessen the stench.

"Sleeping?"—her voice muffled by the handkerchief she held over her nose and mouth.

Theo yanked the ropes as he began unlacing them, shaking the box, keeping an eye on Brown. Theo begged for a shoulder to twitch, for his head to roll, for a muffled grunt through the duct tape. He yanked the rope again, and the box squeaked along the floor.

"Easy," Colleen said, placing scissors and fresh gauze neatly on the slab. With the handkerchief still held to her face, she finally looked into the box.

"Noooo——" she whispered.

She reached slowly over the plywood edge and stopped her fingers inches from Brown's cheek. She was shaking her head. There was no sweat on Brown's skin, no movement in his chest. Colleen's hand hovered above his face. "No, no, no," she chanted, and Theo willed her not to touch him. He wanted for them to remain as long as possible in the state of not knowing for sure.

Her fingertips touched his cheek, and she jerked back her hand as if she'd been bitten.

Theo did not meet her eyes. He slipped his hand under Brown's suit coat, pressed his palm to his chest. The clothes were damp. The body was warm, but it must have been a hundred degrees in the locker. Theo snipped the duct tape at the bridge of Brown's nose, and peeled it away from one eye. He raised the eyelid with his thumb. He slapped him sharp on the cheek.

Damn it.

Sweat stung Theo's eyes.

Colleen had collapsed into a ball on the roll of carpet. "We didn't—" Theo began, but Colleen's head fell to her knees, and he stopped. She made a strange mewling noise. Theo wiped his palms on his pants and slid close to Colleen, putting his arm around her. The noise vibrated through her back, her sweaty shirt. He embraced her more tightly, trying to squeeze the noise from her in one final gush. It was a sound like nothing she'd ever made before. How could his wife of twenty-five years make a noise he'd never heard?

Theo felt dizzy. When they rented the locker that first morning, it had been cool, but if it was this hot at five o'clock, then at two-thirty or three . . . Colleen had been right.

He began to say something to console her, but as if she knew he was about to speak, she gasped for air, and the mewling tweaked higher. He realized that the sound was like nothing he'd heard from her before because the two of them here . . . like this . . . was nothing she'd ever considered.

He pulled her face into his chest. He did not want his wife to see the dead man tied up in the box that he had built. He did not want her to remember that the pink and white comforter that was soaked with the dead man's piss and sweat was once spread across their bed. He'd tried for twenty-five years to protect his wife and family from the horrors of the world. That was the point. What else had these last three days been about? Theo knew that a woman expected a man to save her.

He watched a fly drink from a bead of sweat on his wrist. The fly took off and buzzed zigzags over the body, then landed on Brown's shoe, black wing tips that had lost their sheen. But on the tip of the toe where the fly hunkered down, the leather was as shiny as a polished plum. Theo used to love plums. For the last twenty years, every time he saw a plum, he'd bought it, but he hadn't tasted a good plum in years.

He pulled Colleen closer, begging her with the strength of his embrace to release into him. He pulled tighter around her narrow back, and he felt her curl away.

Don't do this to me! Don't turn on me! he wanted to scream at her. *Please.* But he only pressed his face into her hair. All he ever wanted was to take care of her.

Theo finally removed his sweaty arm from her back, then he stood by the open door, looking out. Even with the cool, fresh air creeping in, it was hard for Colleen to breathe. Heat radiated from the floor and walls. The roof creaked. Sweat wormed along her scalp under her hair.

Colleen wished Theo would roll down the door and leave her here with Mr. Brown. She wanted to stay in the locker with his body, his stench, his death. She wanted to lie down on the floor and sleep. A dreamless sleep because her dreams were lies, delusions that she was good enough to deserve her fantasies. She knew now who she really was: a woman who abducted a man for money, tied him up in a coffin, and day by day watched him die.

Today was Sunday. Did he usually go to church with his wife? What would he be praying for today? Praying to love his wife and children better? Thanking God for his blessings? Asking forgiveness for his sins? And for Colleen's? Would she ever be forgiven? Or would Tiffany and Brook inherit the shame and guilt—pass it to their children, and on and on for generations? Colleen prayed that Malcolm and Dot would endure. Thank God her own parents were gone. She prayed Tiffany was strong enough to survive this, but in her heart she knew that Tiffany wasn't. What little stability she provided for Tiffany, inadequate as it was, kept her daughter from a plunge into disaster. Tiffany would be Colleen and Theo's second victim.

Her throat was sore. She'd been wailing, or humming, she wasn't sure, but now she'd stopped. Theo was beside her again, suddenly dropping the lid of the box and snapping the padlock. He took Colleen by the elbow and lifted her to her feet. She could hear a fly, trapped inside the box, scrabbling along the plywood.

He opened the door of the Mercedes and helped Colleen into the seat. Then he locked the storage unit. The sun glared off the hood of the car and through the windshield.

They sat in the car with the windows and doors open. Theo gripped the top of the steering wheel. She could hear the highway in the distance. A few birds. But mostly silence. If she could only hold on to the comfort of silence.

"He must have had a weak heart," Theo said. "No way we could have known. You did all you could for him. Above and beyond. You shouldn't blame yourself."

A pickup truck with a table and chairs heaped up and tied in the bed came toward them. As it passed, Theo raised two fingers from the steering wheel. A cloud of dust floated through the car and settled over Colleen's sticky skin.

"We'll have to bury him," Theo said. "It's safest. It's the decent thing."

"What have we done?" Colleen murmured.

"Don't beat yourself up over this."

She looked at him and shook her head.

"Be fair to yourself. The man was a heart attack waiting to happen, and you took great care of him."

"You said he wouldn't get hurt."

"It's not our fault."

"Of course it's our fault." Her voice was rising. "If we hadn't taken him, if we hadn't shot him, if we hadn't forced him—"

"If the sun doesn't come up tomorrow—"

"Shut up, Theo!"

She looked out the window at the steel door closed tight. Then Theo spoke again. "We made a decision based on all the information we had, and it was the right decision at the time. The only logical thing for us to do. We agreed, and we were right. You can't regret that later."

"It might have seemed like the right thing then, but it's obvious now we made plenty of wrong decisions."

"No way."

"The man's dead, Theo."

"So you regret it just a little. Christ, Colleen. Either you regret it, or you don't. And if you regret the entire thing, you're a very negative person is all I have to say about that. Very negative. I thought you believed in yourself."

Theo started the engine. "We've got to keep moving," he said. "It's too late to stop this thing. We can't stand by and watch our lives grind to a halt."

For Christ's sake! Could *anything* go right? Once? Theo drummed his fingertips on the counter of E-Z Auto Rental. He'd gotten two fake credit cards and a fake Colorado duplicate driver's license a couple weeks ago. He had a file with hundreds of names, birth dates, and Social Security numbers from his work as a financial adviser in Vail, and that was all it took. He'd used the first credit card for the van at Garden State Rentals without a hitch. But the charge on the second card wasn't going through.

"Listen, Stanley," Theo said, reading the nameplate pinned to the kid's shirt pocket, "I'd give you cash for the damn thing, but I dropped a couple C-notes on my daughter's limo for tonight, and to tell you the honest truth I don't have time to go to an ATM and get back here. Do the paperwork. We're talking chicken feed."

"I'm sorry, I can't do that, sir." The kid behind the counter was small with narrow shoulders and a clip-on tie. Theo could pop him like a zit. "Could you put it on another card, sir?"

"This card is for the *business* account. All the *business* transactions have to go on it, or else my accountants give me grief." It would be too risky to use the first card again.

Stanley swiped Theo's card for a third time and waited for approval.

"But you wouldn't understand about the workings of a successful business. What do they pay you here, Stanley? Eight bucks an hour? Eight-fifty? What's that come to . . . sixteen K a year? Eighteen K max?" The kid was nailed. Not a kid, though. A few years younger than Theo, and working this job. "Stanley, if you saved every dollar you earned, you'd have to work over twenty years to buy my boat." He remembered the sloop: thirty-eight feet, solid teak deck, racing winches, roller furling, white and blue sails. The federal marshals wouldn't even let Theo get his Ray-Bans off it. "Half your working life to buy my boat. Does that mean anything to you?"

Stanley backed away from the counter, putting distance between himself and Theo.

"About respect, for example?" Theo said.

Stanley carefully placed the credit card on the counter. He said, "I'm sorry, sir."

Theo rushed around the side of the building, nearly catching his eye on the corner of an air conditioner, and got back in the car.

Colleen was crying.

"The credit card doesn't work," he said through his teeth. "We'll have to deal with it tomorrow." He started the engine.

"You mean *leave* him?" Colleen's voice cracked.

"We'll deal with it first thing."

Tears streamed down her cheeks as she unsnapped a cloth case that she used for carrying tampons in her purse. She unfolded from a tiny square three one-hundred-dollar bills. "It's all there is."

Theo wrapped the hundreds around the seventeen ones in the money clip. He stuffed the wad in his pocket, then pulled it out as he sailed back into the office.

"What about cash?" Theo said, the money filling his hand. "Does cash work for you?"

Stan punched his adding machine. "That's forty-six for the rental. One hundred fifty cash deposit, totaling one ninety-six, plus an imprint of a credit card. But there doesn't need to be approval."

Theo snapped two hundreds from the clip, creased them long-wise and held them in the tips of his fingers, pointing the money at Stan until he took it. "Keep the change," he said. "And I'm in a hurry."

When Stan laid a contract and a set of keys on the counter, Theo slipped the rest of the cash from the money clip. He held the corner of the wad—eighteen bills with a hundred-dollar bill show-ing—held it out to Stan. At first Stan didn't take it, but Theo stared him down. Theo willed him to grab the money, and then he did, and he held it in both hands, a look on his face like, *What's this?*

"Get yourself out of this friggin' job, kid. You're going nowhere." Theo calmly dropped the empty clip into his pocket. He snatched up the keys and the contract, and he slapped the counter. "Life's short."

Malcolm had called Golden Bay Yacht Club again; the presi-dent, he was told, was in a conference. Malcolm implied it was a police matter, and the president, he was assured, would call him back. He'd spent the afternoon going over details in his head. So much didn't line up. Could Theo's knowledge of sailing and yacht clubs be so great that he'd be taken in as a partner without capital? Why would a partner build a locker for life jackets?

Malcolm was sitting on the breezeway watching Tiffany and Dot through the kitchen door. Dot was spreading frosting on an angel food cake. Tiffany danced up behind her and reached her arms around Dot's middle. Music clattered from Tiffany's earphones, her Walkman fastened to her belt. She was wearing a birthday hat. She hummed and moved Dot's hips with her own, then spun her around. Tiffany plucked out one of her tiny earphones and stretched the wire to Dot's ear, and Dot's face came alive. Their hands were pressed together, their noses nearly touched. As they danced in front of the stove, Tiffany's backside knocked kitchen chairs against the table. Malcolm had never seen anything of the sort. "I got your number, girl," she said to her gramma, rolling their shoulders, dipping side to side. The smile across Dot's face was a brighter smile than Malcolm had put there in years. He knew damn well he should talk with her, but how did he phrase such things when he'd said it all over the years? *Always loved you real special. Was a good life. Never went needing. Raised a fine boy. Grandkids.* Dot knew before Malcolm did that he was dying, and now he felt like he was bringing her down with him. Malcolm prayed to God they didn't put him in an oxygen tent and shove in a tube for his urine and another for his crap and keep him going on machines. He'd pull the plug himself if he had the strength.

Tiffany laughed, tossing her head like a rag doll. The two of them huffed deep breaths, drowning out the tinny clatter of music from the earphones. Tiffany peered over her shoulder, pointed at Malcolm, then she pressed her cheek to Dot's, and with the frosting spatula pointing the way, they tangoed out to him on the breezeway. Dot's bottom spread beneath her housedress and apron, accentuating his granddaughter's brittle twig of a frame. He wanted to take Tiffany in his arms and feed her. *Eat,* he'd hum, the way he hummed songs to her when she was a baby. *Eat.* The way he'd held the bottle for Theo, rocking the boy while Dot made breakfast.

They danced for Malcolm in front of his chair. The floor swayed. Maybe the back steps were not the worst of it—the joists under the porch could be rotting. Dot was looking him straight in the face, and Malcolm couldn't remember her beaming like this. Had they spent their lives avoiding each other's gaze, looking away for fear some private thought might be exposed? As Tiffany swung her hips and swished her arms like a hula dancer, Malcolm saw the bigness of Tiffany's heart like a halo around her. He knew she'd have challenges in life, financial or health problems, but he didn't have to worry about her, because she was someone who made her gramma smile when her grampa was about to die.

She reached for Malcolm's hand. "C'mon, birthday boy," she sang, but he pulled his hand away and shushed her. "On your feet!"

"Nonsense," he said.

Dot reached for his other hand. Why did the Lord shine on Malcolm so bright?

"Don't be silly," he said, and groped beside the chair for his paper.

"Dance, birthday boy," Tiffany sang. "We got our sights on Y-O-U."

Malcolm felt his paper on the side of the chair and pulled it over his lap. Tiffany and Dot danced back to the middle of the breezeway, and with his head angled down to the *Gazette,* Malcolm never took his eyes off them. To see the two most important women in his life smiling on his birthday, Malcolm's chest went soft.

Suddenly, he heard the front door slam. "Happy seventy-fifth!" Theo shouted from the living room, and Malcolm got up and went inside after him.

Theo was rounding the newel post behind Colleen when Malcolm called him back.

Theo stopped, and Colleen disappeared at the top of the stairs.

"I only wanted to offer my congratulations," Malcolm said. "No meddling intended. I tried to reach you at the yacht club to be the first to say——"

"You *what*?" Theo turned and came slowly down the stairs, his face twitching with rage.

Father and son stood in the darkest part of the living room, behind the front door. Malcolm gripped the doorknob, and it rattled in his hand.

Theo clenched his teeth. "What did you do?"

"The secretary couldn't locate you. The president was in a conference."

"When was he in a conference?"

"An hour ago."

"Who do you think he was in a conference with?"

"With you was what I imagined. She said he'd call back."

Theo took a deep breath. "What percentage of business transactions do you think are for public consumption?"

Malcolm didn't answer.

"Few to none," Theo said. "Information is not handed out to anyone who feels like calling on a Sunday afternoon. You could have been the press. You could have been anybody. Did I not say from step one that this was very hush-hush?"

"You did."

"If you get a call back, I want you to say wrong number. Period."

Theo turned and took deliberate steps up the stairs. "If you've blown this for me . . ." He shook his head. "I don't know what."

Malcolm was back in his chair on the breezeway when Theo came into the kitchen. "Colleen'll be down in a minute," Theo said. "Let's get started."

"We can wait," Dot said. "No hurry."

"Let's do the cake. She won't mind."

"She won't want to miss the singing." Dot was lighting the candles.

"Pop doesn't want to wait for his seventy-fifth-birthday cake." Theo rubbed his hands together and looked out the door at Malcolm. "Eh, Pop?"

"Dad," Tiffany said. "Don't be a butthole for once."

"You watch your mouth!" Theo slipped the cake off the counter and started singing "Happy Birthday." Dot and Tiffany reluctantly joined in when he got to the breezeway, holding out the cake on one palm and conducting with his other beefy arm. He set the cake on top of the newspaper on the hassock in front of Malcolm. Tiffany blew a noisemaker, the paper tongue unfurling and recoiling. Seven candles on the cake formed a heart. A little short stub of a candle was stuck in the middle.

"Give it a blow, Pop," Theo said. "No cake unless you blow them out."

"I'm afraid I—"

"Don't give me that. Big breath." Theo filled his lungs.

"It's all I can do to—"

"If I slumped like you, I wouldn't be able to breathe either."

"Dad—" Tiffany said.

Malcolm's lungs felt emptied out.

"Theo dear," Dot said. "Papa doesn't have to blow them out."

"Yes, he does. You want cake, you've got to play the game. Blow!" Theo said, looming over him.

Malcolm fumbled through his sweater pocket.

"Cut it out, Dad!" Tiffany shouted.

Malcolm's throat was raw. His lungs felt filled with cement. Finally, he got a grip on the inhaler and brought it to his mouth.

"Now you're cheating," Theo said.

"That's enough, Theo!" Dot stepped between them, forcing Theo back against the screen.

Theo was quiet.

"You are citizen low," Tiffany said to her father; then she kneeled beside Malcolm's chair, put her hand over his, and blew out the candles.

"And now you ruin his birthday," Theo said.

"Tiffany, why don't you cut the cake." It was Colleen, standing in the kitchen doorway. Her eyes were red. She walked to Malcolm, careful steps like an intoxicated woman, and kissed him on the forehead. "Many more, Papa."

Malcolm took a slice of cake from Tiffany and set it on his lap. Theo ate his in big forkfuls. He said, "Dee-lish and nu-trish. Makes you feel ambish." Colleen stared out the screen into the yard.

"Something wrong, honey?" Dot asked Colleen.

"She's fine," Theo said. "Little anxious about tonight. Make-or-break time on the yacht club deal."

"Presents!" Tiffany said, and pointed her chopsticks at the gift from Dave Tomkins.

"Wish we didn't have to go so soon." Theo looked at his watch. "But everything got moved up a couple hours." He turned to Malcolm. "You understand."

Malcolm nodded.

"We didn't get you a present yet," Theo continued, "but after tonight . . . When you see the kind of figures we're dealing with . . ." He was scraping frosting off his plate and licking the fork.

"Are you feeling okay?" Dot asked Colleen again.

"That time of the month," Theo said. "She'll be fine."

"Open this one," Tiffany said. "Is this from you, Gramma?"

"No," Dot said. "Dave Tomkins stopped in—"

"Here?" Theo jumped to his feet.

"—to wish Papa a happy birthday."

Malcolm tore the gift wrap. It was a book. *The Photographic History of New Jersey Crime.* He held it up for everyone to see. On the cover was a picture of the Lindbergh baby.

Theo went white and dropped back into his chair.

"Here's your first present from me," Tiffany said. She plopped an awkward-shaped package wrapped in homely brown paper on his lap. "That's hemp paper," she said. "And a hemp bow."

"I'll be." Malcolm smiled, and he split open the gift wrap at the bottom, but the package twisted out of his hands, and five rolls of duct tape rolled down his legs and scattered across the floor.

"A lifetime supply!" Tiffany said. "For your—"

Colleen gasped. "What's that for?!" Her hands covered her mouth.

"Just some insulation downcellar wants patching up." Malcolm tried to calm her.

She fought to hold back tears.

"It's a gag gift, Mom. Relax. You should really try meditating. Or yoga."

"Colleen, what is it, dear?" Dot asked.

But before Colleen could reply, Theo took her by the arm and hustled her through the kitchen.

Something was obviously wrong, Malcolm knew. Something that felt more wrong than wrong things in the past.

Out through the screen, down the yard, two baby squirrels followed their mother to the edge of the moss-lipped hole in the hull of the Chris-Craft. A low branch dipped with the mother's weight as she leaped to it. The babies scurried around the edge of the hole, then dashed back inside the hull. Malcolm held a plate of his birthday cake on his lap.

The phone rang.

He jumped up to tell Dot not to pass the yacht club president on to him, but Tiffany answered. He was too late. As Malcolm rushed into the living room, she was saying hi to Dave Tomkins.

She handed Malcolm the phone.

"Is everything all right?" Dave asked.

"Fine. Fine," Malcolm said. "Just out of breath."

After a long pause, Dave said, "I called the chief of Golden Bay PD, and the yacht club checked out. Very reputable. Stable."

"Sure it did. Sorry to have troubled you on that. You're much too busy. Theo cleared it all up. And thanks for the book, Dave. You shouldn't have——"

"Is Theo there now?"

"No. He's gone back to the yacht club to close the deal. All very confidential was the problem."

"Malcolm," Dave said. "You mentioned Theo rented a van. Was it an Econoline?"

"Yes, the four-point-two-liter. He said the power was there—good enough for a rental—but I can't believe a guy would buy one."

"What day was that?"

"Friday."

"Early?"

"Practically dawn. Like I said, they've been going full-bore—"

"A dark blue van?"

"Yes. What is this, Dave?"

There was a moment of silence. "We located the kidnappers' vehicle. And it matches, Malcolm. There's prints and biological evidence of at least fifty men—too many to follow up on. But the plywood fragments and threads of duct tape are fresh, and in the bed, Malcolm, there were deep, very recent scratches. And that tire track on your—"

"Dave, I taught you better than that." Malcolm's breath was quick and shallow. "Just because Theo worked for Petrochem . . ."

"You and I know there's nothing to this, Captain, but if there's evidence—"

"Circumstantial. Look at the context. You know Theo."

"Which is why I'm giving it a cursory look. A once-over—"

"Rule it out, Dave."

"Extremely low-profile. I went myself to show Theo's photo to the rental agent. Has he grown a beard?"

"Theo was right. You've got some kind of competition with him. A rivalry."

"Is he at Golden Bay Yacht Club right now?"

"This is my son!"

"I want to help him."

"Don't bother our family again."

"There were powder traces, Malcolm. And Stona Brown's blood. If it's Theo, he's in deep."

Malcolm slammed down the phone. He took a puff of his inhaler. Then another. Theo couldn't be involved. Malcolm picked up the phone again. The Tac Frequency. The pillows. The Ensure. A box the size of a casket.

He dialed Golden Bay Yacht Club.

Her husband had no capacity for contradictory emotions. When they were engaged, she'd had doubts about their love, cold feet she'd decided finally, but she'd wondered about Theo's own doubts. "None," he'd replied, as if the question were absurd. "None at all." Colleen felt it wasn't fair to bask in his absolute devotion, then ask that he understand her hemming and hawing. Theo was all-or-nothing. His commitment to Colleen, to their family, and to his financial responsibilities left no room for second guesses, excuses, regrets. She had loved him for it.

When he turned onto the dirt road, the shovel scraped across the metal floor of the van and banged into the plywood box. They'd come south on the Garden State Parkway, almost an hour. It was getting dark.

The road was bumpy. He slowed, and the stench that had been kept off them by the wind slopped forward. The final evacuation of the bowels. Decaying flesh. Were they smells that people innately feared? Like the smell of burning hair? Smells that protect us from ourselves, warning us that we've gone wrong.

They had made a terrible mistake, but she'd never convince him of that, and to try, especially now, would mean the ruin of even more lives. She had to go through the motions. In two hours they'd have the money, and then, for the rest of her life she could struggle with her conscience. Theo was right. Turning themselves in would destroy everything important to them. Aborting their plans would mean that Mr. Brown's suffering and his death were in vain. She would push through, then she'd pray, for however long it took, to decide what to do. When Tiffany and Brook were set up financially, when her in-laws had passed on, she could turn herself in. Suicide was also an option.

"Can you remember?" Theo asked her. It was an enchanted area of scrub pines and sandy ground. They'd gotten lost on bicycles in here five years ago—the Sunday after Tiffany's eleventh birthday. They'd left the kids with Malcolm and Dot on the beach and ridden off on rented bikes for much of the afternoon, turning down this deserted old road. They'd kept riding until the trees squeezed the road down to a path, and she and Theo had made love on a bed of pine needles in a clearing in the sun. "In front of God and everyone," she'd giggled, rehitching her bra.

"That way." She pointed. He'd stopped the van, headlights flooding a fork in the dirt road. The deeper they moved in the trees, the darker it got. He gunned it left. Branches snapped against the van, leaves flinging in the window, slapping her face. The smell of pine needles and spring mixed with the smell of Mr. Brown's death.

Theo muscled the van between two leafy bushes and turned it around. "We got thirty minutes max," he said, and opened his door. The weak domelight cast a watery light on his face.

Colleen held the lantern, and with his fingers Theo raked away dead branches, leaves, and pine needles to the dirt. "We'll spread this back over the top real good," he said to himself as much as her. He paced out the hole and marked four corners with a slice of the shovel. Then he cut a sharp rectangular outline. How was it that he knew exactly what he was doing?

He dug furiously, biting into the ground with the full length of the blade, heaving off the soil. It landed on the ground with the thump of dead weight. The grave would be squared up and deep. They'd lower the box. Colleen would remember Mr. Brown with a few words. It was anonymous and despicable, but she would try to make the best of it. When she turned herself in, he could be exhumed and properly laid to rest.

Theo threw down the shovel and dropped to his knees. With his fingers he pried up a bowling-ball-sized rock, like buried treasure. He resumed digging, more slowly now, chopping at roots, chipping into the dirt. It had been sandy at first, but now the ground was dense as clay.

He paused for a breath, leaning on the shovel. "I don't think I can do the whole box."

"Another spot might go easier."

"Jesus, Col." He tipped his watch toward the light, then he stepped up on the shovel, riding it like a pogo stick. She held the light higher, as if that would soften the ground. They would not put Mr. Brown in a hole without the box, cover his body with dirt. It was unthinkable.

"That's it," Theo said, planting the shovel upright in the pile of dirt. The hole wasn't two feet deep.

A bitter taste rose in Colleen's throat. "Please, Theo, more. A little bit more."

He clapped dirt from his hands, then the knees of his pants. The hole was shallow and oblong, the shape of a body bag. He gripped her arms below her shoulders, squeezed, lifted. "In two hours we're going to have eighteen and a half million dollars. When the dust settles, we'll have lots of options. One option will be to call in a tip, and they'll come get him. Another option will be to let him rest here in a beautiful place. In nature. Like spreading your ashes in the mountains. Without the box his body becomes part of the earth sooner. Without the box there's no trail of evidence." He released her shoulders. The frame of her torso settled back in place. "It's usually best to let a soul be."

Colleen did not believe that exhumation rattled the spirit, and neither did Theo. She did not believe that Theo really cared. She cracked open her mouth and rounded her lips, not knowing if she meant to say "Oh," or "Okay," or "No." Except for a click in her jaw, no sound escaped. Theo turned away from her. He hauled open the back doors of the van, leaned inside, and dragged the box halfway out. Like beetles creeping over her skin, the stench of death crawled up her nose and down the back of her throat: it was the reek of her sin.

She set the lantern on the ground. She hooked her fingers under the bottom of the box. She lifted and stepped backwards, and they jockeyed sideways. The box was strangely, horribly light. They set it down alongside the grave.

"I'll take it from here," Theo told her.

She picked up the lantern by the wire hoop handle and swung it to him. She took careful shallow breaths. She didn't want to look, but when Theo flipped the lid open and light filled the box, she saw the sight that had become so familiar—his gray suit and black shoes, the pink comforter and stained pillow, the silver bands of tape.

She backed up against the van and squatted beside the tire,

holding her head between her legs, covering her eyes. She felt as if someone had methodically punched her ribs, her stomach, her breasts. She tried not to imagine Theo grabbing the duct tape like handles and heaving Mr. Brown into the hole. Theo's keys jingled as he removed the handcuffs. Then Theo grunted, and Mr. Brown's body hit the ground with a thud. The blade of the shovel bit into the pile of dirt, clacking against a stone. The first shovelful flopped onto Mr. Brown's chest, and Colleen heard the tiny beep of his watch.

Twenty miles before their exit, Theo pulled off the Parkway. He doubled back along the access road, then turned left between two auto junkyards, their fences topped with razor wire. They drove for five minutes on a dark road with reeds on both sides, until they came to a deserted area with a boarded-up factory. They turned past a rusty sign warning *No Trespassing, Keep Out,* past a stripped station wagon, a washing machine on its side, mattresses. The factory was black brick and huge, shaped like a chapel with tall sides, a pitched roof, and what resembled a bell tower running the length of the peak. Behind the factory was a yellow wooden house with a big porch, its roof collapsed, and then a row of decrepit yellow shacks.

Theo stopped the van at the first shack, where a workingman and his family had once packed in tight. The front door flapped open, attached to the frame only by the lower hinge. He dragged the box and the roll of carpet inside. The lantern filled the one-room shack with light, and through the broken window Colleen watched him step inside the box and try to kick out its ends. He kicked violently, fiercely. He put the box on its side and jumped on top of it. But the box did not come apart. He looked out of the shack at Colleen sitting in the van, and although he couldn't see her in the darkness, he shrugged. He was breathing hard from the effort. In the silvery-white light of the lantern, his eyes were very alive.

He rushed back outside. The van rocked as he swept it out; then he carried the broom, shovel, ski masks, everything, into the shack along with a jug of gasoline. He was moving around excitedly. Colleen felt she might never budge from this seat. If she could just go to sleep and not wake up—

She heard a pop. Orange and yellow flames roared up from the box with such force they seemed to come from a place deep down below. Through the flames, distorted by the fire, she could see Theo, splashing still more gasoline up the walls.

At 9:31 Theo made the call to Jackson's third pay phone — a booth in front of the police station in Rahway. Colleen was driving the Mercedes, fifty-five miles an hour on the Eisenhower Parkway. Jackson answered. "Go to the phone booth in the post office parking lot in Metuchen," Theo said over the cell phone. "There's a note taped under the shelf below the phone. Twelve minutes."

Theo and Colleen now had twenty minutes to get to Riverside Marina. Their location   because Jackson's next instructions would come from a note and not a cell phone call—could not be triangulated. While Colleen drove, Theo gave her a talking-to, tried to give her a shot of confidence.

The crowd at the marina was better than he could have hoped. There had to be more people than Friday night. This was what he meant about the magic of the plan. He directed Colleen along the road facing the marina. God damn—the swarming masses. Jay-walking, littering, public drinking. You couldn't count the crimes.

A cop threw up his palm at a crosswalk, and Colleen kicked the brake too hard: a chirp from the tires. People flooded around the car like a riot. "I'm getting out right here," he said to Colleen, and squeezed her knee. "I love you, baby." A teenage kid with an American flag painted on his face pressed his hands to Colleen's window and screamed, "Kill Saddam!" Colleen shrank back like she could break into tears.

"A-hole!" Theo yelled, much too loudly in the closed-up car, and gave him the finger in front of Colleen's face. She put her hands to her ears.

Theo hopped out, and with one hand leaning on the roof of the car, he ducked back inside, kissed his thumb and fingertips Italian style and flung the kiss to Colleen. "Hang in there, we're gonna do it," he said, and with the gym bag over his shoulder he joined the flow of pedestrians just before the cop signaled Colleen and the cars behind her to proceed.

Theo looked at his watch: 9:52. Eight minutes until the flyover and the start of the fireworks. Theo took it all in: this was the place, the situation he'd imagined over and over. He'd stood at this spot a dozen times in the last two months, the plaza deserted, the bricks glazed wet from rain, the marina vacated. But now, the Memorial Day weekend crowd was stretching the plaza and the Riverside Marina to its limits. Tonight was even better than Friday night's flame-jumpers, who could easily have been five minutes off their mark. But the Blue Angels were military, and if they said twenty-two hundred hours, that's what they meant.

"Fuck me," he said out loud. They'd even had time to leave the van at E-Z Auto Rental and toss the keys in the night drop. His plan was too good. The backup, forty-eight hours later, surpassing the original.

Who's good?

That's right.

A cheer rose up to his left. Skateboarders were zipping down the edge of a sloped concrete retaining wall, jumping a deep pedestrian access way, then landing on top of the narrow wall on the other side. Dangerous as hell. Kids with tattoos and earrings in oversized blue jeans, cut off midcalf. Fourteen-year-olds were smoking marijuana openly. For Christ's sake. This is what you get in a public facility. Throw up the gates, is what Theo wanted. They had whole private towns now. Your own marina, golf course, and private mall. Clean roads. Clean as Disney.

He passed the information kiosk. There was a girl working—not his first choice, but at second glance he decided she'd be perfect. She had a hairy-pits, no-deodorant, college girl look—like an environmental activist should. She was talking to an older man and when she raised her arm to point, her nipple poked through her Desert Storm T-shirt. This was what Theo meant. With every breath, he sucked in another sign of good luck. His heart revved when he heard her say to the old guy, "Porta potty."

He moved toward the pay phones. The drop-off drive for boaters was open, as he'd been told it would be. He looked at his watch. Seven minutes until Jackson arrived. At the foot of the pier where the fireworks were set up, an Elite security guard was standing at his post, his cheap blue uniform with a gold braid on the shoulder from the back of the police supply catalogue. Although Elite had a reputation for drinkers, it was not a bad company—they tested for drugs and wouldn't hire ex-cons. He was black, about thirty-five, and he wore a well-stocked duty belt with cuffs, a pager, nightstick, two speed-loaders, and an old revolver.

Goddamn, Theo was hyped. 10:01. It was almost happening without him. From downriver he heard jet engines roar, a crack splitting the air. The crowd hummed. Strangely, like a breeze dying, the roar subsided for a moment as Theo turned out his pockets at the telephone as if looking for change. He glanced over his shoulder at a thousand people staring into the sky, and then an eruption hammered off the water, echoed around the plaza, rattled the plastic and steel telephone stand. The Blue Angels thundered up the river. Four jets, their wings and bodies outlined in blue lights, streamed red, white, and blue sparks that lit up the hundreds of boats bobbing on the water. As the jets banked into a vertical climb in front of the plaza, Theo pulled from his jacket pocket the napkin-wrapped envelope containing a note and a worthless minimicrophone. He pinched the envelope under the steel shelf beneath the phone and slipped off the napkin sleeve.

The roar of the jet engines faded, and he hustled to the gangway where his boat was waiting in a slip. As he keyed the gate, the jets approached again. Theo pounded down the gangway as they ripped low over the water and the crowd cheered at his back. After the second pass, a rocket shot up. Red, white, and blue starbursts exploded over the river, and rock music blasted from speakers around the plaza. The falling sparks were like floodlights on the mass of boats drifting on the river.

At least half the slips were vacated; everybody was out on the water for the show. Theo jumped in his little fourteen-footer, lowered the outboard and started it: 10:03. He left the chain and padlock on the steering wheel, cast off the bowline, released the stern down to two loose wraps. The rock and roll spread out over the water, lost its beat.

It was 10:05 as he wheeled a dock wagon out the gate. He had three minutes, maybe five. He scanned for Jackson. He glanced at the security guard to his right, then took the rubber Halloween mask from his bag and slipped it over his head: General Norman Schwarzkopf. He approached the information kiosk and leaned his palms into the counter. The braless girl touched her tongue to the corner of her mouth and raised her eyebrows. "Can I help you, General?"

He opened his jacket enough to reveal the stock of his .45 sticking out of his pants. "There's another man behind you," Theo said, and fear blossomed in her face. "Don't move." Leaning in closer over the low counter, he could smell cigarettes in her hair, on her breath. "Things are going to happen fast." He pulled the headset from his jacket. "Put this on, gorgeous," he said.

She hesitated. "Do it! My friend behind you is aching to stick a bullet up your ass." She took it and spread the earphones around her head. "Now stick the end of the wire in your pants like it's doing something." She did as he said.

"The security guard over my shoulder by the gangway," Theo said, and she looked. "He's with me too. If you fuck up you're a dead girl, but if you listen up that won't happen. In two minutes a brown Buick Regal's gonna pull in and park by the pay phones. From the moment you see the driver you do not take your eyes off him. He'll walk to the phone. He'll open his trunk. He'll walk toward you but stop twenty feet away. You keep your hands below the counter like you're pointing a gun at him. You stare at him mean. You hate him. You do not take your eyes off him for five minutes. You don't blink, or that guard'll drop you." Her eyes were watery, her face sweaty, her lips trembling. She looked like Theo had fucked her silly.

When he turned around—the magic working with him—the Elite security guard happened to look their way, just gazing around, girl-watching, trying to keep awake. The pissy snaking type of fireworks hissed in the sky, then a triple explosion showered down silver and gold.

Back by the dock wagon and the gate to the gangway, Theo tugged at his beard under the Schwarzkopf mask. He glanced at the girl in the kiosk doing her job. He felt the possession of the money: the out-of-your-mind rush before coming, the coiled-up feeling of all the force in the world funneling through him, a force of such fierce hunger and momentum it obliterated any obstacles. It was the feeling of the rest of his life.

Then the brown Regal came speeding down the circular road. Jackson was one minute late. He slowed past the skateboarders, then accelerated. Green and gold showers reflected off his windshield.

Jackson pulled up to the pay phones and hopped out of the car. I'll be damned, Theo thought, *he's a black man.* He dashed to the phone and reached under the shelf for the note. Theo wasn't more than fifty feet away. *Jackson,* the note said. *Do not speak into your wire. The security guard to your left is with us.* Jackson looked at the guard. Fuck, Theo was high. *The information kiosk attendant is also with us. Clip our mike to your collar. We're already listening. Do not speak into your wire. If you do, you die. If your lips move, you die. Open the trunk, then turn around and walk back toward the kiosk. Stop twenty feet in front of it and do nothing but watch the attendant behind the counter. Do not look over your shoulder. You'll be told when you can move. To put a bullet in your head and get lost in the crowd would be too easy. We are professionals.*

Jackson clipped the microphone on his collar. He glanced at the guard and at the girl with the headset; then he opened the trunk of the car, keeping his head down but his eyes up. He walked back across the driveway and stepped up on the curb. The girl watched him, and he watched her. He stopped and stood facing her with his back to the car.

Theo rolled the cart to the Buick like any drunk New Jersey boater in a stupid mask unloading provisions. He kept an eye on Jackson.

The cart bumped over the bricks. The guard lit a cigarette. The girl was a pro. The crowd cheered at the fireworks. He saw the laundry bags heaped up in the trunk. Sweet Lord. The sky popped behind him, flashes of color lit the plaza. The trunk was packed with bags. Holy shit. He'd had no idea. The cart jumped as the front corner cracked the red plastic taillight of the Buick. Theo lifted a laundry bag in his fists and slung it into the big wooden cart. Christ, it was heavy. He grabbed another just as he'd grabbed Brown's suit and heaved his body into the hole. Colleen was right, he did regret that the man had died, but the guy wasn't young, and he'd had more than his share of the good life.

Theo had hoped the transfer of cash would take no more than a minute, but the trunk was so full of bags. The drawstring on the second bag came loose, and bundles of cash spilled into the trunk. The music got louder, and a deep explosion flashed blue and white, blindingly bright. He stuffed the bundles of cash back in the bag, wasting valuable time. The crowd oohed and aahed and the blue light flashed again. He'd have to leave this bag behind. He reached for the one next to it, and the blue light cut oddly across his face. He turned toward the top of the plaza and saw the blue lights spinning and wigwags flashing from the roof of a police car.

He was running for the gangway, leaving the bags of money behind, when he saw the second squad car speeding into the plaza.

He keyed the gate, sprinted down the dock, unlocked his steering wheel, and flew full throttle out to the middle of the river. Without his money. "Wake," boaters yelled at him. "Asshole," as Theo wove between them. He tossed everything overboard—his .45, a gift from his father when he earned his first stripe, his calf holster, the cell phone and handcuffs. He threw the rubber mask, the pages of phone numbers and directions for Jackson, along with the anchor, into his high school gym bag and tossed that overboard too.

When he was inconspicuous in the jumble of boats, he killed the throttle too abruptly—a back wave sloshed over the stern, dumping a few inches of water on the floor. "Dick!" a guy in the next boat yelled, and threw a beer bottle that smashed on Theo's bow.

He turned the boat toward shore and set the engine idling. Four rockets shot up at once, exploding fiery red one after the other. Blue and red lights flashed from the plaza. The distorted rock music wafted across the water. When Theo reached under the steering column for his binoculars, he saw that squeezed in his left hand was a bundle of twenties: two thousand dollars. He smelled it. Used bills. The sexiest smell he knew. He flipped through the stack with his thumb, then he bit into the wad of bills. When he dropped the money into the river, his heart popped.

He raised the binoculars to his eyes, focusing. It would take the cops a few minutes to get a boat. He had time to think. They'd never be able to question these hundreds of boaters, drunk and belligerent New Jersey river trash. He could slip in with any of the boats motoring along the river.

He focused the binoculars on two police cars, but they were nowhere near the Buick Regal. They were not shining searchlights on the river. They were both parked near the top of the plaza. Two cops were holding people back while another directed an ambulance backing in. They were beside the wall where the kids were skateboarding, and Theo could see through the binoculars a kid in flappy-legged jeans lying on the cement.

Jackson was standing like a statue in the middle of the plaza faced off with the girl.

And a crowd was growing around the trunk of the Buick—ten or fifteen people shoving each other to get a peek, for the only time in their loser lives, at eighteen and a half million bones.

His boat nearly capsized as Theo grabbed handfuls of the black river water, but the band of twenty-dollar bills had sunk.

Colleen's hands were rust-stained. A bitter iron smell of corrosion twitched in her sinuses. Theo had squirted some oil in the padlock, but the chain hadn't been handled in years. She'd used his old police master key, driven the car in, then relocked the chain in place.

She wiped at her palms and fingers with a McDonald's napkin, and through the windshield she watched the fireworks reflect off chops of river water. A large boat nosed down the center of the river; screeches of delight rang out over the water's cold surface. Around the big boat's deck, paper lanterns glowed the color of pearls—hollow and brittle. She heard a champagne cork pop. She heard laughter. She heard cheers and clinks, wet kisses, strawberries plopped in crystal flutes. She heard the sound of fingers running through hair. She heard heartbeats accelerating, breath deepening.

The next explosion illuminated a small powerboat heading for her. As planned, she flashed the headlights twice. She popped the trunk and stepped out of the car onto the cracked concrete of the deserted boat launch.

The last time they were here, twenty-seven years ago, Theo had wrecked his father's boat. The launch had been well used and maintained. But in the eighties, when anybody could buy a boat, the big marina was expanded with a public launch, and this site was chained off and left to decay.

A rat-a-tat of six explosions showered the night with colored light, as bright as searchlights. She saw her husband in the boat speeding toward her. Then a huge blossom burst in the middle and little sizzlers spun around the edges—it was the grand finale: a red, white, and blue Memorial Day as spiritless as waking up in front of the TV at two a.m. to "The Star-Spangled Banner" and an American flag heaving in the wind.

Theo approached too fast and scraped the bow on the launch. One glimpse of him and she knew that he didn't get the money. They'd never have the money. "Had to abort." He was breathless, climbing out of the boat. It was not piled up with laundry bags. Not one laundry bag. None. He did not look at her. "Nothing we could do." He was shaking his head. "Nothing anybody could do. Goddamned kids."

He pulled the plug on the boat and water mushroomed through the bottom. He was sloshing through water up to his knees, turning the boat back out to the river, the engine idling. After tying off the wheel he punched the throttle. The boat for which he'd pawned their wedding rings, sinking already as it puttered away from shore.

Twenty-seven years ago Colleen had been standing where she was now, with Malcolm beside her, as Theo came zipping at them in the Chris-Craft, weaving back and forth, kicking up rooster tails from the stern. He'd taken a wide arc to swing in and splash her and Malcolm, but he cut in too close to the concrete launch that sloped out under the surface of the water. Theo had cocked the wheel left, and Colleen had backed away to avoid the coming spray while Malcolm stood firm. When he curved in front of them, the edge of the launch caught the bottom of the boat. The sound was like a huge wooden crate dropped from the top of a crane to the street. Theo was ejected as if from a cannon. He hit the water feet-first. The varnished mahogany stern board painted with *Theo's Joy* was ripped off the boat and flipped into the air before landing flat on the water. The engine died, and rainbows streaked across the growing gasoline slick on the water's surface. In the quiet, she'd thought Theo was dead. Water silently filled the boat until only the windshield and the tops of the gray leather seats were above the surface. Then Theo's head popped up, and he swam to shore. Standing in water to his chest, he yelled, "That goddamn throttle stuck again. I told you, Pop. You're lucky I wasn't killed."

Now, Theo waded out of the water. "Fucking kids. Goddamn delinquent skateboarding kids." He hurried past her, wet shoes slapping the cement. "Can't control them. I always say it. You know that. They'll be in jail before they're sixteen." His face was red and furious. "And who supports them their whole lives? That's right. Forty grand a year to lock them in prison."

He was already at the car. She stepped nimbly across the busted slabs of concrete, over weeds and the broken-off necks of beer bottles.

"Come on," Theo rushed her. "We'll go again tomorrow night. I've got it worked out already. Here's no good. But down the shore, near where we put him. It's a big heap of change. You won't believe how many bags, a dozen at least. Stuffed. Holy shit. I was holding them in my arms. The weight of it. Sweet Jesus. Tomorrow night though. We'll need a car. No more rentals. I'll get one."

She started the engine and shifted into drive. Not much road remained with all the weeds. They crept through the darkness, the woods pitch-black on both sides. "They shouldn't even *be* skateboarding over there. That kid's parents'll sue the city for millions." He punched the dash. "Fucking people."

Their headlights shone on the drooping chain. Theo snagged his police master key from where it hung by a string on the cigarette lighter.

When she'd thought Theo was dead—for that one quiet moment twenty-seven years ago when Malcolm's boat was filling with river water—they were eighteen years old, the summer after high school graduation, Colleen heading for Providence College in the fall, Theo to the police academy, he'd proposed marriage in a panic he'd lose her, she'd accepted without serious consideration— when she'd thought he was dead, she felt a tiny breath of relief; she'd been backed into a corner, and now she would have a fresh start. The loss, the sadness and mourning—it would be glamorous. It was the mark Colleen had longed for, the extra currency to set her apart from the other girls at college. Her high school sweetheart, her fiancé, her first and only lover, killed tragically in a boating accident. A deep emotional river would flow through Colleen that others would regard with delicate respect.

Theo bent over the chain in front of the car, and as he clutched the padlock, blinding lights hit them. Colleen shielded her eyes. Looking out between her arms, she couldn't see Theo at all through the glare of the dirty windshield. A man's voice ripped over a bullhorn. "Hands open and visible!" "Do not move!" "FBI." And her first thought was that she wished they'd be quieter so that everyone wouldn't know this was happening.

They converged on the car. Her door flew open. Before she knew what was happening she was outside gripping the edge of the roof. Hands moved brusquely over her body. Flashlights searched under the seats. The trunk popped open. The glove compartment. Her jacket. Everything opened. Exposed.

Then she heard her husband's voice: "It's a little embarrassing. A little surprising in this day and age. If I have to explain what a couple of lovers are doing in a car by the river with fireworks, then I don't know what."

Colleen looked into the lights. The silhouettes of men kept appearing out of the darkness. Dozens. Thirty, fifty men. "I'm a police officer," Theo said. "*Was.* Thirteen years of service. I'm on disability pension. I have the key. We come here now and then. See? I have the key. No problem."

He said, "If we could keep this a little hush-hush, I'd appreciate my wife didn't find out. Or this one's husband, more importantly. Who beats her." His thumb jabbed toward Colleen. His voice sounded as confident and true as heart-to-heart in their bedroom.

Cars rolled in closer. She felt the heat off their engines. "Worth the risk I tell you for this gal, though." He lowered his voice as if a hundred men weren't listening, a hundred men with shadowed faces looking her up and down.

"Why's this in your pocket?" a man said.

"Jeez. I've had that for years. I worked security for them till recently. Management job. Which, you're considering leaving the bureau, I do *not* recommend." Colleen saw the FBI man holding it up in the light: an empty money clip.

"Where is Stona Brown?"

"Who?"

The money was supposed to make the emptiness go away. With her fingernails scratching the paint on the roof of the car, Colleen held on, trying to hold her body together, because she was a woman so empty she could collapse like a paper lantern.

"What are you doing here?" another man asked Colleen.

They were leading her husband away.

"Where is Stona Brown?" he demanded.

"We're not what you think."

There was a tense stillness in the house. Nunny had taken a shower. She had tweezed her chin and brow, made up her eyes, put on lipstick. She had dressed in her blue Armani slacks and white ribbed top, the gold Tiffany pendant—all gifts from Stona. He'd be exhausted and hungry. He'd want a shower. Before he slept he'd insist on a briefing from his secretary, Marilyn. Nunny hoped he'd take at least a few days off. She'd already instructed Bradford Ross to keep the press away.

She sat in the living room in a banister-back chair looking through to the dining room at the four men who remained. Everyone else, except for the town policeman parked at the foot of the drive, had spread out over central and north Jersey. Jackson was delivering the ransom. The four men sat at her dining room table, two with headphones, two without. Their gossip and sports talk had ceased. Complete silence. The refrigerator kicked off, and the silence was thicker.

Nunny felt fresh. Her mind was clear of the murky dread and

fear that had wandered like sleeplessness around her head the past three days. She was clean and dressed for Stona's return. When he stepped in the door she'd wrap her arms around him, kiss his whiskery face, then throw out the FBI men and their equipment. While Stona was sleeping in the early morning, she'd have the service in—a dozen Merry Maids—to clean quick and quiet.

The chandelier over the table had been dimmed. One man exhaled, his arms folded over his chest, staring at a spot on the wall. A magazine page ruffled. A chair creaked.

Nunny's perfume surrounded her. She'd put on the Issey Miyake which she usually took on vacations. The perfume of Praiano, of Tahiti, of discovering dungeons in Crusader castles on the coast of Turkey, of lying under a palm tree in a hammock on St. Barth. Nunny was at her best, to welcome back her husband in ways he didn't know he needed.

One of the men was quietly writing, and she could feel—they all could—that something big was happening somewhere else, and that they were connected to it. They all seemed to feel that their silence and intensity could somehow effect a positive outcome, that their usual crass humor and shallow chatter could cause a derailment.

And Nunny was afraid too, secretly, that her own thoughts could cause something to go wrong. She was afraid of the shift that had occurred in her, for which she hated herself. Had her love for Stona diminished since Friday morning? *Confiding in someone makes you vulnerable to them,* she'd told Jane. *Relationships grow through a series of disclosures.* Or deceptions? Had her love for Stona grown over the years because of what she *didn't* know? Had her disappointment returned with the possibility that his kidnapping was a result of Oakville? How was Nunny to reconcile a situation in which her love for her husband impelled her to do anything to gain his release, but her unshakable public loyalty to him prevented her from telling what she knew? She had no answers for these questions. The fact that on this night, in her living room, she was asking them at all made Nunny loathe herself, and therefore Stona.

But at least, the kitchen was clean. And the bedroom. She and Jane had changed the sheets. She'd removed his nightstand to the guest room to air out, and replaced it with her own. The warm night air flowed over their bed.

She had put new candles around the house, thought about some meals she could whip up, tidied his study, laid out his magazines . . . The phone rang. All heads jerked. "Palmer," one of the men answered, and Nunny thought she could hear Stona's voice on the other end, and a broad smile expanded over Palmer's face. "Got'm," Palmer said to the men at the table, and it *was* Stona's voice. "Jackson's fine." Nunny couldn't contain her joy, gushing with relief and laughter, actual laughter. She rushed to the four smiling men, reaching for the phone in Palmer's hand, she rushed to welcome her husband home.

The kitchen was lit up bright. The whole house. Brighter than daylight. Floodlights were set up in the yard where men searched through the work shed, the garbage cans. Just kids really, revved up on too much caffeine, eyes on a promotion. The staircase sagged with six racing up and six pounding down.

Malcolm had been waiting in a Sunday shirt, wool trousers, and his boots. He'd woken up Dot and told her to make the bed, told her to sit quiet and wait for Tiffany on the couch. He sat in his chair with his hands folded on the kitchen table. Dave Tomkins examined a framed photo of Tiffany that Malcolm had brought in from the living room. Then Dave sat in Tiffany's chair, folded his own hands like a man praying. It was well past midnight.

"She's sure grown," Dave said.

"I wish she'd eat more."

"She's going to be a stunning woman."

"Smarter than you and me put together."

Malcolm's gun collection went by in the hands of federal hotshots not much older than Brook. His Shattuck palm pistol. The old Richmond carbine, an evidence tag wired to the trigger guard.

The extension cord that he'd used on the pickle, cut up with wires exposed, went by in a clear Ziploc evidence bag. Electrical torture, the agent was thinking. It made Malcolm want to spit.

One of them stomped up the cellar stairs with the plastic bag from Discount Hardware. He had Malcolm's rolls of duct tape, the store receipt, and three empty cardboard spools. Daisy went to the top of the cellar stairs and started barking so that Malcolm had to call her back. She squeezed between the rungs of his chair and growled as a man brought up her canine carrier and banged it through the kitchen.

"Hot as the dickens last few days," Dave said.

"Early summer. Bad for mosquitoes."

"How's the fishing lodge?"

"Haven't been . . . this'll be the third year. Needs a roof real bad."

"There'll be another bunch of fellas poking around there by now."

"Can I get you a cola, Dave?"

"No, I'm fine. I had——"

"Or a cup of coffee. I'll get Dot to—"

"No, thanks. Really."

"Dot," Malcolm called over his shoulder into the living room. "Pot of coffee for—"

"No, Malcolm. Thank you." He raised his voice. "Thanks, Dot. No need."

Deep booms rose from the cellar as someone banged on the oil tank. "Hello? Oil man?" There was laughter. They'd be real anxious to find him, but they kept their sense of humor.

Flashlight beams sliced between the breezeway floorboards. Chrissake, those boards were tongue-and-groove. They'd dried up and pulled apart worse than he'd thought. He'd never get this house put right before he died.

"Did I mention Stevie Roskoe's boy got married?" Dave Tomkins said.

"I'll be damned."

"Up Lake George. Middle of last month. Real nice. Real nice girl too. From Paterson."

"I'll be."

Furniture bumped along the floor upstairs, bureaus moving away from the walls, beds sliding to one side to get a look under carpets. So many possibilities for hiding a man in a house. He took a puff off his inhaler.

An agent was going through the kitchen cupboards the way cops do: touching everything. Didn't matter it was a cupboard of drinking glasses. His hands slithered over them, tinking and touching the rim of every one. He tipped a few. Reset them aright.

Another man was under the kitchen sink with a monkey wrench. He was removing the trap from the drainpipe to test at the lab for biological evidence: a trace of blood or hair from the missing man. The sinks would be useless until Malcolm could get the traps replaced.

The first man moved on from the cupboards to the freezer, searching for a weapon. Then he pulled open the fridge, where the four remaining cans of Ensure were lined up, shameful as adult diapers. Dave Tomkins saw the Ensure, glanced at Malcolm, then looked down at the napkin holder, fingering the corner of the stack as if he hadn't noticed at all. Malcolm remembered the belligerence of the hundreds of people he'd searched over the years. Cars, homes, offices, boats, bags, and pockets—didn't much matter. Nobody welcomed the invasion.

"The wife turns fifty this July the seventh," Dave Tomkins said. "We'll be sure to have you over to that one. The kids say you rent a hot tub these days. They're gonna put a Jacuzzi right in the backyard for the party."

There was an old man Malcolm had searched once on what turned out to be a bogus tip. In the kitchen of the tiny apartment, clean and well kept despite the building falling down around it, Malcolm made the man remove his prosthetic leg for inspection. In front of his grandkids. When Malcolm had come up empty, the man said, "Lord have mercy on you," his leg lying across the kitchen table, a slipper stuck to the foot.

"Well, I never," Malcolm said to Dave.

The two agents were whispering in front of the sink; then one of them, a Hispanic man who couldn't have been over twenty-five, squatted down and examined the floor. He duckwalked toward Malcolm, practically under the table. Daisy growled. The agent stood up and snapped open a large evidence bag. "Bud," he said. "Give up the boots."

Dave Tomkins's fist slammed down on the kitchen table, and

the table hopped. He jumped from his chair. "Captain Wolkoviak is this man's name!" he bellowed. Daisy cried and skittered from the kitchen; then the house was silent. Men stopped midstep, desk drawers frozen halfway out. Somewhere in the house a man paused partway through a letter, a credit card bill, a doctor's report he had no right to be reading. Dave's voice echoed in the walls. The agent under the counter popped the tight lid off the percolator, and the aluminum rang.

Dave Tomkins sat back down, fuming. "A little respect!"

"Dried grass cuttings on the suspect's clothing and on the floor of their vehicle," the agent said. He touched the linoleum then flicked dried grass into the plastic bag. "Dried grass cuttings plastered to Captain Wolkoviak's boots."

The other agent, holding the percolator basket in one hand, looked away when Malcolm caught his eye. At first Malcolm thought it was a look of suspicion, but as he scraped back his chair to inspect his boots, he realized that the young agent, with his whole career ahead of him, a Glock .45 automatic on his belt, strong legs and good eyes, was looking at him with pity. Malcolm yanked at his bootlace.

It was one o'clock. Where in God's good name was Tiffany? She was an hour late. She was a girl with some convoluted notions, but her heart was solidly in place, and she was reliable. If she said it, she'd do it on time and the best she could. He could say that about Dot, and he loved her for it. He could say that about Dave Tomkins when he served as Malcolm's deputy. But he could not say that about Theo or Colleen.

"I'll be down in Benson Bay as usual for the Fourth. Maybe you and Dot could make the drive. We'll do some fishing."

Malcolm hadn't fished for years. He used to love passing the time looking out at the water. He'd forget about the stress of the department and his ongoing cases. Theo's thirteen years on the force had been the most stressful period for Malcolm. He was putting out fires surrounding Theo what seemed like every day. Three suspensions and five reprimands; Malcolm had his butt chewed up and spit out four times by the mayor on the subject of Theo.

"Benson Bay. They still got real people down there," Malcolm said. "You walk down the beach, a guy'll tell you what he's using for bait."

It wasn't easy for Theo or any cop on the beat in the seventies. Until then, drugs and minorities had not been a factor in the Ludlow department. Excessive force had not been an issue. How was it that no one ever heard of a thing, and then it became an issue? Feminism, then homosexuals, then cholesterol. Whoever heard of a girl as smart and beautiful as Tiffany not eating, and when she did, if he understood correctly, forcing herself to vomit? Whoever heard of a man with a family leaving a good-paying job at a stable company like Petrochem to live beyond his means on a golf course in Hilton Head, South Carolina?

What had happened to the world that regular good people routinely did the wrong thing? When was it going to stop?

Malcolm took a breath as deep as he could get it. "There's something I want to tell you, Dave." Malcolm looked at his hands. "Theo's disability . . . I signed it, and Doc Manning. . . . It was fake." He felt a physical rush, like he did from his inhaler.

They held up their heads, face-to-face, Malcolm and Dave.

Malcolm's upper lip trembled.

"I'll have the new rod and reel by then," Dave said. "You ought to try to make the drive. It would be good for Dot."

He had done it out of his absolute love for his son. It was the wrong thing. But he couldn't say he would not do it again.

"Is Brook in a dormitory?" Dave asked.

Malcolm nodded. Evidence boxes marked *Bedroom,* brimming with books and clothing, were carried through the kitchen.

After a minute Dave said, "Brook's got a telephone in his dorm room, does he?"

"I think he does," Malcolm said.

"Does he have a car at school?"

Malcolm shook his head. Dave was right. Before the morning papers.

"I'll send a car," Dave said.

"Give him till dawn. These kids love their sleep."

"He needs it. Studying like that."

They were quiet for a minute, listening to an agent rummage through the pantry.

"Is this a mistake, Dave?"

"I'm not going to lie to you."

Malcolm felt the veins rush in his eyes.

The screen door shot open. Tiffany. Her grim expression turned to relief when she saw Malcolm at the head of the table. She ran over and threw her arms around his neck. The side of her face pressed to his. "I thought something happened," she said. Then she lurched back. "Gramma!" And the fear rose back to her face.

"I'm right here," Dot said, from behind Malcolm in the kitchen doorway.

"What's going on?" Tiffany said. "Where's Mom and Dad? Was there an accident? Are they okay?"

"No accident, honey," Dot said.

"Where are they?"

Dot pulled out a chair for Tiffany. No one said a thing.

"Are these guys really the FBI?" She looked from Dot's face to Malcolm's to Dave's. "Why are they looking at our food?"

"It's important to stress," Malcolm began, but his chest constricted. Tiffany pulled at her hair while she waited for Malcolm to breathe on his inhaler. "Important to stress that nobody knows anything for sure." And he stopped, thinking it might be enough, thinking he wouldn't have to poison his granddaughter's life.

"Anything about what? Grampa, what's going on?" Her voice was rising.

"Your parents are only suspects," Malcolm said. "It's probably all a mistake, some coincidences, bad leads. Departments get embarrassed by things like this all the time. And I assure you the Feds are not exempt from mistakes. Chief Tomkins will support me on that contention, I'm sure. Nobody's immune from seeing a thing wrong." She waited for more, fiddling with her hair, patient as could be expected. "So don't worry is all I'm saying. Don't even think about it till we see what this nonsense is about—"

"It's that kidnapping, sweetheart," Dot interrupted. "The Petrochem man." And the relief that Malcolm didn't have to say it himself sank through him with the weight of his love for Dot. "They think maybe your parents might know something about it."

Tiffany laughed out loud. "*That's* a good one. Are you serious?"
Malcolm nodded once.

She eased back in the chair, a twitchy smile on her face. "Chief Tomkins," she said. "My parents? Ecoterrorists? What a joke. They couldn't care less about the environment. They're Petrochem's dream consumers. They only care about material things, stuff. They'd trade the redwoods for a BMW any day. I mean, I love them, but their values are warped—sorry, Gramma and Grampa." She twisted a strand of hair around her index finger. "They don't care about anything but money. Sometimes I swear they'd trade me and Brook for a life like Jackie O.'s. They're blinded by money. They'd do *anything*—" She cut herself off. She fingered her hair for a split end. Tore the hair up the middle.

W e're indigent," Theo said. "We'll need a public defender. We're working people. Trying to get our heads above water. A boy in college. A girl with medical conditions."

Then he said, "Is Murry Polson still with the Bureau in Newark? Talk to Murry. Murry and I go way back. Can I kindly have a word with Murry?"

He said, "For that matter get Dave Tomkins on the horn. Chrissake, like an uncle to me. Like a brother."

"I *am* cooperating. Big time. But to a degree. Then I begin to feel my rights are abused. I start to think false arrest, lawsuit, heads rolling."

They had left him alone in the interrogation room. Or they wanted him to think he was alone, but they were watching him. Who did they think they were dealing with? As if they could leave the room and Theo would lose his shit, show his guilt.

Theo knew that careers were riding on this case, from the DA on down. This case picked a man up by his collar and set him down in Washington. Or bumped him over to Manhattan. This case meant rank for a few federal boys. Bonus checks. Pictures in the paper.

Every man who walked into this room wanted something

from Theo, something for himself. But Theo Wolkoviak was nobody's meal ticket.

The lights were bright. There were no windows, no clock, but he figured it had to be almost dawn. He remained righteous as he sat, as they watched him through any number of peepholes. His dignity assaulted. Two blisters from the shovel stung his left palm.

They'd been out of the room at least fifteen minutes when they sent in a girl with coffee in a Styrofoam cup. She set it in front of Theo, smiled at him, said, "I think your wife will be okay," and walked out. On the inside he was laughing. When you're dealing with Theo Wolkoviak, nobody succeeds with the personal reference designed to shake him up. Nobody gets him nervy on police house coffee. Nobody pumps up the pressure in his bladder, then refuses to let him piss. Nobody gets him to lower his guard by dangling a piece of ass in front of him.

If they were watching him for a sign, it meant they had nothing on him. The perfect plan doesn't leave a trail. What was traceable? What single piece of evidence did they have? The Petrochem money clip? Check the records. Check this one for Brown's prints. Good luck.

Time passed. He cradled the coffee cup in both hands, raised it to his lips. He took a small sip so they could believe he wasn't onto their Cub Scout tricks. They could look through their peepholes and think, *He's a frightened and falsely accused man concerned for his wife and family.*

The only reason Theo was sitting here, if he read correctly between the lines, was that the Feds got lucky with hundreds of men on the case, listening to Jackson's wire, floating. The perfect plan does not account for hundreds of men. The perfect plan thinks thirty men. Fifty men max. But this was precisely Theo's meaning: Jackson signed overtime for hundreds of men. Jackson needed a bust. Jackson was a black man in charge of the biggest thing to hit the Bureau in fifty years. He was thinking career advancement, a black man in over his head.

If they had any evidence—photos of Theo at the Buick Regal or popping the note under the phone, if the info kiosk girl could identify him—it would be on the table. Because even more than a bust, Jackson needed Stona Brown alive. If it meant he could free Brown in time for the morning papers, Jackson would settle for a plea bargain. He'd use his evidence as leverage instead of standing with a hard-on at a peep show waiting for Theo to show him a tit.

They were so desperate that they'd told Theo his father had tipped them off. They'd said his father had told the Feds about the box, but Theo knew they'd found some plywood scraps in the work shed, some packaging from the hinges. And that ploy was their biggest mistake, because Theo knew that family meant something to his father, just as it did to Colleen, and they were, all of them, tight as a fist.

Theo was a step ahead. He thought about Tiffany in the hospital down to eighty-seven pounds, a jumble of bones barely making a mound under the blanket, force-fed through tubes; he let his sorrow and helplessness color his face and shudder through his largeman frame. He remembered the tube coming out of her mouth, her lips black and so chapped they were scabbed. Over the sound of machines hushing and beeping to keep her alive, she had whispered to Theo with all the strength she could call on, "Sorry, Dad."

Theo was shaking. Tears darkened two spots on the orange jumper. *Look at me, you cocksuckers. My vulnerability, my violation, my innocence.*

m o n d a y

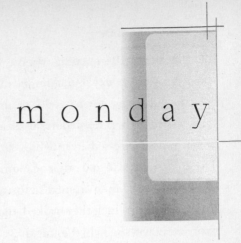

Dawn had spread through Nunny's house with a feeling of possibility. But as the day stretched longer, so did the waiting, and suddenly the gentle swirls of dust illuminated by shafts of sunlight became still.

Sitting in the yellow wing chair, Nunny thought of her journal, which she hadn't written in since Thursday morning, and her poetry, which she had neglected for years. She remembered a girl, a poet, from college.

Nunny had barely known the girl who had laced a rope around her neck and kicked the chair out from under her. But she had fascinated Nunny. Nunny remembered one poem in particular that the girl had written and they'd read aloud in class. The class discussed the rhythmic shortcomings of the last line, "I sometimes feel all dead inside," the gracelessness of the sounds, its failure to close the stanza.

On that early morning when they found her, all the girls in the dorm were awake, bunching in rooms, collecting in the corridor, their dressing gowns and hair unfixed. One girl collapsed in grief, and the others hoisted her up, laid her on the nearest bed. The dorm mother, dressed all in white, appeared with a tray of coffee. The police moved in and out, and Nunny felt suddenly as if she were in a convent, the men seemed so foreign. She remembered mostly the weight with which they walked, the heaviness of their shoes, the clumsiness with which they drank coffee from fine china cups. Their thumby hands.

Did all the girls imagine how those men got her down? One hefty policeman wrapping his arms around her suspended form, embracing her, his whiskered cheek pressed to her cool silk nightie, her cold, young-woman's abdomen. *I sometimes feel all dead inside.* He lifted her skyward, and her head dropped over his shoulder like a sleeping child, so another silent man could loosen the rope, and together they laid her gently on the stretcher, tucking in her hair and arms. Nunny wished she could ask the girl now whether any wisdom had come with her agony, because now Nunny herself had no words more rhythmic or poetically viable than the girl's. There was nothing more to say but *I sometimes feel all dead inside,* and relief would only come if she were floating in the air, then squeezed with a strong-armed embrace, a whiskery face to her abdomen, and lifted.

Racing the setting sun, they sped down the Parkway, escorted by police cars with their lights flashing. Colleen slouched in the backseat of the Buick to hide the orange prison uniform from the people in the cars they passed. A young couple in a minivan peered curiously out their side window at Colleen. A family drove past with two kids in the back and bikes tied to the roof. The little girl waved to Colleen, and Colleen tried to wave back, but the chains pulled at her wrists and ankles. She tried to smile. An elderly woman with blue wash in her hair leaned into the wheel, clutching it tight as she stole quick glances at the speeding motorcade. The people Colleen passed expected to catch a glimpse of the vice president, Bill Gates, or the Dalai Lama.

Her car led the way down the overgrown bumpy road, through the dwarfed pines. Garbage and broken bottles were strewn everywhere, which she hadn't remembered seeing in the dark last night with Theo, or five years ago when they'd pedaled down this road thirsty, warm, and in love.

At the fork, the car stopped. Agent Campbell looked over his shoulder at Colleen. He trusted her now. He understood her in ways that he hadn't during her interrogation, during the eighteen hours that she denied her guilt. "To the right," she said, lying, and they slowly veered away from the grave. She was not ready to betray her husband.

She looked out the back window at the serpentine line of cars following with the patient obedience of a funeral procession over the rutted, narrow lanes of a cemetery. Colleen opened her hands, spreading her fingers. Her skin was dry, chapped on the knuckles. Except for the band of skin at the base of her ring finger which was white and soft, her hands—the crooked pinkie and cracked cuticles—belonged to a middle-aged woman.

"Mrs. Wolkoviak, you need to be looking."

The car had stopped. She raised her head. "It was dark," she said.

"And it's getting dark now."

What would Theo do if Colleen showed the agents Mr. Brown's body? They'd told Colleen she'd have to testify against Theo in court if he didn't plead guilty. Step by step, she would have to explain to a roomful of people, to the press, to a jury— "I think this is it," she said. Agent Campbell opened her door, and Colleen got out and walked among the small, white wildflowers dotting the dead leaves and pine needles. She tried to imagine telling the jury about buying the ski masks, surgical gloves, padlocks, and duct tape. Describing the gas station coveralls. Explaining how she'd wanted to release Mr. Brown after Theo shot him, how she'd pleaded with him not to load his gun in the first place. She would describe locking down the plywood lid on a man forced to sleep in his urine. She tried to imagine looking across the courtroom at her husband, a man with a beard whom she didn't really know, describing the competence with which he'd dug Mr. Brown's grave, the casualness with which he'd slung Mr. Brown into the hole. "I don't know," Colleen heard herself say. "It's around here somewhere." She walked farther from the line of cars, the chain between her ankles catching on dead branches lying on the ground.

In a patch where the sunlight cut low through the trees, she turned and searched the ground unconvincingly. Twenty or thirty men were standing beside their cars, leaning their elbows on top of open doors. They understood that Colleen was a woman with unlimited potential and boundless dreams that would remain forever unfulfilled. These men watched Colleen wading through the brush, and each one thought about how he'd disappointed his own wife. The suburban house, the reliable car, the ten days in Virginia Beach last summer—it hadn't satisfied them as they'd thought it would when they were young. They recognized Colleen, an attrac-

tive woman just past her prime in an orange prison suit and handcuffs, who was not unlike the women they'd go home to tonight.

Agent Campbell was at her side; he touched her lower back.
"You've got to focus, Colleen. Don't lose sight of the right thing."
His face was close to hers, as it had been for much of the interroga-
tion. He was whispering. "You're better than that."

She turned away from him. "Back there. At the fork," she said.
"It might have been to the left."

The cars backed out in a cockeyed jerky stop and start. The sun
had gone down. The gray, even light calmed Colleen as her car led
the way down the left fork. She was calm because from this point
forward in her life she would do the right thing, starting with a
proper burial for Mr. Brown and closure for his family. She'd made
a deal for twenty years in prison. It wasn't a sure thing, she understood, but it was what the DA would ask the judge for. She wanted
to provide for her children. She'd heard of people running GoodLife
businesses from prison. At sixty-five she could have grandkids and a
self-sufficient business working beneath her. From this point forward, Colleen's life would be dedicated to others.

"Stop," Campbell blurted out. He pointed through the windshield, grabbing for the radio. "Get a forensics guy." His excitement
was palpable. "You let us know when we're there," he said to
Colleen. Campbell and two men, one with a camera and one with a
video recorder, got out and walked ahead of the car, recording the
rental van's tire tracks.

Colleen's side window was completely blocked by spring
leaves pressing against the glass, smoothing over it like sudsy
brushes at a car wash. They inched ahead until Colleen said,
"There," and the driver pulled even farther into the foliage so that
she had to hop along the seat and get out the left-side door.

Theo had blanketed the freshly disturbed ground with pinecones and dead leaves. Their crime would have been erased by the first hard rain. But now, as Campbell and the two cameras converged—to the click and whir of auto-advance—tire tracks, loose dirt, and the gentle mound over Mr. Brown's body seemed as obvious as a lynched man swinging from a tree.

Behind her, agent after agent emerged from cars with coffee cups, stuffing half-eaten sandwiches in their mouths, one man marking his stride with a shovel.

As dusk settled through the trees, the agent shooting video snapped on a powerful light. Several men using what looked like children's garden rakes slowly began to remove the leaves covering the mound. Every moment was recorded on film.

Lights on metal poles were unloaded from a van and erected around the site. Finally, a man took up the shovel, and the blade clattered through stones and dirt. The man tipped the dirt into a screen box, which another man shook, sifting, one tiny shovelful at a time.

Far off, she could see headlights bouncing down the road. She watched the car approach through the darkness, past the line of parked cars, then swing into the woods and stop. "Let's give a hand to the digging crew," she heard someone say, and when she looked, the cameraman was moving in close to take a snapshot of Stona Brown's left hand sticking from the dirt at an angle that made no sense, as if it were only a hand and arm planted there. Light glinted off his wedding ring. A corner of gauze was dirty at his wrist.

Agent Jackson had arrived. He stood with Campbell in the floodlights. The two men talked quietly as the agents on their hands and knees painstakingly dug around Mr. Brown's shoulder with tiny garden trowels, scooping the dirt into the sift. Jackson's arrival brought a solemnity that settled over the men. Everyone was quiet and efficient. Campbell pointed at Colleen, then made a backhand motion like shooing away a mosquito. The artificially lighted area where they worked reminded her of the empty yellow Colonial chair in Mrs. Brown's living room minutes after she'd made her plea.

"In the car," the driver ordered Colleen, pinching her elbow. He opened her door and shut her inside. The front door was ajar, though, so the domelight was on. Colleen looked down at her hands and saw they were trembling. The driver stood by the car with his hands behind his back, making sure Colleen didn't try to escape but also, she felt, protecting her. She had done the right thing.

She could still see the grave clearly. Colleen's entire body began to tremble. She could see a shoe, the leg of Mr. Brown's suit pants, and now she realized what was wrong with the angle of his hand and wrist: Mr. Brown's heel was sticking up, his knee was stabbing down into the ground. Theo had buried the man facedown.

The window glass was getting steamy. Her eyes were hot with tears, and she rubbed her cheeks against the glass. Mr. Brown's back was being swept with a whisk broom as they uncovered him, taking pictures of the bands of duct tape wound around his ankles, corkscrewing up his legs, binding his arms at his sides. It was brutal what they'd done. From where he stood, Jackson turned his head to Colleen, lit up in the car on display for public humiliation, and the complete disgust that rose through him chilled the heat of her tears.

It had been only a few days, and it seemed like a lifetime. The agents had cleaned away the dirt from around his head, photographing the angle of his head in the grave, bent sharply back— like a man on his belly shrieking as his neck is snapped.

Colleen rolled her forehead over the glass. She wanted to be touched. Would she wait twenty years to be held again by a man? On this spot she and Theo had made love in the open air. He'd gently taken off her shirt, and the sun had warmed the white skin of her breasts. Theo's strong arms had raised her up by the hips—it had been a promise that the emptiness inside her would be filled. Three men lifted Mr. Brown from the hole in the ground, and the foul smell filled the car. She had killed a man.

Jackson glanced coldly again at Colleen as he stepped toward his car. She turned her eyes from him, staring at the glossy black opaqueness of his car windows, and when he opened the door and the domelight illuminated the inside of his car, Colleen was staring into the eyes of Mrs. Stona Brown. Colleen blinked back her tears, and Mrs. Brown turned slightly away, calmly, to speak to Jackson. Beside her sat a pretty, young woman with long dark hair. Then Mrs. Brown turned back and looked across the night at Colleen.

Mrs. Brown would want to know about the last days of her husband's life. She'd want to ask Colleen if he'd been cold, if he'd suffered. Mrs. Brown would ask Colleen what could possibly have caused her to risk destroying two families, to risk not seeing her own children become adults.

Jackson closed the door, and his car went dark again. But Colleen continued to stare at the dark window, and she felt that Mrs. Brown was watching her. Colleen wanted to tell Mrs. Brown about the mornings and afternoons caring for her husband. She wanted to let her know that her husband had been comforted. She'd sat with him, and he'd spoken of his wife. His concern was more for his wife than himself. His love for her was great. She wanted to try to explain.

If they could meet like two old friends for tea, Colleen would confide in her about Tiffany's anorexia. She would seek Mrs. Brown's advice about dealing with the disappointments of life. She wanted to ask Mrs. Brown why life is not what it's promised to be, why we're told to dream when our dreams have no chance of coming true. She wanted to ask how a woman can believe she has loved a man for twenty-five years and then find that she never knew him at all. She wanted to ask why Theo hadn't been killed in the boating accident. How she was expected to go through life without a mark that would set her apart. She would ask to speak to Mrs. Brown. She would beg for forgiveness.

She looked into the black glass. There was so much Colleen wanted.

The fingers of Nunny's left hand were laced with Jane's, clamping Nunny's wedding band to the bone. Nunny squeezed more tightly. She stared out the window of Jackson's car at the woman, lit up in another car. The woman had known Nunny immediately when Jackson opened the door to say that there was a body confirmed, unidentified, where they dug. But Nunny had already recognized the woman. It had taken exactly one stride. The woman had been standing in handcuffs and leg irons when they pulled up. Then an agent had turned her around and walked her to the car. When she took a step—slightly pigeon-toed, swinging her leg out from the hip—Nunny could suddenly hear the sound of water overflowing the terra-cotta pot on her front porch and splashing down the steps. She could hear Stona's ship's clock strike. She could see the woman's pink-suited legs.

Jane stroked her mother's forearm. She fingered Nunny's ring, the three diamonds—the large one for Stona and smaller ones for Victor and Jane. Jane did not let go of Nunny's hand when she called Joe at the house on the cell phone, but her grip loosened, and Jane cried when he answered. She was a beautiful, brilliant, sensitive woman and her strength had carried Nunny through. Even though the first claims on Jane's heart were shifting to Joe, Nunny would never lose her. Jane would be the closest person in the world to her. Nunny had lost Victor years ago. Tonight, she was losing Stona.

She couldn't see past the pair of scrub pines that Jackson had parked behind. What had they unearthed so far? Stona's shoe? His knee? She stared at the woman—blond hair, rounded shoulders, mother of two—whom she'd first seen Friday morning in pink running pants in front of her home. And who, since then, had destroyed everything Nunny had. She had not only taken Stona from her; she had stolen from Nunny the last days and hours of Stona's life.

She would never think about Oakville again. She would not remember that she had thought her love for Stona might be fading. She would only remember the strength of their love and her unshakable loyalty.

The woman was crying. She had murdered an innocent man, destroyed a family, and betrayed her husband. A woman was nothing if not loyal to her husband, if not dedicated to her children, if not devoted to God. This woman was none of those things. She had confessed because she was weak, because she did not have the courage to accept the consequences of her actions.

Jackson finally came to Nunny's door and asked again if she was sure she wanted to identify the body. She freed her hand from Jane's, but Jane clutched at her arm. "Don't, Mom—" Jane was too young to understand why Nunny could not wait another few hours to know for sure, could not wait for Victor to arrive and identify Stona for her. Nunny had insisted that Jackson bring them here, despite his adamant opposition. She'd had to argue with him. She'd had to remind him that she'd followed his advice at each step, and how did he think things had gone? She looked at her daughter beside her in the backseat, looked at her full-faced, squarely.

And Jane released Nunny's arm. Jackson's hand was at her elbow as she rose from the car, but she shook him off. She was glad the woman was watching. This weak woman would see Nunny walk over the brush and fallen branches to the grave where the woman had dumped Nunny's life. The woman who would not have the courage to do this herself.

When Jackson stepped to the left around the pair of scrub pines, Nunny went to the right. She entered the lighted area strewn with bags of equipment, plastic tubs and envelopes marked *Case #2871*. Only when she saw several men holding handkerchiefs to their mouths did she notice the smell. The men stood perfectly still.

The hole in the ground seemed too small, but she wouldn't allow the folly of hope. She had only a pinch of energy left, not nearly enough to squander on delusion. A man motioned gently to her, and she saw that it was not a sack of lights and shovels at his feet, but a black plastic body bag.

Nunny kneeled on the pine needles and dried leaves as the man squatted so close to her she smelled spearmint on his breath. She nodded to him, and he pulled on the zipper. When he spread the long slit, the gray shrunken face of her husband seemed to lurch toward her. She reached into the bag and touched her hands to each side of his face. A dirty bandage was wrapped around his forehead. As her face dropped closer, she could smell, even through the smell of his death, the sweet oily scent of his scalp. His collar was brown with dirt, and he still wore the tie, the burgundy foulard from Victor. His face was coated with a fine dusting of dirt. Dirt was packed in his nostrils, the corners of his eyes, between his lips. She did not allow herself to think about the bandage on his head, to think about how he died, to imagine his suffering, because she had the rest of her life to think about those things. Stona was a very handsome man. She thought of their last morning, of the two hairs she'd plucked off his shoulder. She kissed him fleshy and wet on the lips, tasting salt and the earth, his lips meaty and cold. As she pulled away, her tears dropped on his face and washed streaks through the dirt, streaks on his skin glowing white.

t u e s d a y

Malcolm stood on the breezeway. Through the screen he watched his grandson cut neat passes across the lawn with the mower that Malcolm had sent him to Discount Hardware to buy this morning. The droning of the motor followed him into the kitchen. In the center of the table several crisp white paper bags from the deli stood in a bunch. Dave Tomkins had stopped by with the sandwiches and a pan of lasagna that his wife had baked. All the sinks in the house were still unusable. This afternoon, when Malcolm's lungs felt up to it, he'd crawl underneath the counters and install new traps.

As Dot ironed a shirt for Malcolm to wear to the arraignment, Malcolm thought of the widow, Mrs. Stona Brown, standing at her husband's closet today looking over his business suits. He imagined her lifting down a suit hanging pressed and floppy from a wooden hanger and passing it to the undertaker. He imagined Dot, a few weeks from now, doing the same thing.

He thought about trying to fix things—a letter to Mrs. Brown and her children. Some way to account for the destruction.

The lawn mower cut off. Malcolm sat down at the kitchen table, and Tiffany fell into the chair beside his. Brook bumped up the back stairs, through the breezeway, and he and Dot took their places.

No one made a move for the food. Daisy scraped into the kitchen and slumped against Malcolm's feet. The quiet stiffened. Malcolm looked down at his patrolman's shoes. "When your father was a boy," he said to his grandchildren, "about seven or eight years old, he'd walk down to the station house and shine everyone's shoes for a nickel a pair. On one occasion, I was so busy with paperwork I didn't have time to take a break and put my feet on his shoeshine kit while he worked. So I took my shoes off and handed them to your father, and there was a hole in my sock—my big toe stuck right through. One of the guys razzed me about it, and pretty soon the whole squad room was getting a laugh. Good-natured, mind you, but your father didn't realize that, and his face went beet-red. Later that afternoon—after I'd seen him set up his kit outside Fulsom Hardware to add to his usual station house take—he spent the whole handful of nickels in Woolworth's and delivered to me on the sly, so no one in the station took notice, a brand-new pair of socks."

Malcolm took a puff off his inhaler; then he stood up and smoothed Tiffany's hair with his unsteady hand. He moved around the table and squeezed Brook's shoulders. He rubbed slow circles on Dot's back. She was crying, soundlessly, her face in her hands.

Then he sat back down and reached into a deli bag. He slid sandwiches wrapped in white butcher paper across the table to

Brook and Dot. He set one down for Tiffany and one for himself. Dot lifted her head and wiped her eyes.

"I'll want to go through some matters with you all," Malcolm said, his hand hovering over the stack of financial records on the table. "After we've eaten."

They unwrapped their sandwiches. They unwrapped dill pickle spears, and Dot peeled the lid off a pint of potato salad. Brook popped open a bag of chips. Malcolm took a bite of his sandwich and so did Tiffany. She sipped her milk. A warm wind, carrying the smell of fresh-cut grass, blew in through the breezeway.

Keith Scribner lives in Corvallis, Oregon, with his wife, the poet Jennifer Richter, and teaches creative writing at Oregon State University. He is at work on his second novel.